Slow Living

Also by the author in reading order:

Destiny: Union Station

Date Night on Union Station

Alien Night on Union Station

High Priest on Union Station

Spy Night on Union Station

Carnival on Union Station

Wanderers on Union Station

Vacation on Union Station

Guest Night on Union Station

Word Night on Union Station

Party Night on Union Station

Review Night on Union Station

Family Night on Union Station

Book Night on Union Station

LARP Night on Union Station

Career Night on Union Station

Last Night on Union Station

Independent Living

Soup Night on Union Station

Assisted Living

Freelance on the Galactic Tunnel Network

Con Living

Empire Night on Union Station

Space Living

Traders on the Galactic Tunnel Network

Orphans on the Galactic Tunnel Network

Swap Night on Union Station

Slow Living

Book Five of EarthCent Universe

Foner Books

978-1-948691-34-5

Northampton, Massachusetts

One

"Learn anything interesting in class this morning?" Harry asked his part-time assistant.

Bill made a face as he donned a clean apron. "Flower is making me study Customer Relations Theory. I thought I had a deal with her to only take practical courses, the stuff I can use when I open my own café, but now she's whistling another tune."

"Competency exams? Even a degree?"

The young man nodded glumly. "She claims I already know as much about commercial baking as any of the students on her Open University campus so it would be a waste of time to stick with the vocational track."

"Don't go blaming me," Harry said with a laugh as he stirred a pot of bubbling beans. "I'll be the first to admit that I never used ninety percent of what I learned at school, but without a time machine, there's no way for a young person to know which ten percent they're eventually going to need. Besides, I met Irene in college."

"I've been engaged to Julie for a year so I don't need school for a social life. I had no idea what the instructor was talking about today, but afterward, the other students were complaining that he was going too slow. Have you ever heard of reverse psychology?"

"If I said, 'I'd let you stir these beans for me but you'd probably just make a mess,' that would be an example of reverse psychology."

"Because I'd want to prove I can do it?" Bill asked, and then he noticed that Harry was looking at him expectantly. "Do you really want me to stir the beans?"

"Another five minutes should do it," the baker told him, letting go of the composite mixing spoon and stepping aside.

"I thought you said that wooden spoons were best for stirring beans," Bill said as he took over the job.

"I'm expecting a Frunge guest," Harry said. "You know how sensitive they are about anything involving wood or paper."

"And if they're traditional, they don't eat wheat or cereal crops because they believe their ancestors made a treaty with the grasses to share their homeworld. Razood explained it all to me when I was working as his assistant in the blacksmith shop."

"Can you keep a secret?"

"Seventeen minutes and twelve seconds," Flower's artificial voice exploded from an overhead speaker grille. "Next time I have something I want to keep private I may as well just announce it over the public address system."

"I won't tell anybody," Bill said, keeping up a circular stirring motion. "It has something to do with the Frunge, right?"

Harry glanced up at the speaker grille, and the Dollnick AI said, "Oh, go ahead."

"Have you been to the Blue Tea Café?" Harry asked his assistant.

"A couple of times. Vivian likes it so she takes Julie there a lot, but it's kind of expensive for what you get. Razood did all of the iron work for the tables and chairs."

"It's a good example of an upscale café, though I doubt you'll want to go into business selling baked goods from Frunge tribute recipes."

"Are you going to tell him or am I?" Flower put in impatiently.

"Did you meet the owner?" Harry asked Bill.

"No, but there was an article about her in the Galactic Free Press last year and Julie pointed it out to me. The owner used to work for the Frunge diplomatic service investigating internal problems or something like that. The guys," he tilted his head towards the swinging door that led to the cafeteria where the alien spies came for meals, "talked about inviting her to eat with them when the story came out, but I never saw her here."

"Did Razood say anything when—"

"You're turning into an old woman playing twenty questions," Flower interrupted. "Fandaz just exited the lift tube so give him the quick version."

"Flower wants to fix them up as a couple," Harry said. "The Frunge take dating seriously—I suppose all of the aliens do—but Flower says that the Frunge usually work through professional matchmakers and there are none on board."

"Are they as strict as the Drazens?" Bill asked. "Jorb and Rinka had to pass a live-action-role-playing test on Union Station before they got engaged, and his parents are still against the marriage."

"The Frunge are stricter," Flower said. "Do you remember how Jorb and Rinka met?"

"He said he fell in love at first sight when she presented her idea for a remedial singing school back when he was on a committee with Samuel and Vivian at the Open University."

"And he waited quite a while after he got here before asking you and Julie to help bring them together. I need you to do the same for Razood and Fandaz."

"I don't think Julie knows Fandaz that well," Bill said. "And I remember from that Galactic Free Press article that Fandaz had been working for their diplomatic service for a long time before she quit. Isn't she too old for Razood?"

"Fifty years was the fastest anybody has reached the rank of Inspector General in their diplomatic service, and differences of a hundred years or more are common in Frunge marriages. I need you to make friends with her to be the middleman between the two of them."

"What am I supposed to talk to her about?"

"The café business," Flower said. "The Blue Tea Café is one of the most popular spots on board and I'm thinking of copying her loyalty program for my LARPing studio. She's entering the cafeteria as we speak."

"So I guess I can drop Customer Relations Theory." Bill's attempt to sound nonchalant while bargaining with the twenty-thousand-year-old AI failed miserably.

Flower hesitated for a moment. "Deal."

The door from the dining room swung open, and an alien with green hair vines twined around a low-rise trellis on her head backed into the kitchen. Then she turned and they saw she was carrying a large tray loaded with small bowls of what might have been spreads or pastry fillings featuring every color of the rainbow.

"You must be Fandaz," Harry said. "You can put the tray on the counter there. I hope you didn't walk all the way from your café carrying all of that."

"It's nothing," the Frunge woman said. "Back in the Shrub Scouts we used to practice carrying each other down mountains in case of a medical emergency. Our muscles are much stronger than yours."

"I noticed that when I apprenticed in Razood's blacksmith shop," Bill said from where he was stirring the pot. "His arms aren't any bigger than mine but he can swing a heavy hammer all day."

"You know Razood?" Fandaz asked, and both men noticed that her hair vines darkened with a rush of chlorophyll.

"The captain got me a job working for Razood when I first stowed away on board. But now I work for Harry and Flower, and I plan to open my own café one day."

"Are these fillings or dips?" Harry asked the Frunge. "I've never seen such an attractive display."

"Thank you," Fandaz said. "I'd like to take credit for the idea, but Frunge chefs have a tradition of color samplers that goes back at least a million years. If I had used the standard ingredients from our cuisine, I would have produced the basic set of one hundred and twenty-eight, but as I limited myself to Earth exports and produce grown on Flower's ag decks, I only managed thirty-two. To be honest, I couldn't have gotten past twenty-six without the liberal use of beet juice and saffron."

"You didn't use any artificial food colors?"

"I never heard of such a thing. Do Humans really add chemicals to their food to change the color?"

"It's almost universal in pre-packaged foods," Harry said.

"But how can people judge whether or not the food is any good before purchasing it?" Fandaz asked incredulously. "Next you're going to tell me that you have fake flavors as well."

"Artificial flavors, and I'm afraid they're used even more extensively than artificial colors in manufactured foods and snacks."

"Like the products M793qK tests for All Species Cookbook certification," Bill put in. "The Farling doctor comes in once or twice a month and I spend a day assisting him. He has a pretty low opinion of most of the food we analyze, and around half of the products sent to us get rejected."

"If artificial coloring and flavors are the norm, I'm surprised he doesn't reject them all," Fandaz said. "Out of morbid curiosity, may I ask if M793qK has ever praised any packaged foods from Earth?"

Bill stopped stirring for a moment and took a quick look around the kitchen to make sure that the stealthy Farling hadn't come in unnoticed. "Most of the manufacturers send us far more product than we need for the lab work and taste testing, and I've noticed that the leftover potato chips and pretzels usually go missing."

"Then I'll have to try potato chips, but of course, I'm here for the opposite reason today," the Frunge said. "When I announced that the Blue Tea Café would begin catering special events, the first request for a quote came from Flower. I was surprised when it turned out to be for an old age home she caters."

"It's an independent living cooperative, and many of us still work," Harry said. "Flower provides the food services under contract, and she features alien cuisine nights on a regular schedule."

"Really? What was the main course the last time she offered a Human interpretation of Frunge cooking?"

"Sashimi. Primarily fish from Earth that she's started farming in a section of the reservoir deck she partitioned off for saltwater."

"It's hard to go wrong with raw fish," Fandaz said, bobbing her head in approval. "I know that you're the Harry behind Harry's Fruitcake, and I was worried that her request was a ploy to steal my vegetable spreads for Flower Foods. Now I understand she chose you to evaluate my sampler because you're also a member of the old—I mean—independent living cooperative."

"Unless your spreads freeze particularly well, Flower wouldn't be interested," Harry said. "The reason she got into the fruitcake business is that the high alcohol content gives them a long shelf-life without refrigeration or artificial preservatives. Bill, that's enough stirring. Turn off the heat, cover the beans, and help me evaluate these spreads."

Bill did as he was told and joined the baker at the counter where Fandaz had set down the tray. "Do Frunge really eat a lot of vegetable spreads, or did you come up with these special for the catering job?" he asked the alien.

"Vegetable spreads are very popular, especially on raw meat. You understand we have no tradition of breads or crackers, though some Frunge have decided that the puffed rice cakes exported from Earth by Drazen Foods are acceptable. Unfortunately, they're also tasteless, so a good vegetable spread is practically a requirement. Flower said that she's tried introducing rice cakes to the independent living cooperatives as a healthy snack food but it ended up having the opposite effect."

Harry chuckled. "I remember Dave loading his with peanut butter, and after a few of the women found a source for chocolate spread, Flower stopped pushing the puffed rice." He pulled open a drawer under the counter and brought out a freezer bag full of tiny plastic spoons. "Think M793qK will mind if we use these, Bill?"

"You don't have to keep bringing it up," the young man mumbled, the tips of his ears turning red.

"Am I missing an inside joke?" Fandaz asked. "I was a diplomatic inspector in my previous career, so I hope you'll forgive me if my question is intrusive."

"It was just an ordering mistake," Bill said. "The doctor got tired of me raiding his supply of tongue depressors to use at public tastings so he told me to order a thousand of these sampler spoons from a catalog. I got the scientific notation wrong and ordered a million. The shipping from Earth cost as much as the spoons themselves so it wasn't worth returning them."

The Frunge picked up one of the tiny spoons and examined it closely. "That's an interesting concept. I've been giving out free vegetable sticks when customers in my café want to try a spread from the display case, but a little spoon like this would cut down on wastage."

"So it's win-win," Flower joined the conversation. "I'm in business with the Farling doctor doing the All Species Cookbook certifications and the spoons were purchased on my account. Take all you want and we'll just say you owe me one."

"I'd prefer an invoice, if you don't mind," Fandaz said dryly.

"Smart," a voice came from the door, and they turned to see that Jorb had entered the kitchen. "I know that I'm late for lunch but—are we sampling spreads?"

"Let me and Bill try them first," Harry told the Drazen. "This is an official testing to see if they're suitable for Alien Night at the independent living cooperative."

Jorb picked up one of the tiny plastic spoons and inspected it dubiously. "It's no wonder Humans shrink when they get old if you make them eat with these. You probably use more energy spooning up the food than the calories it replaces."

"Let's go in order and try the same ones so we can share our opinions, Bill," the baker told his assistant. He took a tiny spoonful of the black paste. "Oh, that's surprising."

"Not good?" Fandaz asked.

"It's excellent, but I expected something bitter because of the color."

"It's sweet," Bill agreed. "Did you use octopus ink? One of my instructors last semester said it's the best natural black coloring."

"Activated charcoal," the Frunge told them. "I make my own. I priced the octopus ink exported by Drazen Foods and it was outrageous."

Harry moved ahead with tasting. "All of these browns are going to be a major hit. Did you use different grades of cocoa for the coloring?"

"And a type of organic coffee bean that Flower is growing experimentally. It has a wonderful aroma with dark chocolate undertones."

"They're all really good," Bill said, passing the small bowl of the lightest brown to Jorb before joining Harry in sampling the maroon color. "This one tastes a little like blueberries."

"The base is a purple sweet potato, but I did use blueberries and grape juice to change the flavor profile," Fandaz said. Then she scolded the Drazen, who was licking out one of the small bowls. "Mind your manners, Jorb."

"You know each other?" Harry asked.

"Rinka likes the Blue Tea Café and we usually go early in the morning on the Human clock when Fandaz is there working on the special of the day," Jorb said. "Hurry up and get to the red ones. I'm hoping they have a bit more bite to them."

"Did you use red cabbage for the blue?" Bill asked the Frunge.

"I got the idea from the appendix of the All Species Cookbook," Fandaz said. "It's an excellent resource for learning about Human foods."

"I'm going to get a little club soda to clean my palate because I know I'm starting to miss some of the subtle flavors," Harry said. "So far I would recommend all of these without reservation."

"Say you'd love to see how she makes them," Flower privately prompted Bill over his implant.

"Are these recipes all secret, or could I maybe visit your café one morning?" Bill asked Fandaz. "I just dropped my Customer Relations Theory course to make room for more independent study."

"Would I have to grade you?" the former inspector general asked, and her hair vines paled noticeably. "I don't do that sort of thing anymore."

"There's no grading involved. I think I just have to write a paper—I mean—a report," Bill corrected himself hastily.

"You don't have to mince words around wood products and grains with me," Fandaz said. "My customer base is ninety-nine percent Humans, and some of the recent arrivals from Earth like to lecture me about paper bags being more environmentally friendly than plastic. I tried to explain to them that Flower recycles everything in a closed system, but it's hard to overcome cherished biases."

"Here," Harry said, giving Bill a glass and then pouring in a bit of seltzer. "Do you want some, Jorb?"

"That tasteless stuff? No, thank you. I'll just go out to the minibar and grab a beer."

Fandaz answered more questions about colorings and ingredients as Harry and Bill worked their way through the samples. Just as they reached the brilliant white coconut spread, Flower announced, "Time's up."

"I was hoping to rinse and dry the bowls before heading back," the Frunge said. "Do you have somebody else coming in to use the kitchen?"

"Time's up for Harry, not for you," the Dollnick AI said. "I have to keep a tight lid on his working hours or he'll overdo it."

"Drain those beans and mash them up for filling," the baker told Bill while removing his apron. "The dough for the red bean buns is in the proofing cabinet, and you know how to steam them the way the captain likes. There's a potluck reception for the new executive officer this evening, and there was almost a mutiny when Captain Pyun brought spoon worms to the last one."

"He should have given them to me," Jorb said, setting his beer on the counter. "I love spoon worms, and they'd go really well with some of that green spread."

"Chili," Bill told him. "That was the only one that was a bit strong for me. When you make these in your café, do you only serve them with vegetable sticks?"

"That's just for samples if people want to try one before buying a takeout container," Fandaz replied. "Keep in mind that we serve Frunge tribute food, and many of the ideas come from recipes that Human contract laborers on our worlds have developed. They're extremely clever about coming up with baked goods that can be made without flour, and I'll admit to trolling through some old gluten-free cookbooks in Humanese for ideas."

"I've heard of that," Bill said. "If you ask Flower to ping me the next time you're baking gluten-free, I'd love to come and learn."

"Only Humans would put so much effort into finding ways to make substitutes for perfectly good food," Jorb said. "Hey, any chance you've gotten in a new batch of Ramen for testing? All of these cold vegetable spreads have given me an appetite for hot noodle soup."

Two

"When are you going to stop working?" Julie asked Vivian.

"Why would I stop?"

"Isn't it, I mean, what did the doctor say?"

"To have Flower ping him when my water breaks, which shouldn't be for another two months," Vivian replied. "I'll probably take a couple of weeks off afterward, and then I'll start bringing the baby to the office. One of the perks of working with my husband is I won't have to change all of the diapers myself."

"But it's your first baby," Julie said. "How do you know you'll be able to take care of it at work?"

"I never got involved in InstaSitter to the extent that my brother did, but I sat for enough babies to know the score. They sleep more than twelve hours a day until they're at least two years old, and the aliens have developed all sorts of interesting playpen technologies."

Julie caught the eye of the waitress and called, "Check, please," while performing the air scribble she had learned from customers during her own waitressing days at the diner. Then she turned back to her friend and asked, "Don't you miss drinking coffee? I couldn't get through the day without mine."

"That's because you let Flower run you ragged," Vivian said. "And I hadn't missed coffee yet this morning until you brought it up."

"Sorry. Anything new from your family?"

"You know they're all workaholics, right? My mom is busy buying or selling alien rights for books in translation when she's not helping my dad run EarthCent Intelligence, and my brother's cooking show has turned into a big business, just like the All Species Cookbook. He'll be even busier when Sephia has her baby."

"I forgot that Jonah's wife is expecting too."

"Sephia was already as big as a house the last time we stopped at Union Station," Vivian said. "I'm going to be an aunt before I become a mother."

"Bill and I have been talking about children," Julie said. "I thought he would want to open his café first, but when I asked, he said that as long as I'm happy, he's happy."

"Talk about pressure. Were you planning on getting married first?"

"As soon as Flower stops nagging," Julie said. She glanced up at the nearest speaker grille even though the Dollnick AI had permission to listen in over the girl's implant. "Flower told me there would be a surprise for me in my office when I go back. I'm afraid to look."

"Let's guess," Vivian said as Julie began counting out coins for the check. "Last year it was a model spaceship because she wanted you to learn how Sharf two-man traders are put together. What's her latest pet project?"

"She's super enthusiastic about the app you're developing for the Human Empire to start keeping track of where everybody is and to locate lost family members, mainly because you're employing so many of the programmers from Bits. But that doesn't have anything to do with me."

"You can participate in the beta test. If you give us a DNA sample, we might even find your father."

"Ugh, no thanks," Julie said, shaking her head vehemently. "He left home before I was old enough to remember his name and he never even tried to get in touch. Why would I want to meet him?"

"Maybe he had a reason for leaving," Vivian said.

"I'm not interested in finding out. Can you sign me up so he won't find me even if he looks?"

"That's the whole point of the new registry. We're building an anonymous messaging system to let related people reach out to each other, but if you never respond, the person sending the message won't know if it's because you're ignoring them or because you haven't registered. They put in a request and we do the matching, eventually with DNA as well as names. The master list of who's in and who's out will never be visible to the public."

"I've forgotten what you decided to call it."

"That's because we haven't yet," Vivian said. "Samuel likes HumanBook, but the programmers are pushing for Bloodster, probably because it sounds like an action game."

"And which do you want?" Julie asked.

"Neither. I'm still trying to come up with an app name that captures the idea of family trees."

"Why not FamilyTree?"

"It doesn't include anything about the genetic testing and we wouldn't be able to get a trademark because it's a generic term," Vivian said. "I know it seems like a silly thing to get hung up on, but brand names have a way of taking on lives of their own, and it's going to be the Human Empire's flagship service."

"I guess as long as you're beta testing you can get away without a catchy name," Julie said. "And thanks for coming to The Spoon with me. The eggs from the griddle here are just better than I can make in a pan back home."

"The pancakes hit the spot, especially with the butter and the maple syrup," Vivian said, rising slowly to her feet. "Next time we'll have brunch at the Blue Tea Café, my treat. And don't forget to ping and tell me what Flower's surprise turns out to be."

When Julie reached the offices of Flower Industries, she would have sworn that the latest co-op student working the reception desk was hiding a smile behind his hand. She walked down the short corridor to her office, swiped open the door, and said, "You have to be kidding me."

"Now don't jump to conclusions," Flower said. "I'm not going to make you take it apart and put it together again."

"I think I'd rather do that than learn how to operate it," Julie said. "I saw the demo hologram before you bought these machines, and everything moved so fast I'd be afraid of sewing my hand up in a seam."

"Don't be silly, the needle doesn't rise high enough, and this is the prototype I had Razood convert to a treadle."

"Is that another name for microwave power transmission or something? Where's the collector antenna, or does the Frunge design work off of a hidden fuel pack or batteries?"

"Look closer," Flower said.

"Do you mean it has an old-fashioned power cord? I didn't think this office had any outlets." Julie studied the Frunge sewing machine, one of a hundred Flower had recently purchased to subcontract production for SBJ Fashions, and she realized that something looked different. "What's with the big shiny wheel on the side?"

"It's a flywheel," the Dollnick AI said. "Razood replaced the motor with a treadle. Look under the machine, near the floor."

"Is that a treadle? It looks like he went overboard with iron scrollwork to make a footrest."

"A treadle translates the up and down motion of your feet into a circular motion for a belt to drive a shaft," Flower explained. "The earliest Human sewing machines were all powered by treadles. It's hard to believe that your people started using them for the purpose less than three hundred years ago, but the basic principle works for lathes and any other type of machinery that can be operated by a belt drive with modest effort."

Her curiosity piqued, Julie sat at the machine and tried pushing down the treadle with both feet. The flywheel at the side turned, but the needle remained stationary and the mechanism didn't make the universally recognizable sewing machine sound.

"Did anybody test this after Razood put it together?" she asked.

"It works perfectly," Flower said. "I told him to build it with a tension knob on the flywheel so you could practice working the treadle without the distraction of the needle going up and down."

"I already figured out the treadle part," Julie said, tightening the knob and pushing with her feet again. The machine made a satisfying sound. "Now it's working."

"Did you notice that the flywheel turned the opposite direction this time? If you were working for real, the thread would have broken, and then you'd have to remove the stitches and start over again."

"Oh." Julie pushed the chair back and lowered her head to study the mechanism under the sewing desk as she worked the treadle. "How do I choose which direction to go? Does it matter where I put my feet?"

"You'll want to keep one foot near the front and the other on the back so you can maintain a steady rocking motion, but the only way to control the direction of the flywheel is to start it with your hand and pay attention that it keeps going the right way."

"Weird."

"There's nothing weird about treadle technology," the Dollnick AI said. "Every bipedal species has used it at one time or another."

"Follow-up question," Julie said, unconsciously mimicking a reporter from the Children's News Network. "Why do you want me to learn how to work a treadle sewing machine?"

"The Alts have agreed to share Earth Two with humanity but they're placing strict limits on the usage of technology to avoid environmental damage. Machinery will only be allowed if it's powered by muscles."

"What about solar power, water power, or windmills?"

"There's an exception for windmills driving grindstones, but water power requires dams, and there are already too many of those on Earth Two, thanks to an accidental release of beavers. As for solar power or advanced fuel packs, the Alts are worried that they would just serve as gateway technologies and lead to backsliding. A list of limited exceptions includes Verlock heat stones, Drazen lanterns, and a few other clean alien technologies."

"Okay," Julie said slowly. "But what does the Alts sharing Earth Two with people willing to agree to technology limitations have to do with your giving me a treadle-powered sewing machine?"

"It's a loan, and Earth Two hasn't been connected to the tunnel network yet because it doesn't meet the Stryx requirements for population or economic activity. I've been negotiating with the appropriate parties to ferry colonists there from Earth and other locations along our circuit."

"And you want me to learn how to sew so I can be your saleswoman for the old-fashioned machines you're going to produce?"

"I wasn't planning on going into the treadle-powered business, but you may have a good idea there," the Dollnick AI said. "Unfortunately, many of the colonists will be from the Old Way movement, and they frown upon using machines that are mass-produced by advanced technology."

"How do you know so much about them?"

"I've digested all of the digital books in our library, including the collection Zick's mother brought from Bits. Earth has a long history of back-to-nature movements and religious communities that reject aspects of modern technology for one reason or another. It's fascinating to observe a civilization at such an early stage of its development."

"So if you don't want me to sell them sewing—" Julie cut herself off with a groan as the realization sank in. "Am I your new head of ferrying services or something?"

"You're my executive assistant, and somebody has to be in charge," Flower said. "The leaders of the Old Way communities may not be comfortable dealing with me directly as I'm an artificial intelligence. I'm hoping that learning how to sew with a treadle machine will help you understand them a little better."

"But what about Captain Pyun and Lynx? Aren't they in charge of dealing with temporary passengers?"

"They work for Eccentric Enterprises, which is a thin cover for EarthCent Intelligence. You work for me."

"I don't know anything about transporting large numbers of people between planets," Julie protested. "And what if they bring their farm animals with them?"

"We have plenty of room, and I've been preparing one of the underutilized ag decks for grazing," the Dollnick AI said. "Thanks to MultiCon and the other events we've hosted, you already know a great deal about providing hospitality as we move between planets. Think of the ferrying service as ColonyCon if it makes you more comfortable."

"You've got to be kidding me."

"Keep in mind that I'll be continuing my circuit between Earth and Union Station with scheduled stops at the sovereign human communities, so most of our guests will be here for weeks, if not months. In addition, not all of the colonists will be familiar with low-tech living, so I'll be offering training to prepare them for their new lives."

"An advanced artificial intelligence is going to teach people how to live without technology?" Julie asked. "Doesn't that defeat the point?"

"I plan to hire instructors from the Old Way movement—it will give them something to do while they're in transit. And don't forget about Colonial Jeevesburg. Razood has already agreed to teach a basic blacksmithing workshop, and the other craftspeople will welcome the opportunity to earn something extra while we're moving between stops and there aren't any tourists visiting."

"I didn't think of that," Julie said, turning the flywheel towards herself with her right hand and starting a rocking motion on the treadle. "Hey, it works."

"Before we go any further, I need to ask if you have any experience with sewing," Flower said.

"Not with a machine. I can use a needle and thread to do minor repairs, but I never did anything fancy."

"Excellent. That means you won't have to unlearn any bad habits."

"Wait a second," Julie said. "The needle only goes up and down, right? How can it be making stitches if it doesn't get pulled through to the other side and then come back from the bottom through a new hole?"

"I'll explain that after you learn how to keep the flywheel going the right direction and move the work under the needle," Flower said. "Since you've never sewn with a machine, it's important to understand that you won't be running a never-ending seam. You need to master the skill of frequently starting and stopping."

"You don't know how the stitching works, do you?"

"That was the crudest attempt at reverse psychology I've been subjected to in my twenty thousand years of existence. I take it Bill told you about his Customer Relations Theory class."

"And that you asked him to help you set up Razood and Fandaz," Julie said, frowning as the flywheel reversed direction after she stopped rocking her feet and tried to start again. "Did people really sew like this?"

"The treadle-powered sewing machine was one of the greatest successes of Earth's industrial age," Flower said. "The manufacturers introduced installment plans to allow housewives who couldn't afford machines to pay for them over time. It was the beginning of the slippery slope of living on credit that eventually led to the Stryx intervening before your species could commit suicide via monetary policy."

"Are you making this up to motivate me? I thought loaning money went back to biblical times, if not further."

"You're thinking about somebody pledging their coat for money to eat and redeeming it at the end of the day. I'm talking about the birth of consumer credit. Humans began making other major purchases on installments at the same time, primarily pianos, expensive furniture, and modern farm equipment, but the sewing machine did the most to get average people around the world hooked on payment plans."

"But that must have been centuries before the Stryx opened Earth," Julie pointed out. "I watched that Grenouthian documentary about the collapse of Earth's monetary system. It's not the fault of women buying sewing machines to make their own clothes that governments started printing money to buy their own debt."

"Not directly, but it was the beginning of the end of humanity's patience with deferred gratification, a fundamental character trait for the advancement of sentients," Flower explained. "Over the course of two hundred years of easy credit, your people lost the ability to make hard choices about the allocation of finite resources. Borrowing from future generations to solve today's problems was presented as a virtue rather than a vice."

Julie halted the rocking motion with her feet and stopped the flywheel with her right hand at the same time. "I've got this down. I'm ready to try sewing something." When the ship's AI failed to respond, she added, "It's not an instant gratification thing—you know I can defer with the best of them. I just don't learn things piecemeal the way Dollnicks teach everything. I need to see the whole picture."

"Fine. Do you still have that sketch pad you bought from Ellen when you were going to try your hand at art?"

"I haven't given up yet. I've just been busy."

"So here's your chance to draw something," Flower said. "Use a pencil to trace an outline on a piece of paper. That plate you keep forgetting to return to the cafeteria would be perfect."

"I never should have agreed to you installing a camera in my office," Julie muttered as she followed the AI's instructions. "And drawing a line around a plate isn't my idea of art."

"Now find a straight edge and draw a couple of lines across the paper, it doesn't matter where."

"Are you trying to teach me trigonometry again? I told you I'd never need it and I haven't changed my mind."

"I don't want to rush into showing you how to thread the machine, and it's easier to learn how to control the feed with paper than with cloth," Flower said as Julie drew three lines across the circle.

"Oh, I get it," the girl said, putting the paper on the sewing table. "What's next?"

"Lift your foot and slide the paper underneath."

"On the treadle? Are you making fun of me?"

"I was referring to the presser foot that holds the fabric against the throat plate while you sew," Flower said. "There's a lever on the back of the sewing head that raises and lowers the presser foot."

"You should have given me a picture with the basic parts all labeled," Julie said, correctly guessing that the sewing head was the business end of the machine housing the needle mechanism. She found the lever and raised the presser foot. "It looks like little teeth are sticking up from that plate thing. Won't they damage the fabric?"

"Those are the feed dogs, and they're an essential part of the design. They rise up to move the fabric forward and then drop back to their starting position while the needle is performing the stitch. When you're sewing at full speed, it all happens so quickly that you won't even notice the fabric is stopping while the needle is poking through, but if you think about it, you'll see that it couldn't work otherwise."

"So I slide my paper in and lower the presser foot on top," Julie said as she carried out the action. "Spin the flywheel towards myself, start rocking the treadle, and—I'm sewing!"

"You're making holes in a piece of paper," Flower corrected her. "When you can land all of the holes near the lines you've drawn, I'll teach you how to sew with fabric and thread."

"Sure, that will give you time to figure it out first."

"The only time anybody ever successfully used reverse psychology on me, it was Stryx Gryph. He said he couldn't blame me if I didn't want to work with humanity because the odds of any colony ship AI succeeding in the job were about the same as winning the lottery."

Three

Jack finished his standard spiel about the buddy system and locator bracelets for members of the independent living cooperative on an outing and added, "One more thing. We'll be handing out our usual recruiting fliers, but instead of an ad on the back from the Farling doctor for discounted medical procedures, you'll see that the Human Empire is seeking colonists with terraforming experience for Earth Two."

"Don't you think people our age are a bit too old for that kind of work?" somebody called out from a few rows back in the shuttle.

"No question about it, but most of the people on this planet have completed at least one long-term contract working for the Dollnicks on an ag world or terraforming," the president of the independent living cooperative explained. "We'll see some folks in their sixties and seventies who are still working, but the average age is probably under forty."

"Do we have a recruiting quota?" a woman seated further back in the shuttle called out. "This is my first field trip."

"The independent living cooperative is already self-sustaining so there's no pressure. At our last board meeting, we considered dropping recruiting on field trips, but it's a good way to meet new people you never would have spoken to otherwise."

"Attention all passengers," Flower's voice came over the public address system. "We will be landing on Kurel in approximately two minutes. Please return to your seats and place the chair backs in the upright position for landing. And thank you for choosing Flower Transportation."

Harry's wife folded down the view screen on the small immersive camera she borrowed from the Grenouthian director whenever the independent living cooperative went on a field trip and slid it under the seat in front of her.

"Aren't you going to put the footrest down?" her husband asked. "Your feet are just dangling."

"We'll be on the ground in two minutes," Irene said. "I hope we'll get to see some farms. The last Dollnick open world we visited was all factory towns, but everybody says that the ag worlds are lovely."

"Jack went back to an ag world for a second stint after a couple of years of trying to make it as an independent trader with the money he saved from his first contract," Dave said from the seat on Harry's other side. "I don't have any regrets about never leaving Earth during my career in sales, but sometimes I think if I had spent more time doing manual labor I might have had less trouble with my health."

"Being a salesman is hard work, and stress does a number on everybody's health," Harry said. "I remember a rep who came into the bakery year after year just to take an order for a few gross of folding cake boxes, and there was even a guy who eked out a living selling specialty paper, like cupcake liners and parchment for cookie trays. I always told him that he was my guy and I'd order from him even if he didn't make the trip. He said that if he'd learned one thing in his life it was the importance of showing up."

"He probably had a half-dozen other customers in your area that he could visit on the same day. Besides, outside salesmen can't spend their lives cold calling or working tradeshow booths. Sometimes it's nice just to see a friendly face and hear how things are going in the industry."

"Harry was always in the back baking," Irene said as she refastened the safety restraint she had taken off while stowing the camera. "I'm the one who worked the counter and talked with our regular customers. It's only since we moved to Flower that he's become such a people person."

"I don't think I've changed that much," Harry said. "It's not like I was ever a loner."

"You're on a first-name basis with more aliens than anybody else in the cooperative."

"Socializing with aliens makes me a people person?"

"I think it's a fair description," Irene said.

Harry shrugged. "I relate to them as if they were people because I'm too old to learn a new way, but it's hard to forget that they're aliens when they do things we wouldn't dream of trying."

"Like what?" Dave asked as the shuttle set down with barely a bump. They were immediately surrounded by the sound of buckles being undone and safety restraints reeling back into their holders, but the experienced travelers remained in their seats rather than standing in the aisles while waiting for the doors to open.

"The other day Brynlan came in and asked if I could boil a large pot of water. It only takes a few seconds on the Dollnick induction stove, and as soon as it was boiling, he stuck his hand in and kept it there for a few minutes. He'd just written a long report and his fingers were stiff."

"Since when do Verlocks write reports on paper?" Irene asked.

"It's the latest fad with the intelligence crowd," Harry told her. "It's especially crazy because the Verlocks probably have the best encryption technology on the tunnel network, other than the Stryx. I try not to pay attention when they're discussing tradecraft in the cafeteria, but Flower has been offering them courier services via her new Tunnel Trips rental franchise. So the aliens have all started playing at doing things like the spies in immersive dramas in order to have documents to send."

"It seems a bit immature for advanced species."

"Aliens know how to have a good time," Dave said. "I've worked with most of them while standing in for M793qK on the anime set at Flower Studios. They're all masters at turning lemons into lemonade, and then somebody always spikes the punch."

"The aisles are clearing," Harry said. "We better get going before Nancy runs out of bracelets."

"Is *Everyday Superheroes* going into its third season?" Irene asked as she retrieved the immersive camera from under the seat in front of her. A quick tap enabled the autostabilizer that allowed the camera to float free, and she brought it up chest-high using the gesture controls. "I've lost track since Harry got killed off."

"I'm not really dead," her husband reminded her. "M793qK's character, the Evil Farling Mastermind, put me in a stasis pod and shot me into space."

Jack and Nancy were standing on either side of the ramp handing out tracking bracelets to cooperative members as they exited the shuttle. "Give mine to Harry," Irene told Nancy. "I don't want to take any chances while I'm guiding the camera."

"The local tourist council has sent floater buses for us and they're offering two options for visiting groups," Nancy said as she handed Harry the pair of bracelets. "The blue floater buses are going into the city, which the original Dollnick settlers built over a hundred thousand years ago, so there's a lot of interesting architecture. The green floater buses are doing an agricultural tour, with lunch at an Old Way community."

"That's the one I want to do," Irene immediately told Harry. "Are you coming with us, Dave?"

"You know me and food," the former salesman said. "I can always study up on Dollnick architecture from a book."

"Go ahead and I'll catch up," Irene told the men. "I want to get some footage of people getting on the bus."

"Does Flower have you filming scenes for a commercial again?" Jack asked her. "She didn't mention anything about new ad spend at the last board meeting for the cooperative."

"I signed up for a course in immersive documentary making at the Open University," Irene said, shooting Nancy a guilty look. "I've always had an interest, but every time you do one of those questionnaires about future courses for continuing education, I'm the only one who puts it down."

"You don't have to apologize about taking an outside class," Nancy said with a laugh. "I signed up with the Open University myself for a series of lectures on Imperial Vergallian history. And if the course works out for you, maybe you can teach it to the other members of our independent living cooperative."

"But nobody will show up."

"There's a difference between the classes people say they want and what they'll actually register for if it's on the calendar," the retired teacher told her, and turned to look back up the ramp. "Was there anybody left on board after you?"

"Not unless they were in the bathroom," Irene said. "Which floater bus are you and Jack taking?"

"The green bus, of course," Jack answered for his wife. "Nancy is always asking me questions about the work I did on ag worlds, and now I'll be able to show her in person." He glanced at the three green busses, two of which were empty, and headed for the one that was perhaps three-quarters full.

Irene split her attention between where she was placing her feet and what was shown on the camera's view screen as she followed the other members of the cooperative to the green bus at the front of the line. The Dollnicks used advanced field technology to protect passengers from the weather, so it was more like riding in a boat than a bus. The sides only came up as high as the seatback, and the top was open to the sky.

"Are you also the tour guide?" Jack asked the driver as the bus began to pull away from the spaceport.

"I'm just here to make sure you don't get lost," the woman said. "There's usually a volunteer on each bus to tell people what they're seeing, but I'm guessing they all went up to orbit to visit Flower. Feel free to jump in if you know anything about agriculture."

"Thank you, I will." Jack accepted the offer of a surprisingly bulky wireless microphone from the driver. "I hope the other drivers aren't losing a day's work because most of our people chose to go into the city."

"They're volunteers too, so they aren't losing out on any pay," the woman said. "If you're planning on standing for the whole trip, safety regulations require that you tie off to the railing. There's a harness in the compartment under the front seat."

Jack retrieved the harness, buckled it on, and tied himself off to the railing before testing the microphone. "Can everybody hear me?"

"Perfectly," Dave called back.

"I guess I'll be playing tour guide even though I've never been here before. I can tell you that the ground we're floating over is typical for a world that the Dollnicks have terraformed for agriculture. I think I can just make out some snow-capped mountain peaks in the distance."

"Why didn't they flatten 'em?" somebody asked.

"Terraforming engineers use mountain ranges as windbreaks and to store excess atmospheric water as ice and snow," Jack explained. "A world like this has weather control satellites, but there's no free lunch in the universe. A planet that can maintain the desired climate without external controls will be more profitable in the long run than one that requires constant energy input from space. Dollnicks are also big on skiing."

"How do they ski with four arms?" Harry asked.

"Better than we do with two," Jack replied with a laugh. "And river systems are important for ag worlds if you don't want to be totally reliant on rainfall and wells. Mountains play a role in that too."

Everybody started talking at the same time, pointing at the fields off the right side of the bus where a team of draft horses was pulling a seed drill that looked like it might have been borrowed from a manor house in Victorian England.

"You never said anything about farming with horses, Jack," Nancy said from her seat.

"They must be from one of the Old Way communities," Jack said as everybody's head swiveled to watch the horses while the floater bus zipped by. "The Dollnicks hire people as farm labor on ag worlds in keeping with the tunnel network practice of minimizing automation wherever possible, but they always provided us with the latest equipment."

"How about the Vergallians?" somebody else asked.

"I've never worked for the Vergallians, but I've heard that most of the planets in their empire operate under partial tech bans," Jack said. "There's another seed drill working in the next field over so they're just putting in a new crop. It will be interesting to find out when we stop whether they're growing for themselves or for export."

Irene finessed the floating immersive camera a little to the side before speaking so it wasn't blocking her face. "I never understood how it can be more efficient to move food between star systems than to grow it locally."

"It depends on the planets. I know we used to export to some mining worlds that didn't even have atmospheres. All of the work was carried out in sealed tunnels, and while the aliens have the technology to grow food in those conditions, it's cheaper to import most things and only grow fresh vegetables."

"What if the world isn't developed enough to be on the tunnel network?"

"Jump-capable container ships can deliver amazing tonnage at a surprisingly low cost," Jack said. "Think about terraforming jobs. Reengineering a planet can take thousands of years before you get to the point that anything would grow there. If there's a colony ship like Flower supporting the job, she could feed a few million workers without a problem from her ag decks. But I think most commercial terraforming jobs start with a purpose-built habitat that gets towed into orbit. If you made the habitat big enough they could grow their own food, but that requires more people."

"How many planets are the Dollnicks terraforming at any given time?" a man called from the back of the bus. "It can't be that big of a market."

"I don't know the number, but it's a lot," Jack said. "The different species all have preferred activities where they invest their excess energy and capital. For the Dollnicks, it's large engineering projects, and it doesn't get any bigger than terraforming a new world and putting in space elevators."

Twenty questions and forty-five minutes later, the floater bus crossed over a dirt road with well-worn ruts from wagon wheels and settled to the ground in front of a large barn. The retirees disembarked with the enthusiasm, if not the speed, of school kids on a field trip. They were met by a tall woman with a black bonnet covering her blonde hair.

"Welcome to New Wisconsin Six," she greeted them. "My name is Imogene and I'll be your guide. Is somebody in charge?"

"I'm the president of our independent living cooperative," Jack said, and introduced himself. "Could I ask why I saw so many abandoned cellar holes with stone foundations as we floated in?"

"Our community is in the process of a division," the woman said. "When the population grows to the point that the adults can't fit in a single meeting house, the Old Way tradition is to start a new community."

"Wouldn't it be easier to put an addition on the meeting house, or build a new one?" Dave asked.

"We don't believe that bigger is necessarily better. In fact, the opposite is often true. But this division marks the first time since we left Earth that the new community is moving off-planet, which is why there are so many missing buildings. They were disassembled for shipping two months ago, and the group that's moving to Earth Two has been sending the containers up on the space elevator so they'd be waiting in orbit when Flower arrived."

"Is there a lack of available farmland on Kurel?" Nancy asked.

Imogene smiled sadly. "No, and the lease terms are attractive, but the Dollnicks…" she trailed off and shook her head.

"They aren't impressed by your old-fashioned farming methods," Jack guessed.

"Let's just say that they're waiting for us to come to our senses. A few weeks after we determined it was time for a division and contacted Prince Drume's land agent about available tracts, a ship landed nearby and we received a visit from an attractive artificial person. It seems that Flower is offering a commission to land agents who notify her about available human communities with experience in low-tech farming or terraforming. Dewey made such an effective pitch for Earth Two that our new division signed up."

"I wondered why we were stopping here when it wasn't on the original schedule," Jack said. "I hope you aren't losing anybody close to you."

"My older brother and his family, but that's always how it is when you live in small communities," the woman said. "If we didn't have these divisions, we'd grow to the point where it was impossible to govern by mutual consent, not to mention the issue of inbreeding. If everything goes well on Earth Two, perhaps we'll follow when our current lease runs out in another five years." Imogene began walking backward to the large barn, frequently checking over her shoulder to make sure she wouldn't trip or slip in fresh manure. "Do you have any questions before I show you the milking parlor?"

"Aren't you worried about stepping on a chicken?" one of the retirees asked.

"They're pretty good about getting out of the way."

"It looks to me like you've established a limited Earth-type ecosystem here," Jack said. "On the ag worlds where I worked, the Dollnicks set up containment fields and facilities so we could grow our own vegetables, but they were very careful to make sure we didn't introduce invasive species."

"Prince Drume is running an experiment on Kurel," Imogene explained. "The Dollnicks take a biological inventory of all the flora and fauna we import for our farms. Occasionally they reject something at customs as too dangerous, but given their experience in ecosystem engineering and advanced life sciences, they're confident that with a little work, they can handle any runaway outbreaks."

"That seems like a risky game to play with a whole planet," Nancy said.

Imogene paused at the entrance of the barn to reply. "Yes, in a sense it is, but in another sense, it's all a sort of game to the Dollnicks. They're natural problem solvers, but like all of the advanced species, they've mastered their environment to the point that life can be a bit dull for those who aren't self-starters."

"I'm not sure I understand."

"Just because they have a greater natural capacity for learning and more knowledge resources than humanity doesn't mean that they're all scientists, artists, or entrepreneurs," Imogene explained. "The average Dollnick may be more proactive than the average human, but it's only when life throws up a challenge that you see them at their best."

"And people in the Old Way movement live with limited technology because you want to make life more challenging?" Harry asked.

"It's more about creating community and building strong families," Imogene said. "We believe that being able to turn on a holographic communicator and talk to somebody on the other side of the planet does the opposite of bringing people closer together. It gives them an excuse to remain apart."

"Can you give us an example of technology that you use?" Irene asked from behind the camera's view screen.

"I can give you several, starting with our fields. Have you noticed how flat they are?"

"I thought that was because the Dollnicks leased them to you that way."

"But the land moves and reshapes itself over time," Imogene said. "When we leased this farm, we paid for a contractor to come in and laser level the fields. It limits the runoff and makes us a little less dependent on the weather control satellites operated by Prince Drume's technicians."

"Anything you use every day?" Irene followed up.

"The equipment in the milking parlor that you're about to see. In addition to providing dairy products for ourselves, we sell the excess in the open market, which means conforming to modern standards for refrigerated storage and quality testing. But we're still an organic dairy and I'm sure you'll taste the difference when you sample our ice cream."

"That's all the questions we have," Dave said, silencing the others with a sharp wave. "Let's get to those samples."

Four

"Is Sam—uh, the First Administrator in?" Bill asked the new receptionist in the Human Empire headquarters.

"Your name?"

"Bill. Flower sent me."

"Don't I know you from the Open University?" the girl asked. "I'm studying hotel management."

"I'm in the food and restaurant track, but mainly independent study," Bill told her. "Is this your co-op job?"

"As of yesterday," the receptionist said as she rose, gesturing for Bill to follow. "Flower has made herself the dean of the hospitality school and she thinks I'll get more varied experience here than working on the Con deck. I'm afraid she's grooming me to take the civil service exam." The door to Samuel's office slid open at her approach, and she announced, "Bill is here to see you, First Administrator."

"No titles," Samuel reminded her. "How much free time do you have this afternoon, Bill?"

"I'm completely open. This was going to be one of my rotation days where Flower has me work in her different businesses just to get familiar with them, but she canceled when you asked for help."

"I hope it's nothing you were looking forward to."

"Shadowing a quality control inspector at Flower Shipyards?" Bill shook his head. "If she wanted me to help pick fruit, at least I have experience with that, but inspecting

Sharf two-man traders isn't something I'm qualified to do. I keep telling her that I don't learn much from spending an afternoon here and there, but she thinks it will prevent me from panicking if she ever wants me to cover for somebody. What's up?"

"Did you hear that Flower took on board an Old Way community for transport to Earth Two while we were stopped at Kurel?" Samuel asked.

"I helped Dewey check in their containers for long-term storage a couple of days ago. They brought a bunch of disassembled barns with them. The timbers were bigger than most tree trunks I saw growing up in the city."

"I want to visit them and show the flag for the Human Empire," Samuel said. "Vivian wasn't feeling up to it today, and our Cayl mentor said that I should never go on official business alone or I'll cheapen our brand."

"It could be interesting," Bill said. "Dewey helped them bring their livestock on board and he said some of the animals were pretty upset about their short stint in weightlessness. There was a lot of cleaning up involved."

"Hold the fort until I get back, Linda," Samuel told the receptionist on the way out. "If any emergencies come up, just have Flower ping me."

When Bill and Samuel exited the lift tube capsule on the ag deck where Flower was hosting the Old Way colonists and their livestock, they almost ran into Lume, the station chief for Dollnick Intelligence who ran a lunch counter in the food court for cover.

"Bill, Samuel," the four-armed alien greeted them. "If you're here recruiting agents you'll have to get in line."

"Seriously?" Bill asked. "Why would you need intelligence sources on Earth Two? There's nothing there, and it's not like the Alts or a bunch of our people living in tech-ban colonies are going to make trouble for anybody."

"I see that Yaem has a lot to teach you about the business," Lume said. "All information is of equal value until it isn't, and the Stryx are the only sentients I'm aware of with the predictive powers to know what matters ahead of time. Signing up casual agents on a pay-go basis is the cheapest insurance policy an intelligence service can have."

"But if they're living in a tech-ban community without access to the Stryxnet, how can they contact you if they have anything important to report?" Samuel asked.

"You've heard of mail, haven't you? It may not be the fastest way to transfer information, but given the number of interstellar ships that will be traveling to Earth Two, I estimate no more than a cycle on average to get a letter."

"To Flower?"

"Exactly," Lume said. "Most ships jumping away from Earth Two will soon visit a Stryx station, or at least a system on the tunnel network. Every package service and post office with a Stryxnet connection receives updated routing information about our scheduled stops from Flower herself."

"The postage will probably cost more than Old Way farmers earn in a month, if they're even using money on Earth Two," Samuel pointed out.

"I provided each of my new recruits with a book of Dollnick first-class stamps. The hard part was teaching them how to use the one-time coding pads for encryption." The Dollnick cocked his head and stared off to the side for a moment, obviously reading a message on his heads-up display. "Sorry, I have to run. And Bill, if you and Yaem need some pointers on tradecraft, I can fill you in the next time we have lunch together in Harry's cafeteria."

"Have you ever sent a letter?" Bill asked Samuel after the lift tube doors closed behind Lume.

"Just last week," the EarthCent ambassador's son admitted. "Did you know Flower opened a Tunnel Trips franchise?"

"She wants me to train there when I have time."

"My family started the business in the hold my Dad rents from the Stryx on Union Station. The rental ships are mainly repurposed space taxis, so they're limited to running between Stryx stations and orbital destinations connected to the tunnel network. Flower is installing lockboxes so they can carry small packages and letters, which means I don't have any excuse not to write home."

"I assumed that with you being First Administrator of the Human Empire and Flower having an unlimited bandwidth Stryxnet connection, you could talk to your family any time."

"My niece, Fenna, needed a pen pal for a school project. I almost gave up on finding an envelope, but Vivian went to the bazaar and asked one of the information desk volunteers. It turned out there's a stationery booth run by a Vergallian."

"You mean the booth never moves?"

"Oh, sorry," Samuel said as they stepped aside to avoid an enormous draft horse pulling a wagon. "It's one of those words that sounds the same but is spelled differently, and there's no reason you would ever have come across it. The 'stationary' that stays in one place has an 'a' instead of an 'e' near the end. I only know about the writing supplies version because I studied Vergallian and they have hundreds of specialized words relating to correspondence."

"You don't have to apologize about being smarter than me," Bill said, and then waved when he spotted Dewey coming towards them. "It would be pretty sad if you didn't know more than I do after spending most of your life in school."

"Flower asked me to introduce you to the colonists," Dewey said by way of a greeting. "I've been spending my spare time here learning about the Old Way movement and I'm thinking of writing something about them."

"For the Galactic Free Press?" Samuel asked.

"Maybe for an academic journal," the artificial person said. "I'm more interested in the evolution of their societal structure than their day-to-day lives."

Bill lowered his voice and asked, "Did you tell them that you're, uh…"

"Artificial intelligence inhabiting an alien-built android body?" Dewey completed the sentence. "Yes, and their elders asked me to give them a few hours to talk it over. In the end, they decided that there was no reason we can't be friends as long as I respect their rules."

"I guess I don't really understand the anti-technology thing."

"It's part of what I find so interesting about their history," Dewey said as he led them towards a temporary encampment. "I'm trying to trace how much of their philosophy originates in Earth's pre-Stryx religious and social movements and how much is simply borrowed from the Vergallians and other advanced species."

"I can't believe that Flower put them in tents," Samuel said. "Did they refuse to occupy regular cabins?"

"The tents were their choice. Flower offered a variety of options, including obtaining natural construction materials and letting them build houses, but the colonists don't expect to be on board for more than a few months. The tents aren't necessary for shelter from the elements, but they provide privacy, storage for their personal possessions, and a place to return to when the lights dim for the night cycle."

"So everybody is treating it like a long camping vacation?"

Dewey shook his head. "They made a deal with Flower to take over all of the agricultural work her bots were doing on this section of the deck. And living on board doesn't change the amount of time they spend preparing meals, making clothes, and doing all of the other things one would expect from a largely self-sufficient community."

"Is that the Grenouthian director?" Bill asked, squinting up the curvature of the deck to where he thought he saw a giant rabbit manipulating a pair of floating immersive cameras.

"He's here to work on an independent documentary," Dewey said. "At first I assumed it was just a cover to let him meet people and try to recruit some sleeper agents for Grenouthian Intelligence, but he appears to be taking the production seriously. I think he believes that the story of the first Old Way colonists being transported to Earth Two might win him a prize in one of the smaller festivals."

"It looks like he's moving to intercept us before we get to the tents."

"You are correct," Dewey said a moment later. "It never ceases to amaze me how the Human brain allows you to perform complex calculations involving analytical geometry and the multiple external factors related to catching a ball or shooting a bow and arrow, all without the ability to solve the underlying equations on paper."

"That's the one advantage biologicals have over artificial intelligence," Samuel said. "Evolution selects for brains that are good at visual processing, extrapolations, and educated guesses."

"What's in the large tent we're heading for?" Bill asked.

"The woodshop," Dewey said. "Oscar, the expedition leader of this community, is a cabinetmaker by trade. He brought along a stock of wood to make furniture and is continuing his apprentice's training while in transit."

"I thought Old Way groups were governed by a council of elders for day-to-day decisions and community meetings for anything major," Samuel said.

"When a group divides and half of the membership leaves to start a new settlement, it's important to have an executive capable of making quick decisions during the transition period," Dewey said. "You won't get far if everybody has to stop and vote at every turn in the road or change in the weather."

"Hold on there," the Grenouthian director called as he closed to polite speaking distance. "I want to capture this moment for posterity."

"I'm just here to get acquainted," Samuel said.

"The head of the Human Empire travels to meet the expedition leader of the first Human community bound for Earth Two and you think it's not a big deal?" The alien shook his head in disbelief. "It's that kind of attitude that explains why you don't have any decent digital records of the period on Earth when your history was actually interesting."

"We've only had film for a few hundred years, and digital imagery for about half that time."

"Then you should have employed sketch artists. I've seen oil paintings of supposedly historical events from your homeworld that were obviously staged well after the events took place. Now just let me get inside first and I'll capture your meeting with Oscar. Try to say something memorable."

"My first words to be recorded for posterity," Samuel said as the Grenouthian director brushed past them and entered the tent. "Anybody have any ideas?"

"I just ran a quick search of famous greetings from Earth's history, and 'Doctor Livingston, I presume,' came out at the top," Dewey said.

"Just say whatever you'd normally say," Bill told the EarthCent ambassador's son. "I was on *Everyday Superheroes* for two seasons and the Grenouthian director always gives instructions like that when he's working."

Samuel followed Dewey into the tent and immediately noticed one of the floating cameras was pointing his way. The second camera was focused on a middle-aged giant of a man who was holding a chisel to a piece of wood that was blurred from the motion of turning in a lathe. Little chips of hardwood seemed to fly off the tip of the chisel, and the sound of the operation was interrupted by a regular thumping. The man was so intent on his work that he didn't notice the newcomers for almost a minute.

"Fantastic," the Grenouthian mouthed in his own language.

"Oscar," the artificial person said loudly when the woodworker looked up from his lathe.

"What brings you back to the shop so soon, Dewey?" Oscar asked.

"I'd like to introduce you to my friends, Samuel McAllister and Bill," the artificial person said.

"Pleased to meet you both," Oscar said, coming out from behind the lathe. He extended a callused hand to each of the young men in turn. "Do you both work for Flower?"

"I'm with the Human Empire, and Bill helps us sometimes when Flower isn't keeping him too busy," Samuel said. "The Human Empire is scheduled to replace EarthCent in another century or so, and Flower sort of works for EarthCent. The Human Empire is still in the startup phase, and we established our headquarters on board to take advantage of the fact that Flower is continually visiting the planets and space structures with large populations of Earth expatriates, including Earth Two going forward."

"I see," Oscar said, though he didn't sound convinced. "So if I have any issues with Flower, I can talk to you?"

"I'd be happy to act as a middleman for you as long as I'm not stepping on Dewey's toes."

"Be my guest," the artificial person said. "As a full-time employee of Flower's, I have a conflict of interest when it comes to representing passengers."

Oscar nodded and took a moment to gather his thoughts. "We're all acutely conscious of the fact that we're guests and that our passage to Earth Two has been heavily subsidized. But we aren't willing to give up who we are in return for saving a substantial amount of Stryx creds, even if the alternative means going into debt."

"Of course not," Samuel said. "Are your people having issues with the ship's rules, like the morning calisthenics and the required team sport?"

"We've always done morning stretching exercises as a community, and Flower has agreed to recognize some of our regular activities as equivalent to team sports. I don't want to sound ungracious, but there are a number of things troubling us, the largest of which is Flower's push to enroll our children in her schools."

"She's probably concerned that you've left your educational infrastructure behind and doesn't want your children to miss out on their studies during the long trip," Samuel said, but he noticed that Oscar was already shaking his head in the negative. "Is it a curriculum issue? I know that Flower is very proud of her schools, but I'm sure she could make adjustments for your beliefs."

"Members of the Old Way movement believe that educating our children is the foundation of our community. The first building we erect in a new settlement is the schoolhouse, which also serves as the meeting hall for collective decision-making. I'm sure we would have differences with Flower over the curriculum as well, but the main point is that all of the adults in our community take turns as teachers."

"Does Flower object to their running their own school here on the ag deck?" Samuel asked Dewey.

"It's more complicated than that," the artificial person said. "There's also the issue of what you might call book-learning versus vocational training. Flower is an old-fashioned Dollnick when it comes to education, and if she had her way, all Human children would have to attend school until they at least mastered the basics of differential calculus and classical physics. The Old Way movement isn't interested in training the academics of the future, and by the time their children reach twelve or thirteen years old, most of them are learning a trade with a parent or working as an apprentice."

"We teach our children what they need to know to live and thrive in our communities," Oscar said. "We don't recognize the right of any outside authority to tell us what constitutes an educated child."

Samuel opened his mouth to ask a question but paused when he realized that a floating immersive camera had approached within an arm's length. He shot an irritated look at the Grenouthian director, who made a subtle beckoning motion, causing the camera to retreat a small distance.

"Did the Dollnick administrator on Kurel enforce educational standards?" Samuel asked. "I thought education was one of the few areas where sovereign human communities on open worlds had to accept some regulations from the alien government."

"There were clashes in the early days, but eventually the Dollnicks accepted our approach, subject to our children displaying basic literacy and competency in math," Oscar said. "We don't object to the governments we live under taking an interest in children's welfare, only that they don't try to force their views upon us."

"I was raised in a sort of a cult on Earth and never attended school," Bill contributed. "Flower kept pushing me to get the equivalent of a high school degree, and when I finished that, she registered me for the Open University. I don't think she believes you can get too much education."

"Let me study up on the relevant precedents when I get back to my office, then I'll talk to Flower and return to see you tomorrow," Samuel offered. "I take it you don't speak with her directly yourself?"

"As long as Dewey is willing to perform as her intermediary, I find it more comfortable than conversing with a disembodied voice," Oscar said. "Can I show you around our settlement while you're here?"

"I have a question about the machine you were using when we came in," Bill said. "What was that thumping noise?"

The woodworker looked over at his lathe and realized that a box of off-cuts was blocking a view of its mechanism from the front. "Come around the other side and you can spin it up," he said. "It's a basic treadle lathe, with a good sized flywheel to maintain a steady turning rate without stutters."

"You run it standing up? My fiancée is learning to use a treadle-powered sewing machine and she works it sitting down."

"It takes more force to work the lathe than a sewing machine," Oscar explained. "I put most of my weight on the treadle with one foot to get it started, and after that, keeping it spun up is good exercise, especially when you're turning against a large chisel. Go ahead and try it."

Bill put his left foot on the treadle, which reminded him of the small foot-powered bellows that Razood would sometimes use when working alone in the forge, and then put all of his weight on that foot as if he were climbing a stair. The treadle went down, gaining speed along the way as the large flywheel on the side of the lathe spun up. When he shifted his weight back to the other leg, the treadle rose, and he repeated the operation.

"So that's what was making the thumping sound," Samuel said. "My father would love this machine."

"You have to remember to alternate your treadle leg on a regular basis or the muscles will get overdeveloped on one side, like the dominant arm on some blacksmiths," Oscar said. "Speaking of which, we only had one smith in our community on Kurel and he stayed behind after the division. We've arranged for a local blacksmith to start training some of our members with an interest in the work. Do any of you know Razood?"

"I started an apprenticeship with him before I decided to focus on baking," Bill said, his breath coming out in huffs as he worked the treadle. "He's a great guy, but you probably shouldn't let him in this tent. The Frunge can be sensitive about wood."

Five

"Let me get you a chair," Julie offered. "I'll ping Flower and have a bot bring—"

"I'm fine standing," Vivian interrupted. "If you keep treating me like some kind of invalid, I'm going to stop inviting you along when I'm trying to get sign-ups for our family database."

"But you're preg—okay, okay," Julie backed down under her friend's scowl. "Should we have covered our hair?"

"Do you think they'll ask us to help serve food?"

"All of the Old Way women I've seen were wearing bonnets or kerchiefs."

"I'll have to ask them why," Vivian said, flipping open her notebook and checking that she had several sharp pencils at the ready. "It's going to double the work to write down all of their information and then input it on tabs back at headquarters. What bothers me is that every transcription is going to increase the error rate."

"Flower showed me the software that Zick and his team developed for your app and I thought you'd need your tab to take their pictures," Julie said.

"My mom sent me some Old Way romances to read, just to get a jump on the culture, and they don't sit for photographs because they consider it vain. The books aren't as steamy as the shifter romances you're trying to write, but if you're curious, I'll lend them to you."

A young woman with a toddler clinging to her skirts approached the table outside the dining hall tent where Vivian and Julie had set up to register people for the Human Empire's family registry. She studied the poster with the bullet-points explaining the purpose of the database and appeared to be puzzled.

"I'm Vivian, and I'm the Registrar for the Human Empire," Vivian introduced herself. "Julie is Flower's executive assistant and she's here keeping an eye on me."

"Emma," the woman said, dipping her head politely. "And my shy child is Josh."

"Could I start by asking you a question?" Vivian continued with a confidence Julie wished was her own when meeting strangers. "Why do you wear a head covering, and will it make people in your community uncomfortable if my friend and I don't?"

Emma touched the silk scarf tied over her head as if she was just noticing it was there. "This?" she asked, pulling it off and revealing a thick chestnut mane. "When you work in the fields it's easier to keep things out of your hair than to remove them after the fact."

"So it's not a religious thing?" Julie asked.

"I'm not a person of faith myself, but some in our community are," Emma said, thrusting the scarf in what might have been a work bag. "Your database sounds like a very interesting idea. I can't imagine using it myself since I don't own any electronic devices, but I'd love to hear from some of my cousins who I've never met."

"Would you have a problem with being photographed?" Julie asked. "It's not necessary, but computer facial recognition can be very useful for confirming familial relationships."

"What would I have against being photographed?" Emma asked in reply. "Haven't you seen that big furry alien with the rabbit ears and his floating cameras following everybody around?"

"He's Grenouthian," Vivian told her. "I thought you only accepted his presence because he didn't ask permission. I was just telling Julie that I've been reading about Old Way communities and I thought that you wouldn't pose for images because it's considered vain."

Emma started to laugh so hard that her toddler joined in without knowing what was funny. "You must be confusing the Old Way with the Old Amish," she said when she recovered her breath. "My father grew up near an Old Amish community on Earth, and he told us stories about their plain ways. If you have a book about their history I'd be interested in learning more myself. It's my turn to teach a class about Earth for the children next week."

Vivian reddened. "They're sort of fictional history."

"Do you mean romances?" Emma laughed again. "That's even better. We don't read on tabs, and the romances in our community library were falling apart even before the division. Is there a good bookstore on board?"

"There's a print-on-demand shop with tens of millions of books in their catalog," Julie said. "It's on the same corridor as the library."

"Thank you. Do I need to fill out a form to be registered in your family database, or will you put my information in one of those tab things everybody on Flower seems to have?"

"I didn't bring mine," Vivian admitted. "I was worried that the technology would offend you."

"Just because we avoid using advanced technology ourselves doesn't mean we want other people to stop," Emma said. "We were happy that Flower brought us up to her ship on shuttles because the space elevator takes all day, and the sprinklers on this deck beat any irrigation system I've ever seen. If it will save time, why don't you come back for lunch tomorrow and bring your tab? Leave the poster and I'll tell everybody at dinner what you're doing so they'll be prepared."

"That would be a huge help," Vivian said. She hesitated a moment before asking, "Are you going to mention my mixing up the Old Way with the Old Amish?"

"If you bring me some of those books, I guess we can keep it between us," Emma said slyly. "And if you want to get to know us better, you're welcome to join our sewing circle at eight in the evening, ship's time, Mondays and Thursdays. Several of us are expecting so we're working on baby clothes. Did you marry with a hope chest or a trousseau?"

Vivian looked embarrassed for a second time in just five minutes, something Julie never expected to see. "I don't actually know how to sew," the expectant mother admitted. "I'm sure our parents will send us more than we need."

"I'm sorry if I offended you," Emma said, reaching down to stroke the hair of her son, who was still clinging to her dress. "Other than what I've read, I know very little about people outside of the Old Way movement, and most of those books were set in Scotland or England in the early industrial age. There's just something about a romance with a man on a horse."

"Is sewing baby clothes something I can learn?" Vivian asked. "Is there something easy, like, I don't know, a blanket?"

"Both of you will be welcome regardless of your skill level. It's a circle, not a classroom, so there's no pressure. I can try to show you the basics myself, but the older women are the ones who know all of the tricks."

"Does anybody sew with a machine?" Julie asked. "I have a treadle-powered sewing machine in my office and I'm not making very good progress. Flower keeps giving me helpful tips, but she's never actually used it herself."

"Your ship's artificial intelligence is trying to teach you how to sew?" Emma laughed again. "That, I'll have to share with the others. All of us know how to use treadle sewing machines, but we have to share because it takes a mechanic so long to manufacture one. The blue tent with the banner is our community crafting center." As she began turning to go, something else occurred to her, and she asked, "Will your family registry accept mailing addresses?"

"Of course," Vivian said, making a note to have Zick add mailing addresses to the app.

"Do they have mailing addresses on Earth Two?" Julie asked. "I remember a weekly postman back on Earth and he had to match the address on the envelope with the address on the building."

"Old Way communities have always depended on mail for communications, and everybody knows everybody else, so the name of the person is enough," Emma said, but she looked a little uncertain. "If we're really among the first permanent colonists heading to Earth Two, I don't imagine there will be a postal system yet, so that could be a problem. If you distribute forms that we can fill out once we know our new addresses, we could mail them to you."

"We'll have to do that," Vivian said. "When we designed the database, we had an app that would work with

Earth smartphones in mind because that's easily ported to tabs or teacher bots. But we definitely need an alternative for people who avoid technology or don't have network access. Thank you."

"Does it have a name I can use when I'm describing it to the others, or should I just say that it's a registration system that—" Emma glanced at the poster again, "—utilizes genetic testing and a ring-fenced database to allow family matching and notification-based central messaging for individuals who opt-in."

"We're still working on a name and I didn't realize the poster was so heavy on the jargon," Vivian said apologetically. "The important thing is that we guarantee your privacy, so you'll be notified of a genetic match when another user is searching for relatives, but they won't know you exist unless you choose to respond."

"That seems like a reasonable precaution," Emma said. "I'll see you tomorrow then."

Vivian began gathering up her pencils.

"We're leaving?" Julie asked.

"I know this is going to sound weird, but back on Union Station, I was assigned to spy on some trade shows for the Drazens. I've watched a lot of sales pitches made to foot traffic from booths, and you only get one chance with the people who stop. It doesn't make any sense to waste that chance today to write down partial information if I can come back tomorrow with my tab and mail-in forms."

"Can you get the forms done that quickly? I helped design fliers and posters for MultiCon and it took weeks just to agree on the artwork."

"Thanks to Samuel becoming pen pals with his niece, I know a place where I can buy envelopes, and I can get a form run off at the print-on-demand place using the

Human Empire logo for the art," Vivian said. She put her notebook in her oversized purse and checked the table to make sure she hadn't left anything behind. "The trick will be getting the right postage on the envelopes. I'll have to study up tonight."

"Because we don't know if Earth Two will use Dollnick stamps, Alt stamps, or Earth stamps?" Julie asked.

"Oh, there's another thing I'll have to talk to Sam about," Vivian said as she started up the path for the lift tube. "We need to start thinking about Human Empire postage stamps, as a branding thing if nothing else. But the problem isn't which stamps to use because the tunnel network treaty provides a rebate mechanism for all of the members to honor each other's postage. If we're going to eventually be providing forms and envelopes with pre-paid postage to all of the Old Way communities, I should get authorized to print the postage and address on the envelopes, rather than wasting our co-op student's time putting on stamps one-by-one."

"Do postal services let people print their own stamps?"

"Sure," Vivian said, stopping to look at a cow accompanied by a calf grazing on the slightly concave pasture that followed the curvature of the deck. "I remember when my mom got authorized to print postage for mailing the alien romances she publishes in translation. I think she said that it all gets billed to her programmable cred, so the Stryx are probably the brains behind the system."

"I'm surprised your mom's publishing business mails books directly to readers," Julie said. "Bianca the Sixth told me that some romance authors experimented with that as a business model, but the retail price for paperbacks is too low to justify all of the overhead involved."

"In some ways, my mom thinks more like an alien than a human," Vivian said with a wry smile. "She's bought into the idea that providing jobs is more important than profits as long as the business can stay competitive."

"I know that my experience running money for the drug cartel on Earth isn't typical for business but they were incredibly competitive. I mean, those guys would kill each other over just about anything."

"There's competition and there's competition," Vivian said, serious now as she resumed the walk to the lift tube. "Take InstaSitter. My mom always made sure I understood that the business couldn't exist without the support of the Stryx station librarians, and it's almost impossible for anybody to compete with us on a large scale for that reason. So InstaSitter can afford to pay well and provide all of the education benefits because it's basically a monopoly. It's not fair to anybody else trying to break into the commercial babysitting business on Stryx stations, but that's life."

"I never thought of it that way," Julie said as they approached the lift tube. "Did you want to come back to my office and see the sewing machine?"

Vivian vacillated for a moment and then said, "I better go directly to the print-on-demand place to check about printing on envelopes and see if he has any experience with metered postage. If I have time later, I'll stop in, and then we can take the same lift tube home."

"All right," Julie said, standing aside at the last moment. "You go ahead first. The Con deck is below this one and the deck with the library is above."

"I've been here almost a year and I still don't have the geometry down," Vivian said, entering the lift tube without an argument. "See you later."

"Change in plans," Flower announced over Julie's implant when the next capsule arrived. "There's a meeting at the shipyard I need you to attend."

"You can't complain about my lack of progress with the sewing machine if you don't give me time to practice. What's the meeting about?"

"A business opportunity. How much do you know about Tunnel Trips?"

"It's a rental business that Samuel's father and step-brother started on Union Station. I forgot the step-brother's name, but he's married to the Aisha who hosts *Let's Make Friends,* so they have really deep pockets."

"Paul McAllister. Samuel's father is currently the president of Tunnel Trips, but that's just a formality. The business is run by Paul and a young Horten named Marilla, who attended the Open University with Samuel. The social networking possibilities in higher education often pay higher dividends than the courses."

"I'm not going back to school, Flower," Julie said firmly.

"I was just mentioning it in context," the Dollnick AI said. "Marilla is the one who I work with on day-to-day scheduling of rentals and special consignments. The point is, the first ship just floated down the new magnetic levitation assembly line that the Zarents copied from the old Sharf production line I bought."

"So this is more of a party than a meeting?" Julie asked as the doors slid open on the manufacturing floor of the shipyard.

"The party will be after working hours," Flower said. "The chief engineer of the current group of Zarents vacationing on board has told me they can have a third assembly line up and running in a month."

"I thought the whole idea of Club Flower was to provide the Zarents with rest and relaxation."

"Just being away from the Wanderers is the real vacation. If I didn't find engineering work for them to do, they'd be miserable."

Julie smiled at a pair of workers heading the other direction with a custom ship wrap carried between them and shifted to subvocing so everybody wouldn't think she talked to herself. "Do you need a third assembly line? I know there's still a backlog of orders for your Sharf two-man traders, but adding production capacity would just mean more people suddenly out of work when you catch up."

"You see, you understand business better than you think," Flower said. "I would prefer that the shipyard operate with a permanent backlog for the sake of planning, and it's also important for maintaining the selling price. We don't have any direct competition selling newly manufactured ships into the Human market because the margins are so low. My Stryx mentor wouldn't be pleased if I disrupted the pre-owned market to the point that buyers found themselves owing more on their mortgages than the ships are worth."

"So why would you even consider a third production line?" Julie asked, heading for the desks where the managers worked in full sight of the production floor. "Are you going to have one vacationing group of Zarents build it and the next take it apart?"

"That would be a waste of resources," Flower said. "I want to create a rental fleet."

"You just signed a deal with Tunnel Trips," Julie said in exasperation. "Don't you think it would be polite to at least wait a few months before going into competition with them?"

"I don't want to compete with Tunnel Trips, I want to leverage their current network and franchise locations for commercial rentals. A fleet of reconditioned Dollnick space taxis is ideal for tunnel network businessmen who value their time more than the savings of taking a regularly scheduled passenger ship, but they have no cargo capacity and they aren't capable of landing on planets or moons. Tunnel Trips is accurately named because the ships are only good for quick trips between space stations, orbitals, and space elevator hubs that happen to be within a few hours of a tunnel exit."

"And you want to—Hi, Don," Julie interrupted herself to greet the foreman she had hired for Flower at the first MultiCon. "How are Laura and little Iris?"

"Couldn't be better," the proud father said. "They'll be here in a minute. Flower agreed to make an exception to her maternity leave policy because it's a strategic planning meeting, but Laura has to go home immediately afterward."

"I heard the first ship came off the new production line today."

"Yes, but we'll still have six months of backlog, and that will probably go up as soon as people realize they won't have to wait that long to get their hands on one. But if Flower does decide that we're going to produce directly for the commercial rental business, it will make a huge difference in the lives of new traders."

"How so?" Julie asked. "I have to believe that renting a ship would be too expensive to justify for the bartering business model."

"But with short-term rentals, anybody with some extra cash will be able to try it without signing on as an apprentice or committing to buy a ship. Even the second-hand models—"

"Pre-owned," Flower interjected over Julie's implant.

"—cost more than a house back on Earth, so it's far and away the biggest investment most people will make in their lifetime. Thirty or forty years ago, when there was still a glut of used Sharf ships available, people were able to buy them for a small down payment and a ten-year mortgage if they worked their butts off. These days, most of our buyers are either getting loans from their families for the down payment or have just finished their first long-term contract working for the aliens and have a nest egg saved up."

A woman in her mid-thirties placed a bassinet with an infant on the desk, offered Julie a handshake, and said, "We still haven't opened the coconut."

"You mean from that giant fruit basket Flower had Bill deliver when you were staying in her maternity center?" Julie asked.

Laura nodded. "Even though Iris is my first, I have to admit that the Dollnick traditions Flower insisted on our following make more sense than what people do back on Earth. I remember one friend rushing home from the hospital with her newborn the next day to take care of the other children. It took her months to fully recover. In the maternity center I got to make friends with several other new mothers, and after two weeks, I felt ready to go back to work."

"Except Flower Shipyards has a mandatory six-month maternity leave," Don said.

"Nothing for fathers?" Julie asked him.

"Flower offered me a cigar, but she said I couldn't smoke it anywhere near Laura or the baby, so I passed."

"The special exception for strategic planning only allows fifteen minutes so let's get started," the Dollnick AI contributed via a desk speaker. "At issue is hiring the Zarents to construct a third assembly line to build ships for the commercial rental market. Does anybody have any objections?"

"You expect it to be up and running in a month?" Laura asked. "I won't even be back from maternity leave yet."

"I haven't begun negotiations with our Sharf supplier for drives and fuel packs, so it's likely that production will have to wait a little longer," Flower said. "I tried pushing them to license us to manufacture fuel packs when we started on the second assembly line but the Sharf are holding me to the existing contract."

"We barely have enough people to man two shifts on the existing production lines, and some days it seems there are more trainees than employees on the factory floor," Don said. "Where are you going to find us new workers?"

"To date I've limited my recruiting to people already living on board to achieve full employment. I'm now cultivating contacts with technical recruiters at all of our stops, and I believe it will be no problem to bring on new workers as long as the jobs are in place."

"What about the internal layout?" Laura asked. "One of our main selling points on the ships we've been building is the custom interiors and add-ons. Won't ships for commercial rentals have a completely different set of requirements?"

"Excellent point," Flower said. "Julie and I will research the market, and your time is almost up. Unless there are any objections, I'll tell the Zarents to go ahead and start fabricating the new machines. Laura?"

"I guess I'm okay with it."

"Don?"

"Sure, the more the merrier."

"Then this meeting is adjourned."

"What about me?" Julie asked.

"Doesn't matter," Flower said in her executive assistant's head. "With three of us in favor, you're outvoted in any case."

Six

"I can't get over the fact that they have the complete set of my *Galactic War College* paperbacks," Geoffrey said to Bianca as they walked through the pear orchard on their way to the next structural spoke. "I thought the terrible anime production completely killed the sales of those books almost thirty years ago. I'll have to ask Flower's lawyer why I haven't seen any mention of them in my royalty reports."

"Maybe the company that bought the anime rights has been publishing the books and not paying you," Bianca said. "I remember that happening to an author who wrote novelizations of pre-Stryx movies. The poor woman was down to her last few eBucks because the entertainment company had changed hands and they were claiming they had acquired the rights to her books without the contractual obligation to pay royalties."

"That's right, but it must have been over forty years ago, and it's slipped my mind how it turned out."

"One of the author organizations I was a member of took it to court, but by the time they got a judgment, the company had changed hands again and the author had passed away."

"If it turns out that these people have been reading a novelization of my *Galactic War College* books based on the anime production, be prepared for them to throw rotten fruit at us," Geoffrey said.

"Look," Bianca said. "That must be the new fence Julie was telling me about at our mentoring session today."

"I never would have expected to see barbed wire on an interstellar jump ship, but I guess the cows would just push through anything else and get into the other crops. How has Julie been progressing with the D'Arc universe lately?"

Bianca, the sixth in line to the D'Arc name, shook her head slightly. "She has the imagination and introspection to become an author, but I don't think her heart is really in shifter romance. Seventh and I thought that her experience growing up in the big city and being forced to work for the drug syndicate would make it easy for her to write bad-boy characters, but I think her early difficulties gave her a yearning for a simpler life."

"Like becoming the executive assistant of a twenty-thousand-year-old Dollnick artificial intelligence who controls a colony ship that could wipe out life on Earth in a blink of the eye?" Geoffrey teased.

"Flower would never do such a thing. And if you think about it, Julie's life today, as busy as it may seem to us, must be far less stressful than carrying drugs and money for violent criminals."

"It is nice being able to go for a walk anywhere on the ship and not have to worry about getting mugged for my pocket change." Geoffrey ran a hand over the stubble of his beard and asked, "Do you think I should have shaved?"

"If these people are anything like the Old Way communities I visited on Earth, some of the men will have full beards," Bianca said. "Are you getting tired carrying the cake?"

"This?" The old author made a show of balancing the cake tray on one hand and then had to grab for it with the other when it nearly fell. "I guess I'd make a lousy waiter. Are you sure they won't have a problem with your baking it in a modern oven?"

"I visited the community after talking with Julie. Several of the men were working on something with one of Flower's maintenance bots, so they must have a reasonable level of comfort with advanced technology. One of the women told me that they relax their rules during travel because they don't want to cause problems for everybody around them."

"It's been years—decades—since I was a guest at a book club," Geoffrey said. "And they really do all of their reading on paper?"

"They maintain a sort of community library without a central location so the books are always in circulation at one home or another. The funny thing is that this afternoon was the first time I've seen a print version of the newspaper put out by the Galactic Free Press. It turns out that you can have them run off at the print-on-demand place, though you pay by the section. I was thinking about getting a subscription to the arts supplement for our writers colony."

"The Old Way community hasn't been here for a week and we're already reverting to reading on paper," Geoffrey said with a chuckle. "Next thing you know we'll have newspaper boys standing in front of the lift tubes hawking the headlines."

"The school where the book club meets has the white flag on top," Bianca said, pointing in the direction of the largest tent. "It looks different from this side."

"Is the next structural spoke closer in the other direction?"

"Yes, that's why the lift tube brought me that way when I came earlier. Flower always chooses the shortest path unless she thinks we haven't been getting enough exercise."

Geoffrey dodged to the side as some children guiding a rolling hoop with short sticks burst past them, and then he had to pay attention to avoid collisions as they navigated through a press of people around the one-room-schoolhouse tent. A tall man in his early seventies, whose back hadn't yet conceded in the battle with old age and gravity, waved to them from the entrance. Bianca led the way to meet him.

"Scott," he introduced himself to Geoffrey, pulling back the proffered hand he had started to offer when he noticed the cake the author was carrying. "We don't expect our guest speakers to bring anything but it's always appreciated. Let's put it on the refreshments table and maybe you'll take something before the talk begins."

"Did you have regular lectures back on Kurel?" Bianca asked. "I pictured a quiet agricultural settlement far from the cities and industrial areas."

"As a Dollnick open world, everybody who wants a floater can afford one, even if it's the most basic sled-type," Scott said. "While we didn't use them ourselves, we certainly made no objection to our guests choosing the transportation of their choice."

"I had the impression that Old Way communities on Earth were set up in part to isolate themselves from modern society."

"There's modern society on Earth and there's modern society on Kurel," Scott said. "The Old Way movement encompasses a full spectrum of lifestyles, from isolationists who are trying to turn back the clock, to communities that accept teacher bots and networked tabs."

Geoffrey set the cake on the table and helped himself to a cup of coffee and a brownie. "What do you think about the deal that the Human Empire made with the Alts to allow Old Way communities to emigrate to Earth Two?" he asked their host.

"I've read the agreement and it doesn't mention the Old Way movement by name," Scott said as he filled a coffee cup from the large urn. "The Alts place limitations on the technology we're permitted to bring to Earth Two, and perhaps more importantly, on our future behavior. Our goals and those of the Alts overlap in certain areas, but they come from very different motivations. The Alts want humans who will live in harmony with the ecosystem, while the focus of the Old Way movement is to live in harmony with our bodies and each other."

"I never heard it put that way," Geoffrey said. "I guess I always thought you were more of a religious movement."

"That's the Old Amish—everybody gets us confused."

"This pumpernickel is excellent," Bianca said. "I haven't had any in ages. Do you have a bakery that sells retail, or does everybody bake at home?"

"Flower provided us with a large brick oven that we can fuel with branches and twigs from the orchards and the inedible parts of plants, so we're doing all of our baking communally," Scott said as he led the way to a pair of side-by-side stools at the front of the tent. "If you look up and in the direction of the closer lift tube when you leave the tent, you'll see a fume hood extending down from the ceiling. I'm not sure how much cooking and heating with wood the Alts will permit us on Earth Two. That level of detail remains to be negotiated."

"No microphone?" Geoffrey asked in dismay. "I don't know how well my voice projects these days."

"Don't worry. Everybody will be quiet as church mice once the talk begins. The acoustics in here are surprisingly good for a tent. It's probably some high-tech Frunge fabric, but we didn't ask. Just relax and enjoy your snacks while I get the club members seated, and then I'll say a few words before you begin."

"Nervous?" Bianca teased.

"You have to admit it's a strange setup," Geoffrey said. "I'm not sure that the same talk I'd been giving the last few decades will work for this crowd."

"Are you implying that you changed your talk a few decades ago? That's news to me."

"How about you?" he challenged her. "Have you moved on from the characters being the soul of every book?"

"No, but at least I have different talks prepared for adults and children. Do you remember the time at the children's book fair where you tried to answer a boy's question about—"

"Don't remind me," Geoffrey cut her off, and then tested his coffee again to see if it had cooled enough to drink.

"You won't be able to sleep," Bianca warned him.

"So maybe I'll finally finish that chapter I'm stuck on. I've been fantasizing about faking an injury to have an excuse to see M793qK and pick his brain."

"Have you written your hero into a medical corner and now you need a miracle cure?"

"It's an action scene, and the Farling knows more about the wars taking place outside of the tunnel network than anyone I've met," Geoffrey said. "The trick is getting him to talk about them."

"I've always thought you were gifted with unnatural skills of persuasion, but I don't suppose they would work on an alien."

Geoffrey lowered his voice as if he thought the giant beetle might be lurking. "I use reverse psychology with him. All I have to do is to claim I came up with a scenario for a battle the likes of which has never been put on paper, and then he's off and running about some incredible interstellar fleet action or another that he participated in."

"Are you sure he's not making them up?" Bianca asked.

"If he is, he's got a better imagination than I do. I change the details enough that I'll be safe if he's borrowing them from an alien writer."

"All settled in?" Scott asked as he returned to where the authors were sitting. "We'll be closing the tent flaps in another minute and everybody should be settled by then—" he glanced towards the buffet table and nodded in agreement with himself, "—so I wanted to ask if you'll be giving a timed talk, or whether you'd consider just taking questions."

"Your club members won't be disappointed if we just answer questions?" Geoffrey asked. "I always thought that paying customers feel cheated if you make them into part of the entertainment."

"But we're not paying you."

"Then there's that. Questions are fine by me. Bianca?"

"As long as we get to ask them as well," she said mischievously.

Scott nodded, turned to the audience, and clapped his hands twice. The conversations died out with a few short sentences, and everybody turned their attention to the front of the tent.

"Welcome to the first meeting of our book club held on Flower," Scott began. "I hope everybody is settling into their temporary homes, and that you'll all remember to take advantage of the offer from the ship's library for one free book per new cardholder, providing they have duplicates. If you can't think of a book to ask for, just check with me."

Everybody chuckled, and there were a few comments along the lines of, "You wish."

"Tonight we have the unique honor of hosting two authors that some of us have actually read, namely Geoffrey Harstang and Bianca D'Arc the Sixth. They've agreed to take questions rather than trotting out the same talks they've been giving for the last half-century, which works out well for me because I get more floor time as the moderator." He took a quick sip from his coffee to let his words sink in. "Who's first?"

A dozen hands flew up in the air, and Scott pointed at a woman in her thirties in the front row.

"Melinda," she introduced herself as she stood. "I'd like to know your thoughts about how the forms of government presented in the science fiction canon line up with the reality of today's galaxy."

Bianca shook her head slightly and nudged Geoffrey.

"Starting right in with the heavy stuff, eh?" he asked. "Well, as it happens, I can talk about forms of government in science fiction all night, but I'll limit the comparison to the tunnel network. I'm sorry to say that my understanding is that many of the empires operating outside of the Stryx sphere of influence act very much like those encountered in the space marines and alien invasion genres."

"The tunnel network is fine," Melinda said.

"The science fiction published before the Stryx opened Earth was way off the mark, but there are reasons for that," Geoffrey said. "Rather than faulting those authors, I think it's fair to say that both then and now, most readers want heroes whose shoes they can imagine themselves stepping into. That means creating plots that allow the heroes to fight epic battles, and the easiest way to do that is through invasions or uprisings against oppressive governments."

"So it's our fault as readers because we get what we ask for," Scott interjected.

"Perhaps I'm oversimplifying, but I honestly believe the market is the main factor. And from the perspective of drama and human interest, it's much easier to come up with rivalries centered on royal families or military hierarchies than on the leaders of democracies. For one thing, regular elections result in too much character turnover, especially if epic timelines are involved. Some of the classic authors, Asimov comes to mind, did speculate about alternative forms of essentially imperial government. In the end, he had to rely on elites with special powers that humanity has yet to develop."

"I don't want us to get too bogged down in governments right now, but we can return to the subject later if there's time," Scott said. "Does anybody else have a follow-up question before we move on? Abel?"

A man of around fifty with a large bushy beard rose to his feet. "Are you saying that nobody wrote about a confederation of empires living in peace with each other thanks to interference from ancient artificial intelligence because it would be boring?"

"Exactly," Geoffrey said, and took another sip from his coffee. "Who wants to read about diplomacy and business? If you look at translated science fiction from some of the tunnel network species, you'll find a romanticized version of piracy, or stories about new colonies outside the recognized bounds of the tunnel network, even in new galaxies. One of the reasons that Vergallian dramas are so popular is they focus on royal intrigues playing out against a faux-medieval background on tech-ban worlds. And most of the Horten and Drazen science fiction I've read is really alternative history that reimagines their early days of conquest."

"I don't think any of us have been reading alien books in translation unless—Naomi?" Scott cut himself off, pointing at a woman in her sixties who raised her hand.

"I just read a Dollnick romance in translation and I plan to get more," Naomi said, rising to her feet in keeping with the Old Way tradition at public meetings of any kind. "The publisher included a note in the back explaining that they have to edit the books heavily because of cultural references that don't map to anything English readers would understand. But I also have a question for Bianca."

"Go ahead."

"A few minutes ago, I overheard somebody say that you're writing books for children these days and that *A Tan Tuber For The Teacher* is yours. They were giving out free copies of that book to those of us who took Flower's school tour today. I have to say it's the best illustrated children's book I've read in years, and I plan to use it in the class I teach. Can you tell us where you got the idea of a Dollnick female teaching humans in a one-room schoolhouse on an alien open world?"

"It was just released last week and I haven't even gotten my author's copies yet," Bianca said. She looked at the woman suspiciously. "Did Flower put you up to asking that question?"

"I haven't spoken directly with the ship's AI since we arrived in her shuttle," Naomi replied, clearly amused by the implication she'd been manipulated into participating in a guerilla marketing campaign. "The book is in my bag. You can have it and I'll buy one when I can."

"Forgive the question. Publishing through Flower Media was a new experience for me, and I'm glad to hear the book came out so well. It's the first time I've worked with a team of artists rather than an individual illustrator, and the process was a bit more interactive than I was accustomed to back on Earth. In answer to your question, the teacher in the story is loosely based on Flower herself, but I changed her into a flesh-and-blood Dollnick because there's no visual way to portray artificial intelligence to small children. Four arms and a feathered crest they can figure out."

"I loved the way that there weren't any explanations about who the teacher was or how she ended up teaching human children on an ag world. I already read the book with a seven-year-old. He never questioned how the alien teacher changed that little boy's life."

"I've always felt it's best not to explain any more than readers need to puzzle out what's going on," Bianca said, "and thank you for the kind words. But now it's my turn to ask a question, and I'd like to know if it's common for Old Way communities to be so literate? No, that came out wrong," she corrected herself. "I meant that I have an image of you working from dusk to dawn and not having time for frivolous pursuits like reading fiction."

"We don't have any electronic entertainment devices in our homes, and most of our communities frown on anything like telephones," Naomi said. "When we finish our work for the day, most of us enjoy reading and playing music, though some prefer athletic activities."

"I think I've heard about people in some farming communities on Earth using old wired phones and keeping them in the barn," Geoffrey said.

"That's the Old Amish again," Scott said. "They believe that having phones inside leads to the sin of gossip."

"But you're not religious and you don't use phones at all."

"Our reason is that phones and other high-tech communications give people an excuse not to meet face to face. Most of our practices that seem odd or archaic to outsiders can be traced to our goal of forming strong communities."

"But when I think about the Old Way, the first thing that comes to mind is self-sufficiency," Bianca protested. "The Galactic Free Press recently ran an article about how many followers of the Old Way on Earth are willing to pull up stakes and move to Earth Two where there will be limited support and almost no infrastructure."

Scott smiled. "We aren't quite the intrepid pioneers you might think because we always travel as a community. None of us are ever truly alone."

Seven

Bill took a bite of the light pastry and his eyes popped open at the explosion of flavors. "It's indescribable," he said, and then hurried to add, "I mean, indescribably good. One of the first special seminars I took at the Open University taught us how to criticize our own work—there were a lot of artists and musicians in the class as well as chefs and bakers—but I don't have the vocabulary to even get started with your Frunge Twist."

"I'm sure you're exaggerating," Fandaz said, but it was obvious that she was pleased by the compliment. "When you open your café, I'll give you the recipe, but you have to agree not to tell Harry or it could end up commoditized by Flower Foods."

"But all of your customers must be talking about your gluten-free pastries. I'm surprised my fiancée hasn't told me about the Frunge Twist. She's in here at least once a week with her friend."

"I haven't started serving it yet. You're the first Human to try it."

"You should definitely put it on the menu. You could charge two or three creds, easy."

"That much?" Fandaz asked. "I thought the average wage on Flower for Humans was on the order of five Stryx creds an hour. I pay my waitresses a base rate of two creds, but of course they get tips and profit-sharing."

"Last year I took a cake estimating course, and I did so badly that I had to do a special report on café pricing to get credit," Bill said. "I'm kind of a dunce when it comes to complicated math stuff, but my friend, Dewey, he's an artificial person, helped me understand the Bridgette Curve. Have you ever heard of it?"

"Something to do with small bridges?" the Frunge hazarded a guess. "I didn't have my implant turned on because I'm trying to become fluent in Humanese."

"It's named after a French woman who owned a chain of famous cafés back on Earth. She concluded that every café should have a featured pastry that was intentionally priced beyond the comfort level of most patrons so they would have something to celebrate special occasions," Bill explained as he looked around the kitchen for something to draw with. He spotted the piping bag that Fandaz had employed to show him how she put the prices directly on some cookies with green icing to simplify the display case. "May I?"

The Frunge nodded, and Bill squeezed out a thin line of icing on the stainless steel counter for the vertical axis of a graph, and then another for the horizontal axis. He continued with a curve starting near the top of the vertical axis that began by dropping steeply, flattened somewhat in the middle, and then turned down sharply again towards the horizontal axis.

"Units sold versus price?" Fandaz asked.

"You got it right away," Bill said. "To generate word of mouth with the house specialty, most experts recommend pricing at the first inflection point, where the curve begins to flatten and the number of units sold is maximized at the expense of a lower profit. But Bridgette concluded that for the café's featured pastry, you should price at the second inflection point, where the curve turns down sharply and it's past the pain point of affordability without being so expensive that it will only be bought by social signalers showing off that they can afford it."

"We have a similar pricing curve for certain government services," the Frunge said. "The idea isn't to make them unaffordable, but to push them past the point where everybody will over-consume because they are perceived as cheap. I didn't realize that Humans were so advanced in economic theory."

"I think we only apply it to pastry," Bill said, using a damp sponge to wipe up the icing. "And a pricing suggestion is a poor exchange for all that you taught me this morning."

"If you're looking for work, I'm thinking of expanding into a second location," Fandaz said, and cast a sidelong glance at Bill. "I've been meaning to stop in Colonial Jeevesburg and talk to the blacksmith about furnishings."

"That's right, Razood made all of your wrought iron tables and chairs," Bill said. "I'll see him this afternoon because I'm helping build a smithy on the ag deck where Flower has been putting the Old Way colonists. Razood is going to start teaching blacksmithing classes for them while we're between stops."

Fandaz considered the offer. "That's very generous of you, but—can you read Frunge emotions?"

"I worked as his apprentice for long enough to tell what he thought of my skill, if that's what you mean. And I've gone LARPing with him a bunch of times, so I guess I have a decent idea of his regular expressions."

"I want you to watch him closely when you ask about working for me and then report what you see. If he agrees to do the job but he doesn't look happy about it, I'll make an excuse not to open another location. I wouldn't want him accepting the commission just because it's another Frunge asking."

"Understood," Bill said. "I've got to meet Dewey at Flower's new ship rental franchise in ten minutes, but if you'd let me come back next week at around an hour before opening, I'd love to see how you manage the final prep."

"I welcome your interest," Fandaz said. "Why don't you bring your fiancée for a snack this evening and tell me about Razood's reaction? I've found when dealing with Humans that it's best to get your impressions while they're fresh."

"Thanks, I'll do that."

On his way out of the Blue Tea Café, Bill almost ran into M793qK, who was carrying what looked like a very beefy hydraulic cylinder of stainless steel.

"What are you doing up at this hour?" the Farling rubbed out on his speaking legs.

"Working on my independent study for the Open University," Bill said. "Fandaz comes in really early in the morning. Are you on your way to do a ship repair or something? I'm going to help Dewey, but I'm sure he can wait if you need a hand."

"This isn't a spaceship component, it's an entropic isolation chamber," M793qK said. "It can maintain liquid Helium at standard atmospheric pressure without refrigeration, or keep Tungsten metal molten without heat."

"Wouldn't the liquid Helium freeze and crack the steel, or the molten Tungsten burn right through it?" Bill asked.

"I see that somebody has been learning, as opposed to just memorizing. The cylinder you see is just a shell for the phase-locked entropy containment field that's a specialty of Farling engineering."

"What do you keep in it?"

"It's empty at the moment, but I'm about to fill it with Frunge tea," M793qK said. "It helps keep me awake while listening to Humans drone on about their aches and pains. As long as you're here, a new batch of product candidates for the All Species Cookbook seal of approval has arrived and I want you—"

"Sorry," Bill interrupted, backing away. "Flower has me scheduled to train with Dewey at the Tunnel Trips franchise before he goes in to work at the library, and then I'll be at the Old Way encampment all afternoon."

"I'll have to speak to her about monopolizing your time," the alien said. "Go."

An hour later, Bill finished welding a new lockbox for packages on the interior bulkhead of a former space taxi, flipped back the protective face shield, and straightened up with a groan.

"Are you injured?" Dewey inquired solicitously.

"I was nervous I'd burn through the deck and that made my muscles lock up," the young man said, hitting the safety cut-off on the rig.

"I would have said something if you started going wrong."

"I know, and thank you for coaching me. Have you done much welding yourself, or did you learn about it through one of those installable upgrades?"

"Flower insisted I acquire the skill through practice," the artificial person said. "It may seem unfair that I can learn new skills as easily as you can purchase a scroll in a role-playing game, but I still need to practice to master any physical ability."

"Why?" Bill asked. "I mean, I thought that you had perfect control over your body."

"Yes and no," Dewey said as he prepared the welding rig for moving. "Every android body is different, and the instruction sets I download are basically templates that I have to customize for my physical parameters. In some cases, I can perfect my control on the job, but I would never try using an upgrade to learn how to milk a cow."

"That seems like an odd example."

"I've been visiting the Old Way community before my shift starts at the library and I'm taking advantage of the opportunity to learn about working on a farm. You never know when the ability to produce food will come in handy."

"You don't eat," Bill pointed out as he followed Dewey out the hatch.

"But I've spent my entire existence in close proximity with Humans and I earn my livelihood in jobs supporting your presence on Flower," the artificial person said. He stopped and looked around the section of the docking deck that had been set aside for the Tunnel Trips rental franchise. "Those three need the lockboxes welded in place, so that should keep you busy until lunch."

"Do you still find working at the library interesting?" Bill asked the artificial person. "I can't imagine the pay is as good as what you can earn working on Flower's schemes."

"I enjoy meeting and helping the wide range of Humans who visit the library, and I come across all sorts of interesting books I never would have known about if somebody else wasn't searching for them," Dewey said. "It's been a pleasure to serve the Old Way members who have joined recently because they're voracious readers with eclectic interests. I'm looking forward to working at Tunnel Trips for the same reasons."

"You think that the people who rent ships are interesting?"

"Retail, not so much, but with the addition of commercial rentals, I expect there will be all sorts of mishaps once renters gain the ability to land on planets. Flower is modifying the bookmobile to serve as a mini-tug should the need arise."

"You mean that the new renters will be able to go beyond the tunnel network?" Bill asked in surprise. "How will Tunnel Trips keep people from stealing them?"

"The Sharf two-man traders Flower Shipyards will be manufacturing specifically as fleet rentals won't have jump capability so they're still limited to the tunnel network," Dewey explained. "But unlike the repurposed Dollnick space taxis, two-man traders can make long trips between planets, moons, and other destinations within a star system, and more importantly, land and take off with cargoes. They'll likely be rented by entrepreneurs testing new business models."

"And you're not worried that I'll do any damage welding those boxes into place by myself?"

"Just don't change any of the settings on the rig and the worst that can happen is I'll have to come back and redo your work," Dewey said. "I've got to run if I'm going to be early, but have Flower ping me if you get in trouble."

The young human watched the artificial person sprint off for the lift tube, envious of Dewey's ability to continually adjust the magnetic field generated in the soles of his feet to allow him to run despite his low body weight on the docking deck. Then Bill grabbed the guide handle on the floating Dollnick welding rig and brought it into the next empty rental, where a lockbox had already been placed in position for installation.

By the time he finished welding a bead along the bottom edge of the last lockbox, Bill was starting to feel hungry. He lifted the protective face shield that doubled as a visor and inspected the job with satisfaction. "Not bad for my fourth try," Bill said out loud.

"I monitored your progress with thermal imaging and the results are acceptable," Flower said over his implant.

"I was wondering where you were all morning," Bill said as he hit the safety cut-out on the welding rig and began winding the cables around the holder.

"You asked me not to interrupt with advice while you're working and I've done my best to comply. They've started serving lunch in the Old Way encampment where Razood is setting up the forge. Leave the welding rig and I'll send a bot to tidy up."

"Works for me." Bill pulled off the heavy leather gauntlets and removed the face shield completely. "When's our next stop?"

"We'll be arriving at Cold Iron this evening," Flower said. "There's a group of sixty thousand contract workers from Earth finishing a fifteen-year stint and I'm going to try recruiting them for terraforming work."

"What does mining have to do with terraforming?"

"In the early stages, almost nothing, but Earth Two was largely finished when the Container Prince took it over. I've been reviewing the plans for the remaining continents, and if they're to be available for anything other than sparse grazing land, we're going to have to do some serious plumbing."

Bill double-checked that his magnetic cleats were still activated before starting to shuffle towards the lift tube. It took another second before Flower's words registered. "Did you say plumbing?"

"Subsurface rivers and reservoirs," the Dollnick AI said. "I've facilitated similar work a dozen times in my former service and miners can be easily trained for the job."

"How long is all of this going to take?"

"A few hundred years, give or take a century. It depends on a number of variables, such as when Earth Two qualifies for a tunnel network connection, how many Human workers I can recruit, and whether or not we run into any regulatory interference from the busybodies who equate terraforming with planet murder."

"Planets aren't alive," Bill said as he entered the lift tube. The capsule set off without waiting for his instructions, but if he noticed, he didn't complain. "Julie told me that EarthCent and the Alts had to jump through a bunch of tunnel network legal hoops to get permission to take over the terraforming, but she didn't say anything about murder."

"There are always sentients who believe that the universe should be frozen at its current state," Flower explained. "Occasionally, an entire species becomes obsessed with the idea of preserving the status quo for future generations, but it always works out badly."

"You mean they lose a lot of money?" Bill asked.

"I mean they go extinct. Progress is a necessary ingredient for longevity. Space-time itself is always changing, and clinging to the past is not a recipe for future success."

"But I had the impression you liked the Old Way people. You definitely rolled out the welcoming mat."

Flower startled Bill by generating a sound like a dry chuckle. "Don't get caught up in labels. The Old Way movement hasn't been around long enough to be old even in Human terms, and it's been constantly evolving during that time. Species who fall into the steady-state trap don't go out of existence overnight—it takes hundreds of generations, and it's not impossible to reverse course."

The lift tube doors opened and Bill emerged near the growing collection of tents that defined the temporary town center of the Old Way community. "The cafeteria is in the white tent with the green stripes," the Dollnick AI spoke in his head. "They don't have a miniregister so you'll have to pay cash. I'll reimburse you."

"I've got to eat anyway."

"But I told Razood you'd pay and he's waiting."

Bill hurried the remaining distance to the tent where he saw the Frunge blacksmith chatting with a couple of old men near the entrance. He hung back for a moment and watched while Razood slipped each of the men the plastic chit that contained his contact information.

"There you are," the Frunge greeted Bill as the two men headed off in opposite directions. "I've been doing masonry work for the last thirty hours and I'm starving."

"I hope they have something without grains in it for you," Bill said. "Did you just recruit those guys for spy stuff?"

"It's not polite to ask. And I already talked to the cook and she's slicing up some raw steak for me. You'll probably like the shepherd's pie."

The cook recognized Razood and handed over a plate of skewers with raw steak, onions, and peppers. "It might be better if you took it back to the forge to eat," she said. "I told my assistant you prefer to cook them to taste."

"Can I get Shepherd's Pie to go?" Bill asked.

"You can get anything to go. Just bring back the plate."

Bill paid the young girl sitting at the end of the serving line while everybody else was walking right past her. "Am I the only one paying?" he asked as she made his change from a small box.

"You and the other guests," she told him. "The members decided to pool our food purchases for communal meals during the trip since we don't have kitchens in our tents. Your suggested donation helps to pay for the extras."

Razood was already halfway to the exit and Bill had to walk quickly to catch him just outside. "How far have you gotten with the forge?"

Razood gestured with a partially denuded skewer at a brick chimney reaching up towards a fume hood a few hundred paces away from the main collection of tents. "They wanted a bit of separation to cut down on the noise," he replied after swallowing. "I told them that Flower could slap an acoustic isolation field over the whole thing, but the carpenter said that noise from the smithy is like the heartbeat of a village, which I would have to agree with."

"Are you going to continue the chimney right up to the fume hood?"

Razood shook his head while chewing on another mouthful. "No, the masonry work is all finished. Brynlan delivered the bellows this morning."

"The Verlock sells bellows?"

"He made them from scratch. His parents are accomplished leather workers and he's thinking about dropping his current business and setting up shop in Colonial Jeevesburg."

"You mean his cover business, not his work for Verlock Intelligence," Bill surmised.

"Of course," the Frunge said. "It always comes as a surprise that somebody who moves as slowly as Brynlan would be any good at recruiting sources, but he stole my hod carrier right out from under my scaffolding."

"I get the general meaning so I'm not going to ask for a translation of the technical terms. What's left to do?"

"After you eat, which could take a while based on your lack of progress, we'll put in the floor."

"Over the ground?" Bill asked in surprise. "Why bother? It's not like Colonial Jeevesburg where if you didn't have a floor you'd be working right on the metal deck."

"Compacted dirt isn't bad, but compacted clay is better. It's also what they'll use for a floor in whatever forges they build on Earth Two," Razood said. He licked off the first skewer and stuck it in his belt like a dagger before starting on the next. "The purple onions are excellent."

"Where are you going to get clay on Flower? I thought it was dug out of riverbeds or something."

The Frunge shrugged. "Flower sent a wagon load."

Bill didn't want to try eating the shepherd's pie while walking, and rather than pestering Razood, he subvoced, "Flower?"

"Clay is what Humans call a blend of hydrous aluminum phyllosilicate minerals," the Dollnick AI said in his head. "I end up with a lot of them in my wastewater treatment plant and creating clay is an efficient way to deal with all of the ions that are left over from the purification process. You can mix in a wide variety of other elements, and if you leave the clay long enough, it will form a sedimentary rock. If I don't have another use for it when it builds up, I dump it on an asteroid."

"So we're going to make clay tiles or bricks and then use the new forge as a kiln to bake them?" Bill asked.

"You're going to trowel it on the floor in a good thick layer," Flower said. "It's not squishy clay, if that's what you're thinking."

"Don't ever try to communicate secretly by subvocing because anybody can read your throat movements," Razood told Bill after polishing off another skewer. "It will take us all afternoon to get the clay down in the form I built for the floor. Then we'll invite everybody to come celebrate the new smithy with a dance."

"You've lost me," Bill said.

"To compact the clay," the Frunge said. "Nothing better for it than bringing in a bunch of bipeds who think they can dance when they're actually just stomping around."

Eight

"This is your captain speaking," Woojin's voice came over the public address system. "We have arrived at Cold Iron and will remain in orbit for the next ninety-two hours. Flower Transportation will be providing direct service to the surface with a shuttle leaving every four hours. For those who weren't with us the last time we visited, Cold Iron is a Drazen open world with several sovereign human communities, in addition to a large mining consortium that employs over five million contract workers. Captain out."

"I wish you would let me come with you," Vivian said to her husband. "I haven't had an excuse to wear my prosthetic thumbs and tentacle in ages. Hey, do you want to borrow them?"

"I'm representing the Human Empire, so going as a Drazen would be counterproductive," Samuel said. "And you know we can't keep on doing everything together or we'll only get half as much done."

"Don't you believe in synergy?"

"Not when I need to be on the surface and you're scheduled for a Stryxnet call with all of the government school academic experts on Earth that EarthCent's president can cram into a hologram."

"I almost forgot about that," Vivian said with a groan. "You're right, though. Flower has been surprisingly reticent about giving us advice on setting up the Human Empire School of Government, and getting input from professionals seems like a logical step. Your mom asked President Beyer to arrange for all of these people to talk to me so I have to show up."

"I won't forget to bring up your family registry with everybody I meet," Samuel said. "We agreed on HumanBook, right?"

"No, and the more I hear it, the less I like it."

"I was just kidding. Don't forget to ask the president if he would be interested in attending our final treaty talks with the Alts for sharing Earth Two. We're going to start negotiating when we pick up the first group of Alt colonists and hope to have it finalized by the time we reach Union Station."

"Julie mentioned that the convention team is working out the details to make it into a big event. There's a tunnel network law about doing these types of negotiations publicly and hosting observers. You know how Flower rushes into business opportunities at the drop of a hat."

"I don't rush, I seize the day," the Dollnick AI joined their conversation. "I was going to invite President Beyer myself but it would look better coming from you. And you might try talking those academics into attending some side sessions. If nothing else, they could provide comic relief."

"I'm going to advise Julie to keep it as small as possible," Vivian said. "After we get the deal done there will be plenty of opportunities for conventions."

"I've got to run if I'm not going to miss the first shuttle to the surface," Samuel said. "You hash it out with Flower, Viv. I'm fine with whatever you decide."

Vivian stuck her tongue out at her husband's back as he fled Human Empire headquarters, and then she spent an exhausting fifteen minutes debating the pros and cons of a large conference with Flower. Then she popped into Krey's office and found the Cayl emperor's granddaughter sewing on a treadle-powered machine.

"Is it time?" Krey asked.

"The holo-conference call starts in five minutes," Vivian said. "Is that the same machine Julie is learning to use?"

"I haven't seen Julie's machine, I got this one from Flower," the Human Empire's mentor said. "M793qK cautioned me to cut back on knitting, and sewing seems like such a useful skill."

"Even though you don't wear clothes," Vivian said to the Cayl, who could almost have passed for a female polar bear during the arctic winter.

"My family has a tradition of making gifts rather than buying them," Krey said, getting up to join Vivian. "When you come from royalty, everybody expects you to give expensive presents, but they can't complain about receiving gifts we make ourselves."

"Ooh, that's so clever."

A hologram displaying the president of EarthCent and several other well-dressed individuals with blurred faces was superimposed over the table and chairs when they entered the room. The only two open spots were a human-sized chair and a Cayl stool, which Krey appropriated. Large numerals in the hologram counted down to zero, and President Beyer immediately began to speak.

"I want to start by thanking everybody for participating, though I was somewhat surprised by all of the requests for anonymity filters. Since your institutions don't want you to be identified by name, I'll just say that I welcome the deans and presidents of the top schools of government on Earth. We're meeting with Vivian McAllister, the Registrar of the Human Empire, and Krey, the empire's Cayl mentor. Are there any questions before we begin?"

"Has our speech been disguised as well?" one of the blurs asked in an unnatural voice.

"Yes," the president confirmed. "Since we don't have a set agenda for the meeting, let me ask if any of you prepared advice for the Human Empire, or if we should just proceed to questions."

A well-dressed man brought out a sheaf of papers from his valise, tapped them on the table to get the edges straight, and said, "I have a few comments prepared."

"Why does everybody from Boston think they have all the answers?" asked the blurred woman next to him.

The man put his papers back in the valise, rose from the table, and disappeared from the hologram.

"Good riddance, he would have bored us all to death," another man said. "We're all busy people. Why don't we just proceed to questions?"

"Vivian?" the president prompted.

"We're in the initial stages of setting up our school, but thanks to the full cooperation of the Open University extension campus on Flower, we don't have any infrastructure or administration concerns. If I could ask each person here one question, what is the single most important thing to get right that we only have one chance at?"

"Naming," a woman answered immediately. "What's the name of the school?"

"For now we're calling it the Human Empire School of Government."

"Excellent," the woman said, and the other administrators all nodded and expressed their approval.

"Why is the name so important?" Vivian asked.

"A generic starting name is perfect for selling the rights down the road," a different man chipped in. "One of the greatest challenges facing universities on Earth today is that we sold the naming rights to every school, department, and building centuries ago. You're just starting out and you'll soon be hearing from philanthropists—" he made air quotes with his fingers, "—willing to help kick-start your endowment with a gift in return for naming rights. My advice is to hold out until the school becomes famous."

"I hadn't even thought of that."

"And don't forget endowed chairs," the woman who had brought up naming said. "Back before the Stryx opened Earth, our university sold hundreds of chairs for a few million dollars each. After the monetary collapse wrecked our endowments, we had to come up with whole new departments to work around the legal obligations before we could sell new chairs."

"Our campus was destroyed by an unfortunate fire not long after the Great Opening, so we were able to reset our naming rights business," a man at the end of the table said smugly.

"Everybody knows you set that fire yourselves," said the first woman who had spoken.

Vivian glanced over at Krey, who appeared to be napping. "Thank you for that. We're currently funded by revenue from the All Species Cookbook, but they haven't asked for any naming rights or chairs, and I'll be sure to drive a hard bargain if they do. What is the second most important thing you could suggest?"

"Location, location, location," another man said. "If you're going to attract top faculty and guest lecturers, you need to locate your school where they want to live."

"Restaurants are the most important factor for visiting faculty," a woman said. "I remember once when the governor-general of—it's not important which city-state—visited our campus. I took him to our faculty cafeteria before his speech. He threw out his prepared text and spent a half-hour ranting about being treated like a nobody."

"Since the school is on Flower, all of the restaurants are only a short walk or a lift-tube ride away," Vivian said. "Maybe we should forget my last question and I'll just ask if you can give me any advice about attracting the best students."

"Do you have a football team?"

"We don't have any teams. Is that the sport where you kick around a ball?"

"It depends which continent you're from," another man said. "But let's not put the cart before the horse. Do you have a school logo for your degrees and correspondence?"

"We have a Human Empire seal."

"No, you need a unique one for the school. That way when students get their wait-listed letter, they'll know who it's from by the graphic, and they can ask a family member or a friend to open it."

"Don't forget a mascot," a woman wearing a pearl necklace said. "Maybe your Cayl mentor would—"

Krey interrupted with a show of fangs and a warning growl.

"Rituals," one of the school presidents inserted into the uncomfortable silence that followed. "You should make up traditions for your students to follow when they arrive on campus or they'll invent their own and you could end up with underwear draped over your statues every fall."

"We don't have any statues, but that's actually not a bad idea," Vivian said. "It's always good to keep the initiative."

"I've got one," a blur-faced man spoke up excitedly. "No tenure. If you keep all of the faculty on five-year contracts from the start, any extra money you have to spend upfront to attract them will more than pay for itself down the road when you aren't stuck with a bunch of relics droning on about how everything was better thirty years ago."

"And that's when their medical expenses are peaking," somebody else contributed.

While Vivian was scribbling down ideas on the surface of her tab with a stylus, the giant shuttle carrying Samuel was approaching Cold Iron. One row behind him, Julie complained to her Drazen friend, "This is the weirdest idea Flower has had yet. I almost wish you had refused."

"Why?" Rinka asked. "I grew up singing mining opera. My first solo was in *Roof Fall*, where my character's parents are trapped underground by a cave-in. It was such a thrill to see how moved the audience was that I forgot to look heartbroken."

"I don't understand why opera singers don't get paid twice as much as other entertainers. You're acting and singing at the same time."

"Drazen opera singers *do* get paid twice as much as actors, not to mention being given better tables at restaurants," Rinka said. "Trust me, this will be fun. All you have to do is act like you're excavating the cavern wall, and then scream on key when you hit your foot with the pick."

"It's the on-key part that makes me nervous," Julie said. "Can I borrow your pitch pipe again?"

"I can give you the right note over your implant," Flower said in the girl's head. "We're going to be landing in ten minutes and the audience is already gathering."

"Who does opera at spaceports anyway?"

"Drazens," Rinka said. "I made a bet with Jorb that we get at least a thousand recruits for the Earth Two terraforming project. Did you bet with Bill?"

"Neither of us are gamblers, and I don't understand why all of the advanced species are so into making bets," Julie said. "Why wasn't the gambling instinct eliminated by evolution?"

"You have it backward," the Drazen choral mistress said. "Evolution selects for gamblers. Playing it safe all the time would only give you a survival advantage in a universe where nothing ever changed."

"Can I use that as a line in the book I'm working on?"

"I thought that Bianca the Sixth still had you doing character sketches and research."

"I'm sort of writing this on my own," Julie said, trying not to look guilty. "I really like the Biancas, and the once-a-week mentoring sessions Sixth gives me have helped structure my ideas, but I'm more into shifter romance as a reader than as an author."

"I only took twenty years of creative writing in school as my alternative arts elective before I swapped to sculpture, but they always told us to start by writing in a genre we like to read," Rinka said.

"I think it's because I can believe in the shifter stuff when I'm reading it, but when I try to write about somebody changing from a human into a jaguar, I feel like I'm faking," Julie said. "Sixth believes that—did you just say you had twenty years of creative writing in school?"

"After I moved to the performing arts track," the Drazen explained. "It's normal to channel a hundred percent of your effort into a single outlet once you go professional, but the schools insist that students prepare a fallback so we won't think that the world has come to an end if our first choice doesn't work out."

"That's pretty smart, I guess, but it was the number of years that threw me. How long were you in school altogether?"

"Your years or our years?"

"Ours," Julie said.

"Around fifty, if you don't count pre-school," Rinka said. "If you aren't going to write paranormal romance, are you thinking about crime thrillers? I know you don't like talking about your time working for the drug syndicate, but it was your whole life until you joined Flower. It seems a waste not to build on that foundation."

"That's what everybody tells me, but the drug business isn't anything like the entertainment industry makes it out to be," Julie said. "Imagine long stretches of boredom interrupted by the occasional minutes of terror. The worst part was working with people who were used to that life. It was like something inside them had already died and they didn't care about how much damage they caused."

"That's how it is in Drazen crime novels, which is why I don't read them. So what do you want to write about?"

"I have an idea for an Old Way romance. I did some research at the library and there hasn't been much published yet. It's not an established genre where if you don't meet the reader expectations they'll hate it."

"I didn't realize that Human literature was so rigid."

"It is and it isn't," Julie said. "You can write whatever you want, but it's nearly impossible to find readers unless it fits into some existing category that people are already looking for. If every author's books were delivered to a random sampling of the reading public, it wouldn't matter, but almost all discovery happens through network-connected tabs or teacher bots. There are so many titles that readers have to decide what they're looking for before they start searching. If somebody's read a few romances with bare-chested Dollnicks on the cover and really liked them, it probably wouldn't do me any good if my Old Way romance came up in their search."

"Why?" Rinka asked. "I don't read as many romances as you do but I've been at it longer. For me, it's all about the emotions."

"Humans tend to get caught up in specific make-believe worlds. Sixth says it's like slipping on a comfortable pair of old shoes rather than trying a new pair that are bound to pinch and chafe somewhere until you break them in."

"We'll be landing in thirty seconds," Flower announced over the public address system. "After disembarking, the Open University co-op students who came along to earn marketing credits will report to Samuel McAllister, the First Administrator of the Human Empire. You can identify him by the yellow umbrella he'll be carrying."

Samuel groaned. "Really? You couldn't have just told them to wait at the bottom of the front ramp?"

"Yellow umbrellas are proven technology for gathering groups on alien worlds. I had one prepositioned in your overhead compartment."

"I can barely reach the overhead compartments."

"Stand on the seat. I made a deal with the spaceport AI to promote a performance by a visiting Drazen choir mistress so there should be a large crowd in the terminal hall. And I've supplied all of the co-op students with handouts for terraforming opportunities on Earth Two. All you need to do is make an inspirational speech and point them in the right direction."

"You do know that I'm here to meet with the leaders of the sovereign human communities," Samuel said in exasperation.

"There will be plenty of time for that, and if you're worried about missing the shuttle's departure, I can send Dewey with the bookmobile to pick you up at any time," Flower told him. "There, we've landed, so grab the umbrella and get out there before the students forget why they're here and wander off in search of a party."

As it happened, the co-op students exhausted their supply of handouts before Rinka's third encore, and the EarthCent ambassador's son had to admit that the Dollnick AI knew how to run a guerilla recruitment campaign. Even better, it turned out that the spaceport AI had tipped off the administrators of the local sovereign human communities about the flash event, saving Samuel from having to travel to their communities just to meet them for a chat. Flower had even reserved the event room for them at the local Human Burger franchise.

"Amanda," a middle-aged woman with prosthetic thumbs complementing her natural set introduced herself when Samuel joined the administrators who were already eating lunch. "I represent the Cold Iron Human Consortium."

"Cork," the short man seated next to her said, shaking Samuel's hand without rising. "Hearts and Hands Labor Community."

"Bartholomew Jackson," a dark-skinned man said. "Somebody had to hold out against going native so I kept my family name. Everybody calls me Bart the Cart because I represent the Human Teamsters."

"Samuel McAllister. It's nice to be able to put faces with the names after reading the electronic notes you sent the Human Empire's suggestion box address."

"I might have been drinking when I wrote that," Cork said.

"So you don't have any members you wish we would kidnap and dump on Earth Two?" Samuel asked with a smile.

"Well I do, we all do, but they wouldn't last. Some people just don't do well with the whole responsibility thing and we end up buying them tickets back to Earth. But Cold Iron is a mature mining and industrial world and some of the younger members in our community are game for a new challenge."

"It's the same with our consortium," Amanda said. "Between our own operations and supporting the local Drazen industries, we have no shortage of billable work, but the under-thirties have developed itchy tentacles."

"And your teamsters, Bart?"

"Our older members have learned to appreciate all of the Drazen safety protocols, but the generation that grew up working here takes it all for granted," Bartholomew said. "It may sound perverse, but it's almost like they want to see a real accident, rather than participating in endless holo-training."

"Something tells me that Flower will kick them off the planet if they cause any injuries, but otherwise she's essentially a consultant on the job," Samuel said. "The workers on the ground will have a great deal of autonomy, though I'm sure she'll hold them to the schedule."

"And the Alts?"

"Their only involvement in the terraforming process is veto power over project goals. The work performed by our people is how humanity will earn equity in Earth Two, and the workers will be paid through the Human Empire."

"I didn't realize you had a revenue stream yet," Amanda said.

"For the time being we're supported by the surplus EarthCent is bringing in from the All Species Cookbook, but some sort of taxes or user fees will eventually be required. I'm sort of waiting until our school of government is up and running to commission some studies of our options."

Nine

"Checking for a thermometer?" the Old Way baker asked.

"I was just curious if there was an opening in the back for the firebox," Harry said as he completed his circle around the brick oven. "There's an old wood stove in the bakeshop at Colonial Jeevesburg that has an opening for loading the wood right next to the door for the oven."

"Ah," Reba said. "That's how our stoves work as well, but they're all in storage for the trip. The brick oven was already here when we boarded and it's an ancient Dollnick design. You burn the wood on the same surface where you bake. Then you bank the embers to one side to make room after it's up to heat."

"How do you keep the temperature steady?" Harry asked.

"That's why we have all the baskets full of little bundles of sticks next to the woodpile," she explained. "It took a couple of days for me to get a feel for it, but I just toss in a small bundle on the side with the embers as needed. The results have been excellent, and the oven is so massive that it never cools down completely. It takes about an hour to get it back up to baking temperature in the morning."

"I loved the slight woody flavor in those rolls we sampled," Irene said from behind the floating immersive camera.

"No talking to the documentary subjects," the Grenouthian director scolded her. "You're breaking the invisible plane and putting yourself in the action."

"A nice flavor is part of the joy of cooking with wood," Reba continued as if the alien hadn't interrupted. "My mother had an old coal stove, but you had to make sure that the firebox was completely isolated from the oven section or the flavor was horrible. I never understood why people considered coal to be an advance over burning wood."

"Coal burns longer and at a higher temperature than the best hardwoods," the Grenouthian director said. "The average heating value…" He trailed off when he noticed Irene looking his way as he shattered the invisible plane. The alien muttered a few words about checking on the other volunteer cameramen and hurried away.

"Something tells me that the last twenty seconds won't survive the editing," Harry said with a grin. "So you haven't had any problems with the longer bakes?"

"No, and we've been using the oven for practically all of our cooking, not just bread," Reba said. "Our elders have approved the use of Verlock lava stones as a temporary replacement for stovetop burners, and depending on the final deal with the Alts, we may have to keep using them for heating and cooking when we get to Earth Two."

"We replaced our home heating system with lava stones when they stopped delivering oil around thirty years ago, but I've never used one of the cooking types," Harry said. "Everybody in our town had electrical appliances."

"If they insist we use Verlock lava stones for heating the house I guess we'll have to live with it, but if they take away my wood stove for cooking, I'll be disappointed."

"Do you think the Alts won't allow wood burning at all?" Irene asked.

"I certainly hope that's not the case," Reba said. "We know so little about them. I've heard that they are deeply committed to supporting the ecosystem, so I can't imagine they would be against burning wood."

"Doesn't burning wood in a stove without a catalytic converter produce more pollution than pretty much any other fuel?" Harry asked.

"I'm no expert on these things, but my husband did a fifteen-year contract as a firefighter for the Dollnicks on Kurel before joining the Old Way. The hardest part of his job was quickly differentiating between fires started by natural causes and those from industrial accidents or simple carelessness."

"Do you mean he was a sort of investigator who analyzed the source of the fire after it was put out?"

Reba shook her head and smiled. "They didn't put out the fires started from lightning-strikes or sparking from natural sources like rock falls. The Dollnicks sent Ernie to special training on a Frunge world to help him make those decisions quickly, and you know how sensitive about trees the Frunge are."

"Now I really don't understand," Harry said. "Are you telling me that the Frunge, the same Frunge who buy forests on Earth just to preserve them from the paper and lumber industries, let forest fires burn if they're from natural causes?"

"Of course. The way Ernie explained it, fires are a natural part of a forest's lifecycle. If you rush to put them all out, the undergrowth and dead wood will keep building up to the point that you're sitting on a tinderbox. Then when a fire does get burning, rather than bringing about renewal, it incinerates everything so completely you're left with nothing but ashes."

"I guess what you're saying makes sense, but that doesn't reduce the smoke you'll get from everybody burning wood in their homes. I remember reading a book about life in London a few hundred years ago when the air was so loaded with particulates that you could hardly breathe."

"I suppose that would happen if the whole population of a big city was burning wood or coal to stay warm in the winter but I'd be surprised if they all could have afforded it," Reba said. "Compared to natural forest fires, I don't think our cooking smoke will amount to much, and my husband says that if we gather deadwood from forests in a sustainable manner, it's actually a positive."

"Do you think he'll be willing to talk on camera?" Irene asked. "I don't know whether the Grenouthian director will use it, but I'm taking a course in documentary film-making at the Open University, and I think forest management would be a fascinating topic."

"I'll ask him," Reba said, though she didn't sound confident in the outcome.

Harry offered the Old Way baker a parting handshake. "Thank you for the demonstration, but I have to get back to my own kitchen or there are going to be some unhappy aliens wondering what happened to their lunch," he said.

"Flower excused me from volunteering in the bazaar while I'm helping the Grenouthian director with his documentary," Irene said. "I'll stay for the morning and keep recording—I mean, if that's okay with you, Reba."

"Happy to have the company," Reba said. "And I'd like to hear more about this independent living cooperative of yours."

When Harry arrived in the kitchen, Bill already had a large pot of vegetable stew going on the stove and was sorting through one of the boxes containing leftovers from the product testing for the All Species Cookbook.

"Did Flower have any special instructions today?" Harry asked his assistant.

"She said it's Avisia's birthday, but we can't let on we know because it's an even century and Vergallians are superstitious about them for some reason," Bill said.

"Even century? She can't be two hundred!"

"She'll look the same at four hundred, at least to Human eyes, but two hundred is correct," the Dollnick AI informed him. "I only found out this morning when she received an encrypted message of congratulations from Vergallian Intelligence. I didn't have time to arrange for a royal vegan chef."

"The ramen is all gone," Bill announced, looking up from the last box of leftover testing products. "Jorb must have snuck in again. I found a jar of peanut butter that has that "V" symbol and some crackers in waxed-paper sleeves."

"I could make vegan chocolate chip cookies and they'd be ready by dessert," Harry said.

"I've already got dessert covered with chocolate-covered truffles from the Blue Tea Café," Flower said. "I asked Razood to pick them up on his way here."

"The Frunge eat chocolate-covered truffles?"

"Fandaz serves tribute food," Bill reminded the baker. "Humans can't eat the tar-coated slugs the Frunge like, so they substituted chocolate-covered truffles and call them the same thing."

"The slugs and truffles are both resistant to farming so they carry a high value," Flower said. "If you make Avisia a tossed salad for the main course with a simple vinegar and oil dressing, she'll appreciate the thought. Wait until right before lunch so it will be fresh." There was a brief pause, and the Dollnick AI added, "Strange."

"What's strange?" Bill asked.

"Lume just arrived with the Grenouthian director, and the captain is exiting the lift tube up the corridor."

"But it's too early for lunch."

"Something is fishy," Flower said. "Go see what they're doing here."

Captain Pyun entered the cafeteria with his three-cornered hat under one arm. His uniform looked a little wrinkled as if he'd napped in it, and he gratefully accepted Bill's offer to make a pot of coffee.

"Did you almost forget your own meeting?" the Dollnick station chief asked the captain. "You look like you're ready for bed."

"I fell asleep in my chair watching a Grenouthian documentary," Woojin told Lume. "If it was my meeting, I would have scheduled it first thing in the morning."

"What was the documentary?" the Grenouthian director asked across the table. "I've never heard of anybody who's fallen asleep while watching one."

"Then you must not know many old humans. The documentary was about Vergallian tech-ban worlds. Lynx wanted to watch it to see if it would help her understand the Old Way communities we'll be ferrying to Earth Two. And to be fair, I probably wouldn't have dozed off if I hadn't served as a foreign mercenary on worlds just like those for more than a decade. Lynx thought it was all fascinating."

"So if it's not your meeting, it must be Flower's," the Grenouthian said.

"I didn't call the meeting," the Dollnick AI informed them via an overhead speaker grille. "I'm as much in the dark as the rest of you."

"The message came over the secure channel on my implant, and I thought you were the only one with the address," Woojin said. "Is Stryx Jeeves visiting? It seems like the sort of prank he might pull."

The Drazen and Frunge spies entered the cafeteria together. When Jorb surveyed the bare table, his tentacle drooped. "Aren't there any snacks?"

"Bill is in the kitchen rustling something up," Lume told him. "Have you forgotten the rule about whoever asks for food first?"

"I was just heading for the bar," Jorb said. "Can I start with something for you, Captain?"

"It's too early for me," Woojin said. "Bill is making a fresh pot of coffee if you'd rather have that yourself."

Avisia entered the cafeteria in a surprisingly drab dress, her long hair up in a conservative bun and covered by a sort of cap none of them had ever seen her wear before. The plain clothes did nothing to hide the Vergallian's inhuman perfection.

"You'll never be able to infiltrate the Old Way community undercover," Razood told her, looking rather pleased with himself. "I'm in for the duration because they've hired me to set up a forge and help train young blacksmiths. And from what I've seen, everybody in the first group knows each other by name."

"I wore this to make them feel comfortable," Avisia said. "I grew up on a tech-ban planet myself, you know."

"In a palace," the Grenouthian director added unnecessarily.

"Be that as it may, I feel a kinship to these Humans, and I just came from a very pleasant session of quilting and gossip."

"And what did you learn?"

"Nothing any of you would be interested in," Avisia said haughtily. "It's a shame the Gem aren't willing to pay EarthCent Intelligence for the privilege of spying on the Humans. Even a cloned female would make a better conversational partner than any of you. And while we're on the subject of male nonsense, whose idea was it to use disintegrating paper to send the notice of this meeting? I was eating breakfast when the envelope came and it showered cellulose powder all over my fruit."

"My notification of the meeting was stamped in a bar of sodium that burst into flames immediately after I read it," Razood said. "I thought it was a bit dramatic."

"Somebody bumped into me while I was shooting a scene of Old Way children playing, and then I found a message about the meeting in my pouch," the Grenouthian director contributed.

The swinging door to the kitchen flew open, and Bill backed through carrying a large tray with a pot of coffee, cold cuts, cheese, and vegetable sticks. "Sorry it's nothing special, but nobody told us about the meeting," he said.

"Are you sure you weren't informed via a telepathic message?" Lume asked. "Perhaps a tattoo discovered on your hand?"

"I haven't even seen Yaem in days and he's the one who always gives me the word. Where is he?"

"Here," the Sharf spy who spent most of his time working for Flower planning anime conventions announced from the doorway. "I stopped to pick up Brynlan."

Everybody nodded their understanding at the delay caused by the slow-footed Verlock, who trailed a few steps behind Yaem.

"I thought I would save time by making the usual rather than taking orders," Jorb said, placing a large tray of drinks on the table. "And I only found out about the meeting because Rinka pinged and told me. Somebody slipped a message into a choral recording she practices with several times a day to recalibrate her range after singing with Humans."

"I suspect somebody is getting carried away with showing off their tradecraft," Brynlan ground out as he took his usual seat at the tables which had been hastily pushed together. "It took me almost an hour to decode the notification I was sent. A very clever encryption algorithm."

"I did get a weird message on my tab while I was doing homework last night when Julie was out," Bill said. "I thought it was just a glitch, but maybe it was in code."

"I spent yesterday evening with your fiancée and Vivian McAllister at the Old Way sewing circle," the Vergallian said. "Neither of them had any clue how to sew. If they were a few years younger, I might have invited them to start sitting in the beginner classes at my finishing school, but the other women in the sewing circle displayed a tremendous amount of patience."

"If everybody is here, and none of us called the meeting, who—" Jorb cut himself short as the Farling physician skittered into the cafeteria.

"I see you all came," M793qK rubbed out on his speaking legs. "I initiated this meeting to address the informal agreement for pooling intelligence information."

"But you aren't part of our agreement," Lume pointed out.

"That hasn't stopped me from participating fully in the past, and you should consider yourselves lucky that I'm willing to provide value in return."

"Informal though it may be, we did seek Captain Pyun's approval since we're all here as paid guests of EarthCent Intelligence," the Dollnick said, crossing all four arms across his chest. "We're all aware that you no longer represent the Farling hierarchy in intelligence matters."

"I'm here on my own account for my own reasons," M793qK said. "I would think that somebody who owes me one would respect that."

Lume inclined his head in acknowledgment of the Farling's point, but at the same time he stretched out his lower arms as if to invite support for his argument from his colleagues.

"Don't look at me," Jorb said to the Dollnick. "I owe him one myself."

"Same here," the Grenouthian snorted as they started going around the table.

"Two," Avisia said with a sigh. "If somebody wants to trade..."

"No takers," Razood said. "We all concede your right to summon us, M793qK, but what is it about our little information sharing club that has your wings popping out?"

The Farling realized that his wings had indeed peeked out of his carapace, the beginnings of a display of mirth in his culture, and he quickly pulled them back in. "May I proceed, Captain Pyun?"

"Now that you have us all here it's a little late to ask," Woojin said, pouring himself a black coffee. "Can I assume you're in attendance also, Flower?"

"Affirmative," the Dollnick AI replied.

"I'm sure you're all aware of my interest in genealogy and all things related to the physical and social evolution of the sentient species," M793qK began. "For some time now, my sources on Earth have been sending me reports about the Old Way movement. I believe it represents a real advance in Human civilization."

"Don't you mean retreat?" Woojin asked. "I was just explaining to the director that I've served as a mercenary on Vergallian tech-ban worlds, and in many ways it was like Earth's pre-industrial age."

Avisia's bubbly pink drink went down the wrong way and she sprayed Jorb and Razood expelling it. "Sorry," she wheezed. "Captain Pyun's comment took me completely by surprise." She reestablished a perfect sitting posture on the edge of her chair and addressed herself to Woojin. "Surely you're aware that the queens ruling tech-ban worlds have chosen that route for their subjects after extensive research, both practical and academic. There are many different ways to judge the happiness and health of a civilization, but the level of technology they choose to employ is not one of them."

"The reduction of evil behavior in a society is a much better indicator of progress than advances in technology," Flower contributed.

"I'm sure you'll get a chance to discuss these ancillary issues at the upcoming conference," the Farling physician rubbed out on his speaking legs before the captain could respond. "Earth Two interests me from an intellectual standpoint, and according to my sources on Union Station, all of your embassies actively intervened to put the Alts and Humans on this course. I'm not asking what side deals any of your species may have had with the Stryx," he continued, raising his top limbs to quell the reflexive protests of ignorance, "or whether your ambassadors were coordinating their actions or acted independently with the same goal. I called this meeting to offer my cooperation in the venture, providing you keep me fully informed."

"I don't suppose you want to sign up with EarthCent Intelligence and pay the hosting fee," Woojin said. Everybody held their breaths while the Farling twiddled his speaking legs, and finally the captain said, "I didn't think so."

"The Sharf don't have an ambassador on Union Station," Yaem said. "And if you're half as good at intercepting and decrypting communications as Flower, you know that my superiors don't trust me so I'm not in their loop."

"Then I'll fill you in," M793qK said. "Your species has deals with both the Fillinducks and the Tharks to represent your interests on the tunnel network, and their ambassadors on Union Station contributed to moving forward the negotiations between the Alts and the Humans."

"The Old Way elders are having a lunch meeting about Flower's education proposals and I have to be there to record it for my documentary," the Grenouthian said. "Are we through here?"

"I've said my piece," the Farling rubbed out. "I hope I can count on your cooperation."

"And then we'll be even?" Avisia said hopefully.

M793qK couldn't restrain his wings from popping out in amusement and beating the air so hard that the captain had to grab for his coffee mug before it blew off the table.

"It wasn't that funny," the Vergallian grumbled.

Ten

"It's too much," Julie complained out loud. "Pick one thing and I'll do my best. I can't help Yaem with the conference, work on a marketing plan and strategic relationships for the new commercial rental business, play hostess when the Alts arrive, recruit new workers for all of your businesses, and master this archaic sewing machine."

The Dollnick artificial intelligence managed a convincing sigh. "If you don't want to learn how to sew on a treadle-powered machine, you don't have to learn how to sew on a treadle-powered machine."

Julie lowered her head to hide a smile while rolling the chair from the sewing machine back to her desk. "I can't be good at everything, you know. And the Old Way women told me that sewing machines just make mistakes happen faster. I'll learn how to do some things by hand first, and then maybe I'll go back to the machine."

"Did you hear me threatening to take it away? The sewing machine will be right there waiting for you when you're ready. Now, we need to talk about the conference planning meeting with Yaem you have scheduled later this morning."

"Why don't you wait for the meeting and talk to both of us?"

"Because Yaem won't be coming," Flower said. "I need him to make the day-to-day decisions at my anime studios.

We have thousands of artists, technicians, and voice performers working on a dozen productions. The business doesn't all come to a halt because the Grenouthian director is following his muse to make a documentary."

"I didn't realize the documentary was taking so much of his time," Julie said. "I've been too busy with your other projects lately to even think about Flower Studios. I'll bet Yaem is happy, though."

"He is, and I'll have to think about making the position permanent. The Grenouthian director was already overworked and he's not really a fan of the medium. Yaem is an anime fanatic, even if he falls a little short on the creativity front. They'll make a good team if I can manage their egos."

"Wait," Julie said, her voice rising. "Does that mean that I'm in charge of this con by default?"

"I'll help, and you can hire assistants," Flower replied. "It's a treaty conference, not a con, so there will be far less work. Samuel and the leaders of the Old Way communities will represent Human interests, and the Alt party will probably bring a contract queen to do most of the negotiating. That's one of the things you need to find out."

"We start loading Alts at the next stop, right?"

"The Alt colonists didn't want me jumping to their homeworld, so they turned to the Vergallians for transportation to stops where I can pick them up. It's all a bit makeshift, but I've been studying the negotiating practices of a dozen species, and I think I have it under control."

"I'm surprised you aren't just following the Princely Rules of Negotiation, or whatever the Dollnicks call them," Julie said.

"My Stryx mentor provided me with some recommended reading, and I realized that Dollnick methods weren't necessarily the best match for either Humans or Alts," Flower said. "Are you familiar with the six basic types of interspecies negotiations?"

"Why ask when you already know the answer?"

"It's considered good manners among Dollnicks. First, there are negotiations between two parties where the balance of power is so unequal that the outcome is never in doubt."

"Do you mean like an unconditional surrender?" Julie asked.

"I was thinking of anything involving the Stryx, but your example is fine," Flower said. "Second, there are negotiations where the outcome is a matter of life or death to one party and a modest loss of business opportunity to the other. An example of this would be anything involving Humans and an advanced species."

"You don't have to rub it in."

"The third type of negotiation is between parties whose rules don't align, which is always the case if they don't belong to the same empire or an umbrella organization like the tunnel network."

"What about variations on the first two types of negotiations, like between unequal parties without so much distance between them? Say the Dollnicks and the Hortens."

"Are you trying to get a rise out of me?" Flower demanded. "There's a gap of millions of years of progress between Dollnicks and Hortens. The exemplars you're looking for are Drazens and Hortens, or Vergallians and Frunge."

"Sorry, Drazens and Hortens," Julie said, again hiding a smile.

"The six types of negotiations are classified by the boundary conditions—what happens at the limits. The trivial case is when the parties and their interests are exactly equal in all ways, and the citation case is when they reach the extremes."

"Okay, I guess I understand that. But why do I have to know all this when my only role at the conference will be arranging for the venue and keeping the coffee flowing?"

"A good host should always be prepared to facilitate negotiations and you can't do that if you don't understand what's going on," Flower said. "Did you understand the third case about misaligned rules?"

"Yes, teacher," Julie said in an artificially childish sing-song.

"The fourth type of negotiations is between parties whose timelines are badly out of sync."

"I thought time travel was impossible."

"I'm talking about timelines in the context of the length of negotiations," the Dollnick AI said. "A thousand years to me and a thousand years to you have very different meanings."

"Oh, I wouldn't have thought of that one. You mean that humanity is always at a disadvantage negotiating with other species because we have the shortest lifespans and that translates into the greatest urgency," Julie said.

"Exactly. Can you tell me the trivial case of the fourth type of negotiation?"

"Well, you just said the trivial case for negotiation types is where all things are equal, so I guess that would mean some sort of artificial deadline that's in the near future for both parties." She paused and looked up at the ceiling suspiciously. "Is that why you pushed to get communities from the Old Way movement and the Alt colonists on board before they've even completed the deal? Now they have a deadline to get everything hashed out before we reach Earth Two."

"It will certainly cause problems all around if I can't disembark both parties when we arrive at Earth Two because no deal has been struck," Flower agreed. "The fifth type of negotiation is distributive, where there's a fixed stake to be divided up, making it a zero-sum game."

"You mean one side has to lose for the other to win."

"It's very common in business, but not recommended in diplomacy for what I think are obvious reasons. The final type of negotiation is integrative, meaning that the outcome creates increased value for both parties."

"That sounds like the win-win philosophy you're always pushing," Julie said. "But it seems to me like all six types of negotiations could apply at the same time in varying degrees. The Alts are more advanced than us—I mean humanity, not you—and from what Samuel told me their interest in Earth Two is very different from ours as well. I don't know how long Alts live, but I'll bet their rules for negotiations don't align with ours, so there's already three types of negotiation rolled into one."

"You're correct that all of the types can come into play at the same table, though if you take them to the upper limit, you usually find there is one dominant requirement driving the outcome," Flower said. "In the case of the Earth Two negotiation, what do you imagine it will be?"

Julie thought for a moment before venturing a guess. "The trivial case of the timeline you mentioned, since the negotiation has to be complete before we arrive at Earth Two."

"I hope the deal will get done, but if I thought that imposing an artificial deadline was a sure thing, we wouldn't be having this conversation."

"So where do you see the main sticking point?"

"In the second type of negotiation, where only one party sees the outcome as a matter of life or death," the Dollnick AI said.

"Because EarthCent and the Human Empire believe humanity needs a second home so our contract workers don't all go native on open worlds and end up as isolated second class communities," Julie surmised. "At least, that's how Vivian explained it when I asked her why Earth Two is such a big deal."

"But I expect the main problem will be that the value system the Alts practice means they're coming to the table with a large number of non-negotiable demands," Flower said. "I've reviewed the transcripts from the preliminary negotiations that allowed the Alts and the Human Empire to move ahead with a joint purchase. While Samuel made the best deal humanity could have hoped for, it was mainly a matter of concessions."

"But the Alts already borrowed like a trillion creds from the Vergallians and handed it over to the Container Prince as a down payment on a planetary mortgage," Julie protested. "They need us to make the economics work or they'll end up defaulting on the loan."

"The Alts find financial dealings distasteful and they left all of that in the hands of their contract queens. What they care about is protecting the current ecosystem of Earth Two and seeing to it that the remaining terraforming work is done in an environmentally responsible manner. They aren't going to make compromises about anything they think pushes back against that goal."

"Then I feel sorry for Samuel and the Old Way negotiators if all they can do is sit there and agree to whatever the Alts ask of them. Do you think they'll back out?"

"No, and I'm hoping that Samuel doesn't choose the path of brinkmanship to get the best possible deal as he did with the Wanderers, or the Alts may be so offended that they simply walk away. But I do think that the negotiations will be hard and that both sides will benefit from any support we can give them."

"Aren't you on our side?" Julie asked.

"As the host ship, I can't play favorites, and as my representative, neither can you," Flower said. "When the Alts arrive, I'll want you to visit them every day just so they know we care."

"What about all of my other jobs?"

"Now do you understand why I keep telling you to hire an assistant?"

"But I'm *your* assistant," Julie said. "Do you really think anybody wants to work as an assistant to an assistant?"

"You're my *executive* assistant," Flower said, putting stress on the word, "and assistants of all kinds are the most common jobs in both diplomacy and the entertainment industry. The Verlock diplomatic service even has assistant trainees nested five levels deep, though that seems like an exaggeration to me."

"Can I just ask Dewey for help if I get overloaded?"

"I'll leave it up to you, but just remember you can hire four co-ops from the Open University for what I pay Dewey for the same amount of time, and the students get an educational benefit."

"I suppose there are going to be observers at the conference," Julie said, unable to keep the dread from her voice. "Samuel told us that when the Conference of Sovereign

Human Communities had to make a decision about starting the Human Empire, they had to host observers from alien species that couldn't have cared less about the outcome."

"The observer requirement only applies to events triggered by the tunnel network treaty," Flower reassured her. "The alien intelligence agents who live on board through their arrangement with EarthCent will all be in attendance, and you should coordinate with Bill about catering for them. Since the conference will be limited to negotiations without any trade show or special events, I don't expect any media coverage until we arrive at Union Station for the final sessions."

Julie let out her breath in relief and brought up the day planner on her tab. She began color coding each item on her schedule in accordance with which one of Flower's businesses was associated with the event. It took her almost two hours of going back and forth to reclassify some activities, the purpose of which seemed to change as she thought more about them. Then she had to run for a blue event, followed by a green, and before she knew it, the day was over and she was sitting down to dinner with Bill.

"I feel like we haven't eaten together in a week," he said, serving up the omelet he'd just made with a side of steamed vegetables and a thick slice of fresh-baked bread. "We're out of those salty olives you like, so I substituted marinated mushrooms."

"It still feels weird that you're a better cook than me," Julie said. "I always thought that the woman was supposed to be responsible for the meals."

"You take care of the laundry and the apartment."

"The machine does the laundry, I don't even have to add soap, and you're neater than I am, so keeping the apartment straight is easier than when I lived alone." She took a bite of the omelet and chewed thoughtfully. "You know, I think the mushrooms are better than the olives. You might want to put it on your list for the café."

"Do you think it works for a light dinner?" Bill asked. "I'm kind of going back and forth in my head as to whether I'd rather run a sort of bakery with breakfast and lunch or go the three-meals-a-day route like Fandaz. She's been teaching me a lot of tricks, but the Frunge can go days on end without sleeping, so I could never work her schedule."

"Have you made any progress on the matchmaking front?" Julie asked.

"You know I'm not good at that stuff. Whenever I'm with one of them, I bring up the other one's name. I think they like each other, but Razood hasn't asked her for a date."

"He isn't going to," Flower interjected over the room's speakers. "That's why I said to set them up the way you did Jorb and Rinka."

"Jorb begged Julie to do that for him," Bill reminded the Dollnick AI.

"And I don't think Fandaz is the board-game type, but I'll ask her," Julie said.

"Jorb invited us LARPing tonight, so if there are enough open spaces, I could invite Razood and you could invite Fandaz."

"You go ahead with Jorb and Razood. I already promised Vivian to go to the Old Way sewing circle with her."

"Tomorrow night is just us, okay?" Bill said. "We can get an immersive to watch on the holo system or something."

"Deal. And I'll do the dishes tonight."

Bill left for the LARPing studio about a half-hour before the sewing circle was scheduled to start. Julie spent around ten minutes of that time putting away some of her things that seemed to have distributed themselves around the apartment when she wasn't paying attention. Then she asked Flower to ping Vivian, and the two young women stepped out into the corridor across from each other at almost exactly the same time.

"Don't stay out too late," Samuel called after Vivian before the door closed.

"He didn't go LARPing with the guys?" Julie asked her friend.

"Samuel is too busy reading everything that EarthCent Intelligence knows about the Alts to prepare for the negotiations," Vivian said. "I'll be glad when this is all over and we can go back to just building the Human Empire, one baby step at a time."

"Do we know much about Alt history? I thought they mainly kept to themselves."

"They do, but they aren't secretive, so the aliens who visit the Alt homeworld have been bringing back books and translating them. The Drazens share the histories with EarthCent Intelligence, but I tried reading one and it put me to sleep."

"The Old Way camp," Julie told the lift tube as they entered, and then resumed the conversation. "It was boring? Aren't they way ahead of us in technology even if they don't use it as much in everyday life as we do?"

"The Alts developed their own interstellar jump ship if that's what you mean," Vivian said. "I don't want to sound like a savage, but they never had any wars or revolutions, the sort of stuff that makes primitive species interesting. If somebody created a game based on Alt history, it would be like that old Earth one the programmers from Bits showed me where you run a farm and nothing ever goes wrong."

"I loved that game when I was a kid," Julie said. "It was my main escape when I couldn't read."

"So, did you talk to Flower about her giving you too much work?"

"Today, sort of."

"Did you bring it up or did she?"

"Flower wants me to be the front person for the Earth Two conference because she needs Yaem to run her animation business while the Grenouthian director is making his documentary," Julie said in a rush. "I used it to beg off mastering the treadle-powered sewing machine for the time being, and then I broke down my schedule for the next two months to see if there was anything I could delegate to an assistant."

"You could use twelve assistants, and maybe a baker's dozen so the thirteenth could keep track of what the others are doing," Vivian told her.

"It's not that bad, really," Julie said defensively as the lift tube door opened on an ag deck. "Half of my schedule is training in her different businesses, which can always be postponed. And I realized that all of my experience hiring people has been to fill jobs for Flower. I've never had to choose anybody for myself."

"You chose Bill," Vivian corrected her.

"I don't pay him so it doesn't count."

"Have the two of you been practicing?" asked a grandmotherly woman who joined the girls on the path. "It's hard to make progress if you only sew twice a week."

"I've been sewing at my desk whenever I get the chance," Vivian said, displaying the tiny red dots on her fingertips from needle pricks as proof. "Our Cayl mentor has been coaching me, but you wouldn't know her."

"Krey? She visited our knitting group last Friday, but she's so advanced I don't think we had anything to offer her. She said she learned from the retirees living in Flower's Paradise."

"Maybe I should have tried knitting first," Vivian said. "The needles are much easier to keep track of and babies look cute in knit caps."

"How about you, Julie?" the woman asked. "Have you chosen a project yet? Learning different types of stitches without sewing anything can only take you so far."

"It's Flower's fault," Vivian said before her friend could speak. "She's been cross-training Julie in so many occupations that the poor girl has trouble settling on any one thing."

"Have I gotten that bad?" Julie asked. "Sometimes I think Flower forgets that I'm not a young artificial intelligence with a perfect memory."

"What a funny idea," the older woman said as they entered the tent where the sewing circle was meeting. "I've heard of people anthropomorphizing artificial intelligence, even those simple teacher bots which are just a cube with a display, but it never occurred to me that the opposite could be true."

"There needs to be a different word to describe an AI who thinks of people as artificial intelligence," Vivian said.

"Arithomorphizing, but don't let it go to your head," Flower said over Julie's implant.

Eleven

Harry whistled in admiration when the president of the Flower's Paradise independent living cooperative answered the door. "I've never seen you so dressed up, Jack. You're making me look bad."

"Cameramen are supposed to fade into the background," Irene reminded her husband. "Jack and Nancy are going to do all of the talking."

"I'll be out in a minute," Nancy called from inside the apartment. "I forgot that we aren't supposed to wear perfume and I had to take another shower."

"Does anybody know why that is?" Harry asked

"There was a briefing at Human Empire headquarters today for people who signed up to participate in the Alt outreach program," Jack said. "First Administrator McAllister told us the Alts believe that people use perfume to project a false impression."

"I suppose that's true, but can't you say the same thing about clothes?" Irene asked. "I'm a little too old to stop wearing support garments because they might offend somebody."

"Sorry for holding everybody up," Nancy said, her skin glowing thanks to the two hot showers and scrubbings in a short span of time. "I'm so excited to be involved in history after teaching it most of my life."

There was a loud beep as Harry accidentally steered the floating immersive camera he was guiding too close to the corridor wall. "I'm turning off the gesture controls and just keeping a hand on it until we get to the Alt deck," he announced. "These beeps are driving me crazy."

"You should keep practicing now while you have the opportunity," Irene said. "Today the Grenouthian director showed me how to slave the second camera to the master I'm controlling to capture a reverse angle view. I'll do it as soon as we get there. Your job will be to stay close and take back control if something goes wrong."

"We need to get moving," Jack said, glancing at his cheap Dollnick wristwatch that was currently emulating an old LCD. The two couples made their way to the nearest lift tube, Harry trailing behind as he tried to corral the recalcitrant camera, which seemed to have a mind of its own. "Alt deck," Jack requested when they were all in the capsule.

"Can we eat their food if they offer?" Irene asked. "The Grenouthian director said that it's traditional for documentary subjects to offer snacks to the camera crew, and I wouldn't want to be rude by refusing."

"The flora and fauna on Alt were all transplanted from Earth when the Stryx rescued their ancestors from ours, so everything they eat should be safe," Nancy told her. "Young McAllister told us that they tend to serve a lot of fruit, so basically the same as Flower."

"Will you be meeting their delegation for the conference?" Irene asked.

"All we know is that the group who came on board are colonists," Jack said. "First Administrator McAllister explained that the point of the outreach program is to give the Alts a chance to slowly adjust to being around humans.

The Alts have a visceral fear reaction to our presence, especially their children and babies. The theory is that they can get over it with repeated exposure."

"So I'll be serving a useful purpose after all," Harry said. "All I have to do is stand there and let them be scared of me."

"Do they avoid using modern technology to the same extent as the Old Way communities Flower is transporting?" Irene asked.

"Supposedly that's a misconception," Jack said. "The Alts have a higher-technology culture than Earth, they just compartmentalize the aspects they see as interfering with interpersonal relationships and individual responsibility. Their technology is all designed with their natural surroundings in mind."

"The McAllisters showed us some intelligence reports about the business ventures the other tunnel network species do with the Alts," Nancy said. "The Frunge made the first breakthrough selling the Alts bicycles with high-tech tires that laid down a random pattern rather than leaving tire tracks."

"Why is that important?" Harry asked.

"Tire tracks create unnatural starter channels for rain, and before you know it, you have ruts and erosion. It didn't stop the Alts from using bicycles, but they were always conscious of the problem. They even experimented with dragging various implements behind a bicycle while they were riding to erase the tire tracks, but they never hit on a good solution until the Frunge came along."

The capsule doors opened on a deck that none of them had ever visited before, but the man wearing the Farling costume who was struggling to pull on the head was familiar to them all.

"Dave, what are you doing here?" Jack asked.

"Waiting for somebody to give me a hand with my head," the former salesman replied. "There's something wrong with the sealing strip at the back."

"Let me take a look." The president of Flower's Paradise examined the edge of the costume's one-piece head and the mating surface on the back of the fake carapace. "It was folded over," he reported, fixing the problem. "There. Now, why are you on the Alt deck dressed as the Evil Mastermind from *Everyday Superheroes*?"

"M793qK asked me to recruit some Alts for a study he's doing," Dave said, displaying a sheaf of handouts. "He's offering all sorts of free treatments to anybody who signs up."

"What's the study about?" Nancy asked.

"Something to do with genetics that I couldn't understand. He said that our scientists are still arguing over how far back you have to go before we and the Alts share a common ancestor, but from Doc's standpoint, we're practically the same species."

"From M793qK's standpoint, mammals are all practically the same species," Harry said. "Sometimes I eavesdrop on the lectures he gives Bill when they're testing products in the kitchen. I worry that he's going to give that young man an inferiority complex."

"The camera!" Irene cried, and her husband realized that he had been too expressive with his arms while talking and accidentally sent the immersive camera floating off over the orchard. "Gesture it back."

"It's too far. It's not responding at all. We better ask Flower for help."

"Hold on a minute." Irene brought her own camera near, touched something in the controls, and then focused on Dave. The stray camera came zooming over to show the Farling costume from the reverse angle, with the output of both cameras showing on the split screen of the one Irene was controlling.

"Sorry," Harry said sheepishly as he went to stand near the camera. "I guess I'm not cut out to shoot documentaries. You better keep the camera slaved and I'll just follow it around."

"Here," Dave said, handing the baker around a quarter of his fliers. "You can help me hand these out."

"What kind of free treatments is the doctor offering the Alts?" Nancy asked. "I was under the impression that they're much healthier than we are."

"I don't know. The fliers aren't in Humanese."

"English, Dave," the former school teacher remonstrated. "It might make sense to say that Dollnicks whistle Dollnick and Vergallians speak Vergallian, but humanity hasn't had time to standardize on a single language, even if we're all expected to know English."

"When in space, do as aliens do," Dave said philosophically.

"It's interesting that Flower put the Alts on an ag deck," Jack said, changing the subject to head off a potential argument. "She's been sending the Old Way communities to camp on the ag deck with the writers colony, which has a few orchards, but it's mainly fields. Here I only see trees."

"For all we know it could be the same deck but the other side of the cylinder," Harry pointed out. "The more important question is, how are we going to find the Alts?"

"Shhhh," Irene said, holding a finger to her lips without accidentally sending an errant instruction to the floating immersive camera. "I think I hear something."

The group stood silent for a moment, and then Nancy said, "Mozart."

"You think Flower is playing classical music to get the Alts accustomed to Human culture?"

"I think that's live," Nancy said. "There, they just stopped and replayed a bar. They must be practicing."

"It's that way," Jack said decisively and pointed at a broad path through a grove of avocado trees. "I know we're expected. Maybe they're playing Earth music to honor us."

"Please guide the camera while we're moving, Harry," Irene said. "I don't have anything to focus on, and even if the anti-collision technology will keep it from hitting a tree, I don't want to exercise that too much. I wouldn't be surprised if the Grenouthian director can download a report about all of the near misses."

"There's something a little odd about the sound," Nancy said as they drew closer to the source of the music. "I wonder if it's the acoustics in here."

"I don't know the piece well enough to tell what's strange, but I'd be surprised if it was caused by the ship's geometry," Jack said. "The Dollnicks are masters of acoustic isolation fields, and I'll bet Flower has the place tricked out like an auditorium."

"There's a campground, but I don't see any Alts," Irene said as the path emerged in a large clearing dotted with tents of an unfamiliar design. "Oh, I think the music has stopped."

Rather than browsing around the deserted tents like potential thieves, the party began to make their way around the outside of the clearing, and soon some teenagers and younger children carrying musical instrument cases came into view. The Alts froze when they saw the visitors from the independent living cooperative, but then a tall boy with what looked like a violin case came closer, circling a little so he could approach Dave.

"Are it alien?" he asked in broken English.

Dave shook his costume head. "I'm a Human stand-in for our Farling physician."

"I can't believe we didn't think of bringing any external translation devices," Jack said. "How are we going to understand each other?"

"I have my ear cuff translator for volunteering at the information desk at the bazaar," Irene said, reaching in her purse. "One of you can borrow it."

"You better take it, Jack," Nancy said.

"It won't help them understand me," he said. "We can ask Flower to translate, but I'm not sure how the Alts will feel about having a disembodied voice talking to them."

"Not worry," the teenager said. "We studying Humanese while waiting Flower. I not so good, but parents is."

"How strange," Nancy said. "I would have thought that it would be easier for youth to pick up a new language than adults."

The boy took a moment to process her words. "We still doing regular homework. Parents only study Humanese."

"Are the adults returning to the camp?"

"They slower we," the boy explained, and then hastily amended himself. "More careful, like. You come guest tent." He gestured for the visitors to follow him, maintaining his distance all the while, and the younger Alts stayed twice as far away just to play it safe.

"They don't seem bothered by the cameras," Harry said. "The Grenouthian director must have been here already."

"He got in contact with them over the Stryxnet weeks ago," Irene explained. "It's just like the instructor told us in my documentary-making class. You have to plan everything ahead of time if you want to end up with a coherent storyline."

Harry and Irene declined to take seats at the table in the guest tent so they could stay with their cameras, and Dave explained that the rigid carapace prevented him from sitting. The young Alt promised to tell the adults that visitors had arrived, and hastily exited the tent as if escaping from a bad smell.

"So far, so good," Jack said, eyeing the bowl of colorful fruit on the table. "If that boy had been dressed like the young people on Flower, I never would have taken him for an alien."

"Their heads are a little bigger than ours," Nancy told him. "I don't know if their skulls are thicker or if they have larger brains."

"M793qK told me something about the pure Neanderthal stock being lost before the Stryx moved them off of Earth," Dave said. "He told me that there was a burst of interbreeding at the end when the Neanderthal population was falling, or maybe that caused it."

"We should avoid the subject until we find out how the Alts feel about it," Nancy said, keeping her voice down.

"Please don't get up," a modestly attired Alt woman announced in clear English as she entered the tent. "My name is Fanli, and I'm the director of our Human outreach program." Her eyes widened slightly when she saw Dave standing off to the side. "Are you wearing that costume to scare away evil spirits? We've heard that you maintain many of the superstitions of your ancestors, but I don't recall insect worship."

"I'm here to hand out fliers for the Farling doctor," Dave said without a hint of embarrassment. "I guess you could say that I'm his mascot. Here," he added, passing her a piece of paper. "I don't know what it says because it's in Alt, but I can tell you that whatever M793qK promises, he delivers. I go to him for all of my medical work."

Fanli took a moment to study the sheet the former salesman thrust in her hand, and she muttered something to herself in Alt before continuing in English, "Interesting. While I don't suffer from any of the conditions listed here, the DNA analysis services on offer are beyond our technology."

"What are you looking at?" asked a male Alt as he entered the tent. Dave hastened to hand over another flier, and if the newcomer was at all put off by the Farling costume, he showed no sign of it. "Forgive my manners," the Alt said after a cursory glance at the list of services. "I'm Hethram, which that ear cuff device you're wearing may translate as a blight that affects certain hardwood trees. I apologize for not being here when you arrived. Our community was caught up in practicing an Earth composition which we hope to perform at the conclusion of the conference."

Jack quickly introduced all five of the party from Flower's Paradise before asking, "Is every Alt a musician?"

"Well, we all play instruments," Hethram replied with a chuckle. "Some of us, myself included, fail to transcend technical competence, but it's important to participate nonetheless."

"Please, help yourselves to some fruit," Fanli said. After Jack and Nancy each chose a piece, she took the bowl around to Irene and Harry before pausing in front of Dave. "You don't want to take the head off?"

"I still have all of these fliers to hand out. I'm hoping you'll allow me to wander about your encampment if you don't think it will upset anybody," he said.

The Alt woman smiled. "Strange as it may sound, your costume makes you more approachable. Especially for our children who will need more time to become accustomed to Humans. Please enjoy yourself."

"Hang on," Jack said, getting up and going over to Dave. "You better take the ear cuff translator just in case." He pulled the head off the Farling costume, installed the device over the salesman's ear, and then replaced it. "Good luck."

The two Alts took seats across from Jack and Nancy. Fanli began by asking, "Are you comfortable talking about the subject of age?"

"I'm the oldest one here and it doesn't bother me a bit," Nancy said. "Do you have a specific question?"

"Only that I would have guessed that you are all above what we're told Humans refer to as retirement age. In addition to learning your language, we have been studying materials on Human society. I had a distinct impression that retired people are—how can I put this politely—encouraged to stay out of the way of younger folk. I'm a bit surprised that the Human Empire allowed you to participate in their outreach program, especially with the emperor being such a young man."

"First Administrator," Hethram corrected her.

"Sorry, yes," Fanli said. "To be honest, we watched a Grenouthian documentary about old age homes on Earth. I was so upset by what we saw that I couldn't sleep that night. I suppose it makes sense that you would want to escape to space."

"We do consider ourselves lucky to be here, but our independent living community is something of an exception," Nancy said. "It wasn't that long ago that elders on Earth were cared for by family members or not at all. As the population shifted to the cities and health care became the biggest industry in many advanced countries, the number of frail people in need of special care grew, and government-supported facilities became widespread. When the Stryx opened Earth, government funding collapsed, and they've sort of muddled through from one bad solution to the next ever since."

"The four of you look alert and active," Hethram said. "If you've found a system that works well, why not replicate it back on Earth?"

"Special circumstances," Jack said. "Our fixed expenses are very low because Flower had vacant space she was trying to fill, and while she encourages us to hire people to provide any services we require, she always has bots available as a backup. And all of our medical needs are taken care of by the Farling doctor, who even makes house calls if need be."

The two Alts exchanged a look, and Hethram said, "I'm afraid we didn't recognize a phrase you used. Does 'house call' mean that the alien doctor contacts patients via a telephony system if they aren't capable of going to see him?"

"He comes to our deck and visits the patient in their cabin," Nancy said with a smile. "I suppose you don't recognize the idiom because it hasn't been used on Earth in the last century or two and wouldn't have appeared in your study materials. Do your doctors make house calls on Alt?"

"We don't have a special term since the only way anybody sees a physician on Alt is when one comes to your home or workplace," Fanli said. "I imagine our medical equipment is much less bulky than yours, and if a patient requires isolation or around-the-clock care, what better place to provide it than at home?"

"Home care was the rule on Earth until a few hundred years ago," Nancy said. "The original hospitals were established by charities to care for the itinerant poor or travelers, and in some cases doctors-in-training even contributed fees to treat patients while they gained experience. It wasn't until the modern era when scientists had a better understanding of the importance of germs and a sterile operating environment that hospitals became the center of medical practice."

"And billing," Jack added. "Hospitals were big business."

"That's the other part we had trouble understanding from the study materials that the Vergallians provided," Hethram said. "The idea of asking for something in exchange for medical care goes against everything we believe."

"We've heard that you don't use money on Alt," Nancy said. "I thought that meant you had an advanced barter system."

"Our economic systems don't line up closely enough to have equivalent terms that can be easily translated. Everybody on Alt keeps track of the work they do and the products they offer outside of their immediate families, but our physicians consider it a privilege to serve and refuse to accept gifts."

"So does the government support them?" Jack asked.

Hethram shook his head. "In most cases, physicians have another career which provides for their needs, though of course, their families and friends support them in such a noble calling." He paused a moment, obviously considering something. "Our educational systems also align so poorly that I don't know where I'd start describing the differences. Anybody studying for the medical profession has their needs taken care of by their community."

"Our way of life may seem strange to you, but I'm sure that Humans are also capable of acting from altruism," Fanli said. "Is anybody paying for you to visit us?"

"We volunteered," Nancy said. "Flower insists that all members of our independent living cooperative who are capable of it put in a few hours of volunteer time every week, but this is something we wanted to do."

"And how about you," the Alt asked, turning to face Irene and the camera she was controlling. "Is the Grenouthian director paying you to be here?"

"I'm studying how to make documentaries at the Open University so I welcomed the chance," Irene said. "I volunteered my husband."

"Perhaps you'd like to visit Flower's Paradise and see how we live," Jack suggested to the Alts. "Nancy runs our lecture series, and she's scheduled some speakers from the Old Way to come in next week and talk about their society. You might find the information useful."

"Is there a monetary exchange involved?" Hethram asked.

"Our lecture series is open to everybody and there's never any charge," Nancy replied.

"Then we'll be there."

Twelve

"I can't believe how much blue tea you sell," Bill said, looking up from the accounting readout on the miniregister. "I guess it's true that cafés all need a low-cost offering that increases the cash flow."

"It would be strange if the Blue Tea Café didn't do well selling blue tea," Fandaz said. "It's one of the only Frunge beverages that's not only harmless to Humans but provides beneficial anti-oxidants. A few mild varieties of tea are our only native food products that Humans can tolerate."

"I used to wonder how you could afford such a large space in the high-rent corridor, but not anymore."

"It seemed like a gamble when I opened, but locating here means I can charge more than if I had opened in the food court adjacent to the bazaar. We have a saying in Frunge that it pays to spend more on a garden plot where the sun is shining."

"I remember poor people back on Earth complaining that it takes money to make money," Bill said. "I'm used to not having money myself, and I'm always thinking about how to keep expenses down."

"Retail is one of the few businesses where if you have sufficient capital or credit, you can start at the top," Fandaz told him. "You'd be surprised how many people come to a café like this to discuss starting a business. Sometimes they ask my advice, and the first thing I tell them is to have their meetings somewhere cheaper, and save coming here for when they have paying clients to entertain."

"I think I get it. Spending to bring in sales is one thing, but spending money to play at being in business is another."

"I've seen boutiques on this corridor open and close again within the space of a few months because they never get any customers. It's always sad to see a business fail, but sometimes it's obvious that the owners are indulging in a fantasy rather than pursuing a dream."

"I'm not sure I understand the difference," Bill admitted.

"A fantasy is unrealistic by definition," Fandaz explained. "As an inspector general, I was trained to draw up psychological profiles of the diplomats on our watch list, and those who overindulged in fantasies were always at the highest risk for ethical violations. Individuals become addicted to the perfect outcomes they create in their imaginations at the expense of dealing with the facts of the real world. If their fantasy world diverges too far from reality they can suffer a psychological collapse. It's a rare condition in Frunge society, but I gather it's quite common among Humans."

"So how does that differ from a dream?"

"The word is more ambiguous in Humanese than in Frunge because you use it in multiple ways," the owner of the Blue Tea Café said. "There's an old tunnel network joke about the Verlocks with the punchline that they have a different word for everything. The opposite seems to be true with your species. Some of us wonder if your working vocabularies are so limited because—but I digress," she cut herself off. "I'm talking about dreams in the aspirational sense, goals to work towards. Fantasists only care about the endpoint, not the process of getting there. Given enough money or credit, a fantasist could pay for something that looks like your dream café, but without you to run the business it would have no chance of success."

"I'm going to need time to think that over," Bill said. "I have to decide if investing in a better location and interior furnishings is necessary, or if it's just playing at business."

"As long as you're aware of the difference, you're more than halfway home," Fandaz told him. "I talked to Flower about bringing you in to train as a shift manager through the Open University and it turns out that the co-op program will handle all of the payroll and benefits. Why don't you start next week?"

"Let me check with Harry and M793qK to make sure they don't need me," Bill said.

"Ask her," Flower prompted over his implant.

"What?" Bill asked out loud, and then remembered to point at his ear when the Frunge gave him a strange look.

"The date," the Dollnick AI said in his head. "The Human Empire is sponsoring a mineral show on the con deck with collections from the Alts and the Old Way communities. It opens in three hours. Tell Fandaz that Julie and some friends will be there, but don't mention Razood by name."

"Got it," Bill subvoced, lowering his hand and trying to look casual. "Would you like to come to the opening of a mineral show on the con deck this evening? My fiancée can get us in free, and I know there's going to be a buffet if you aren't into ore. It's in three hours, and we can meet at the entrance."

The Frunge froze for just a fraction of a second as she was picking up a bowl of sliced carrots to put away. "I love ore. Is—no, don't tell me. Three hours?" She examined her reflection in the door of a stainless steel refrigerator. "What am I going to do with my hair vines?"

"You look fine," Bill said, feeling slightly embarrassed that his mentor was so visibly flustered. "So we'll see you there?"

Fandaz nodded and then pointed at her ear. Something told Bill that she was going to be very busy for the next three hours, so he let himself out of the kitchen and headed for the lift tube.

"M793qK wants to see you," Flower said over his implant.

"Did we get a new shipment of products to test for the All Species Cookbook?"

"No, it's something else, but you can ask about your schedule for next week while you're there."

"I'd already forgotten about that," Bill admitted. "Are you alright with me taking time off from working for you to train with Fandaz? I've never managed employees before so I think it will be double-useful in helping me prepare to open my place."

"If I didn't agree, I would have told Fandaz that the Blue Tea Café doesn't qualify for the Open University co-op program."

"Doesn't it?"

"The rules are flexible," Flower said.

"Hey," Bill said as the lift tube doors opened on the corridor with the library and M793qK's clinic. "You're back to taking me places without asking."

"Does it bother you?"

"Not really, but don't try it when Julie is with me or she'll think that I'm letting you push me around."

The "occupied" sign that the Farling doctor had recently added above his door was lit. Bill continued for a few steps towards the library and then crouched on his heels to wait. A minute later, a little girl came out with a fistful of sugar-free lollipops that had come in for All Species Cookbook testing the prior week. She was followed by a red-headed woman wearing the ship's uniform.

"Third Officer Pyun," Bill greeted her. "I didn't recognize Em, she's grown so tall."

"My father was a big man, and M793qK says that Em will be taller than Woojin if we don't stop feeding her," Lynx said. "I think he's kidding about the second part."

"Is she—were you just here for a regular checkup?"

"Four books, max," Lynx called after her daughter who was skipping down the corridor. "She hides them in her bedroom to make Dewey come visit us." The third officer watched her daughter disappear into the library and then turned back to Bill. "Actually, we were stopping with M793qK to talk about you."

"Me?" Bill racked his brain for what it could be. "Did I do something wrong on one of my jobs?"

"The doctor has a proposition for you and he wanted to clear it with the captain first, but between all of the Old Way communities and Alts we're welcoming, Woojin hardly has time to brush his hat. Besides, I've been with EarthCent Intelligence longer than he has, so I came in his place."

"Is this about my pretending to be an agent for Yaem to get him credit with his bosses? The only thing he's asked me to do lately is practice using one-time pads, but it takes me forever to decode a single sentence. He sent a message to meet him on Monday but I didn't figure it out until Wednesday."

"I hate one-time pads," Lynx said sympathetically. "I heard they were back in fashion, even though I can't imagine the aliens need them for secure communications. And everybody rediscovering mail is driving me nuts. Did I ever tell you about the first time I saw an envelope?"

"When you were a child?" Bill asked.

"I was thirty. The first director of EarthCent Intelligence gave me and my partner our instructions in a sealed envelope. We couldn't figure out how to open it so we tore it in half to get the letter out. But this isn't about your work for Yaem. It's about your work for M793qK."

"EarthCent Intelligence is worried about the products we're certifying for the All Species Cookbook?"

"No, and don't ask me what that glorified alien beetle wants from you because he wouldn't tell me," the third officer said. "I'm just here so you know that M793qK has our permission—and I'm speaking for EarthCent Intelligence here—to talk to you about a job."

"But I'm just about to start working for Fandaz," Bill said, trying not to sound like he was whining. "Do I have to do it?"

"Do you have to talk to him or do you have to accept the job?" Lynx asked with a grin.

"I guess I have to talk to him, but do I have to accept?"

"No, it's entirely up to you, as is what you choose to tell us about it if you do accept. Knowing M793qK, the true purpose of whatever he's up to will be impossible to figure out in any case."

Bill let his head sink towards his chest, bounce a couple of times on the stretched neck muscles, and then looked up again. "Is Flower in on it?"

"Probably, but you'll have to ask her yourself," Lynx said. "Now I have to go catch up with my daughter before she takes all of the books in the children's section off the shelves trying to find one she hasn't already read."

The door to the clinic slid open at Bill's approach, and he entered reluctantly.

"Why are you acting like you just signed up as a medical test subject and you're having second thoughts?" the Farling rubbed out on his speaking legs. "Hop up on the examination table. We have something to discuss."

"I'll just stand if you don't mind," Bill said. "Third Officer Pyun told me that I should listen to you but then I could do what I want."

"Then I won't waste any of my valuable time on long explanations," M793qK said. "Yaem owes me a favor—several favors—and I asked him to loan you to me."

"But I already work for you."

"I need you in your capacity as an intelligence agent, not as a food tester."

"I'm not a real intelligence agent. I just pretend to get Yaem credit. Sometimes I recruit casual information sources for him when there are a lot of people visiting from Union Station, but nobody takes that stuff seriously."

"Do you think you're so different than Jorb, Razood, or Yaem himself?" M793qK asked. "None of them are intelligence professionals. Lume, Avisia, and Brynlan are the only career spies on board unless you count Lynx, and she's on extended leave. The rest of them are here to pursue their passions and collect a second salary as station chief for their respective intelligence services."

"So instead of working for the Sharf as a fake spy, I'll be working for the Farlings as a fake spy?" Bill asked.

"You'll be working for me, not the Farling hierarchy. We had a difference of opinion and I'm on my own."

"I should probably talk to Yaem before answering. You could be testing my loyalty to the Sharf or something."

M793qK grabbed Bill by the shoulders and frog-marched him over to the eye chart on the wall. "Read the bottom line."

"XHUMP BEGER DCZPL," Bill said. "Can I go now?"

"Decode it."

"Oh, no. That will take me all afternoon."

"Give me your pad," the Farling demanded, holding out a limb.

"No way," Bill said, backing up. "And I don't even know what sheet we're on."

"The top sheet. And it doesn't matter because I kept Yaem's sheet after I encoded the message."

"Isn't that a security breach? When Brynlan taught me and Yaem how the one-time pads worked he said we should always destroy the sheet after encoding a message. He even made us do the math on a hard surface with a pencil."

"The Verlock is no fool, but I saved the sheet so I could convince you that Yaem gave it to me," M793qK said. "Here, compare it to yours."

"Turn around," Bill said, feeling a bit childish, but he waited until he saw the back of the Farling's carapace before retrieving his tiny one-time pad from its ingenious hiding place in a drawer built into a five-cred piece. He removed the top sheet and secreted the pad back in the coin, and when he looked up, M793qK was watching with interest.

"Oh, was I supposed to keep my back turned?" the Farling rubbed out on his speaking legs. "I haven't seen the old drawer-in-a-coin trick for ages. It's good to know that the Sharf still appreciate the classics."

Bill shook his head in disgust and set the tiny sheet he'd retrieved on the counter next to the one M793qK had given him. Then he realized that his pocket magnifier was at home. "Uh, do you—?" he began.

"Here," the doctor said, pulling down from the ceiling an articulated metal arm that terminated in an enormous magnifying glass centered in a tubular lighting element. "I use it for examining slides, but don't turn on the light or—never mind."

"What happened?" Bill asked, staring at the wisp of smoke that had replaced the tiny sheets of character groupings.

"The Sharf use nitrocellulose paper for their one-time pads so they can be easily destroyed in case of capture. Between the Xeon lamp and the lens, you incinerated it."

"Brynlan told us to eat the sheets after we used them. They taste horrible, but at least there's not much to them."

"The Verlocks probably like the taste of nitrocellulose," M793qK said. "Did you have time to compare the sheets, or do we need to call Yaem down here?"

"I guess they looked the same, but how am I going to decode the message now?"

"I remember my sheet, which is the same as yours, but it makes no difference since I also know the message that I encoded. The point of producing the sheet was to convince you that Yaem gave his consent."

"I guess I'll see him at lunch tomorrow in any case," Bill said. "Did you really print a new eye chart just for that one line of code?"

"If you ever have to deliver a secure visual message, hiding it in plain sight is always the best approach," M793qK said. "Plus it makes your opponents look bad if you point it out after the fact. Talk to Yaem first if it makes you feel better, but make sure nobody is listening in."

"So we're all set for today?"

"You've grown more assertive this last year, for which I claim partial credit." The Farling placed a limb on the young man's shoulder in an almost fatherly manner. "I play a long game, Bill, and you won't lose by coming along for the ride. If everything goes to plan, thirty years from now your café could be a gathering place for spies from all over the galaxy."

"Uh, thanks for thinking of me, but I was planning on an artistic theme since Julie is going to be an author."

"Spies and authors go together like barbeque and potato chips," M793qK said, confirming Bill's suspicion about who had ended up with all of the surplus bags of chips sent for testing. "I predict that Flower will be stopping at Earth Two at least twice a circuit in the decades to come, and I'll want somebody who I can trust to run a few errands for me on the surface."

"If it's just that, I guess I can do it," Bill said. "I'll have to check with Julie."

"Good idea, work as a team," the Farling said, grabbing a black medical bag and starting for the door. "No, don't thank me," he forestalled Bill's response. "There's an emergency in the second LARPing studio. Some fool brought a real sword to a noodle weapon fight and Flower's bot is having trouble stopping the bleeding."

Three hours later, Bill was dressed in his best shirt and pants and waiting at the entrance to the mineral show with Julie, Rinka, Jorb, and a visibly nervous Razood.

"Are you sure she said she's coming?" the blacksmith asked for the third time. "Maybe you misunderstood."

"I asked if we'd see her here and she nodded," Bill said. "What could be more clear than that?"

"The tunnel network species standardized on nodding millions of years ago and Humans were just lucky that their system matched," Jorb concurred. "It's a fifty-fifty proposition for new members with heads and necks. It took the Hortens and the Dollnicks generations to get their nods right after they joined. The Grenouthians made a classic comedy documentary about all of the problems it caused for the Horten traders when they tried to use sign language."

"There she is," Rinka said, waving her tentacle to draw Fandaz's attention. "Wow, I've never seen her wearing such a high trellis."

"You can't leave us alone," Razood said, grabbing Bill's arm. "And Julie, you have to stay with Fandaz when I'm anywhere near her."

"Don't Jorb and Rinka count?" Julie asked.

"Our parents don't approve of our relationship so we can hardly serve as chaperones," Rinka explained. "If everything works out, Razood and Fandaz can get retroactive approval from a Frunge matchmaker on Union Station. Everybody allows a little wiggle-room for romances that spring up on space voyages."

"I'm so sorry if I kept you all waiting," Fandaz said. "My second shift manager had a family emergency and I had to give a field promotion and a quick training course to the senior waitress."

"That's what it's like working with Humans," Razood said. "My latest batch of apprentices think that seventy percent attendance is a passing grade."

"Why don't you fire them?" Bill asked, ignoring his friend's unintentional slight.

"Flower Entertainment pays me good money to train them so they can create more authentic blacksmiths and ironworkers in the games they're programming."

"Why don't we go in?" Julie suggested. "The Old Way displays are to the right and the Alt displays are to the left. Anyone wearing a green ribbon owns a collection, so you can ask them questions about their minerals."

All four aliens turned out to know as much about minerals as any of the collectors displaying them, but everyone enjoyed the show, and there was even a small gift shop set up at the exit. Julie, Rinka, and Fandaz got caught up looking at the offerings while Bill, Jorb, and Razood continued out to the refreshment area to buy drinks.

"Even I can tell that she likes you," Bill said to Razood while they were waiting for their dates to come out of the gift shop. "Why don't you go back in and buy her a bit of ore?"

Razood choked on his drink, and the violent motion caused him to spill the one he'd bought for Fandaz on the floor. He muttered something about Humans and went back to the bar to get a towel and replacement drinks.

"What did I do?" Bill asked Jorb.

"It's a Frunge thing," the Drazen explained. "They only give ore as gifts for baby showers."

Thirteen

Julie grumbled under her breath all the way from her office to the lift tube. Finally, she asked, "Why does it have to be the bookmobile? You know I get nervous in small spaceships."

"Don't be a baby," Flower said. "We have thousands of potential emigrants to process and we're only going to be here for three days. I don't want you to delay starting until one of my shuttles fills up, and sending you in an empty one would be wasteful."

"Wasteful of what? I thought you said the big shuttles are powered by a miniature version of the same Dollnick pile technology that you run on."

"If we go by your logic, I would be happy to be operating with barely a million inhabitants when my capacity is over five million," the twenty-thousand-year-old AI retorted. "Are you going to tell me your destination, or do you plan to hog the lift tube all day?"

"Sorry," Julie said, realizing that she had entered the capsule without giving a destination. "Docking deck. I know I told you to stop taking me places without asking last year, but when I'm going somewhere *for* you, it seems kind of silly."

"I'm surprised it took you so long to figure that out. Dewey will be piloting, and it's just a ten-minute jaunt to the Sharf orbital. We're going to have a busy visit because

I'll be loading all of the recycled steel they would sell me for use in our shipyard."

"Did they put a limit on your order size to keep you from building so many two-man traders that it depresses the market for their used ships?"

"The Sharf don't have any more old ships to sell or I wouldn't have gotten into the business of building new ones," Flower said. "The problem is that they have existing customers for recycled commodities and I'm at the back of the line."

"I thought that with all the mining worlds there must be more steel being produced than anybody could possibly use," Julie said. "I remember somebody telling me that iron ore isn't even that valuable."

"How many tons of steel do you think went into building me, or the orbital you're about to visit?" Flower asked.

"Alright, I get the point. It's just that we've never had any problem ordering raw materials for the current production line so I assumed there was no shortage."

"I didn't say there was a shortage, just that supplies at any given place and time are limited. If I wanted to pay fifty percent over the market price, some of the other buyers ahead of me would happily pocket the premium for accepting a delay. And speaking of ferrous metals, don't forget to activate your magnetic cleats."

"Right," Julie said, clicking her heels together as the lift tube doors opened. She shuffled out onto the docking deck and spotted Dewey next to the bookmobile trying to get some ship-wrap advertising to lie flat. "What's that symbol?" she subvoced.

"A Farling coat of arms," Flower said. "Getting M793qK to pre-screen potential terraforming workers for Earth Two will save a lot of trouble down the road."

"I never saw you add a coat of arms to one of your shuttles when he came on a trip before."

"It has to do with the size of the ship. Traveling as a passenger on a proper shuttle is acceptable, but it would be bad for his image if anybody saw him disembarking from the bookmobile."

"So how does the coat of arms change that?" Julie asked.

"It symbolizes ownership. Anybody seeing him now would assume that it's the gig from his yacht."

"Could you give me a hand with this?" Dewey called to the approaching girl. "Whenever I get one side flat, a fold appears in the other side. I think the wrap is too loose, but I don't want to take it off again to put a seam through the slack."

"So what do you want me to do?" Julie asked, sliding her recruiting supplies bag off her shoulder and setting it on the deck.

"Keep it taut on this side while I slip around and take up the slack."

"How are you going to do that?"

Dewey flashed an immersive star smile and held up a forefinger, which began to glow. "A line of thermal pinches will do the trick," he said. "The ship wrap is designed to get tacky when you hit it with infrared."

Julie placed her hands to either side of the Farling coat of arms to hold the material flat and found herself studying the intricate artwork while waiting for the artificial person to return. The central image was of a giant beetle in flight, but it was surrounded by all manner of aliens the likes of which she'd never seen, much less encountered.

"Are the creatures surrounding the Farling real, or are they mythological?" she subvoced.

"If you're talking about the coat of arms, they're real," Flower replied. "The Farling hierarchy rules a large number of star systems occupied by other species. Members of the hierarchy derive standing from the quantity and quality of their allies."

"Are you admiring my coat of arms?" M793qK inquired from behind her. "Based on my knowledge of Human optics, I'm confident you would have a better view from a step or two back."

"I'm keeping it flat for Dewey while he fixes the shipwrap," Julie explained without turning her head. "Who are the guys that look like walking sharks?"

"Oosh," the Farling said. "Fierce warriors who consider modern weaponry to be unsporting."

"I suppose it's not surprising given all of those teeth. How about the snaky things with wings?"

"Don't ever let dragon variants hear you calling them snaky. The artwork isn't to scale, and I mean that in the measurement sense."

"How big are they?"

"Picture a dragon you've seen in the LARPing studio," M793qK said.

"That big? How did you conquer them?"

"They're allies, not defeated enemies. Stable empires are built on common interests. The Farling hierarchy is further advanced in the sciences than any of our members, as are the Cayl in their empire. The whole idea of species waging endless wars when there's a gap of millions of years in their technological progress is absurd."

"Oh. Then why does Flower keep telling me that the galaxy outside of the tunnel network is full of civilizations fighting each other?"

"Species who want a war can always find someone willing to oblige them," M793qK said. "Those who don't want war try to find a more advanced species with an empire they can join and leave the fighting to the professionals."

"All aboard," Dewey called from the open hatch. "The two of you can just as easily plan your conquest of the galaxy while we're on the way."

"I don't want to conquer anything," Julie said, picking up her bag and climbing into the bookmobile. "M793qK is welcome to my half. And where is he going to sit?"

"Back here with the cargo," the alien doctor said, lying on the deck. "If Flower has granted you purchasing power for her Tunnel Trips franchise, I wouldn't be averse to a ship with Farling-friendly furnishings."

"Do you think anybody else would ever rent it?"

"Now there's an interesting question," M793qK rubbed out on his speaking legs as Dewey maneuvered the bookmobile out of Flower's core. "Farlings rarely travel the tunnel network unless some urgent business is at stake, but is that because we find the company of humanoids distasteful, or because the accommodations are poorly suited to our carapaces?"

"The chicken or the egg," Dewey contributed from the pilot's seat.

"Are you saying that if somebody built a Farling-friendly resort and provided ship rentals with those reclining bench-things they could make a business out of it?" Julie asked.

"Look at the success Flower has had with Club Zarent," M793qK replied. "Of course, if you did attract Farlings, they would be from the younger generation that places a value on vacations and seeing the sights."

Julie breathed a sigh of relief when the bookmobile began to accelerate away from Flower, pressing her body back in the seat and giving her enough weight that she didn't feel like her face was bulging. "I would have thought the opposite," she said. "I've accompanied the retirees from the independent living deck on dozens of their outings, and they appreciate all kinds of differences that I just take for granted."

"It indeed takes a little living to understand how important small differences can be, but I entered and exited that phase of life long before Humans discovered bronze," the giant beetle said. "Most long-lived species, and I include artificial intelligence in this assessment—" he waved a limb towards Dewey, "—grow out of recreational travel when the places and species all start blending together."

"Isn't that why tourists are always recording holograms, so they'll remember?"

"My memory is excellent, almost on par with that of our AI colleague," M793qK said. "Everything eventually starts looking like something else you've seen because the universe has a finite number of ways to intelligently express higher life forms. Natural selection proceeds down paths of incremental improvement—it doesn't skip from a mouse to a flying octopus in one generation. If any of the mutations between the mouse and the flying octopus aren't an improvement over the previous version, either the process stops, or it heads off in a new direction and you get a horned rabbit. Broadly speaking, there are fewer than a thousand practical templates for advanced life in our galaxy."

"Where do humanoids rank?" Dewey asked. "I put a lot of money into this body."

"Your investment is safe as long as you remain on the tunnel network where the Stryx have ensured that humanoids predominate. Outside the tunnel network, wings often provided a distinct evolutionary advantage, as did natural armor, retractable claws, breathing fire, and various other abilities that Humans would loosely define as magic or telepathy."

"I could have bought wings but I didn't want to stand out in a crowd." The artificial person shook off his momentary regret and said, "Flip time."

Julie felt her stomach rise in her throat as the drive cut out and she experienced Zero-G. Dewey performed the hundred-and-eighty-degree maneuver so that the bookmobile could decelerate the rest of the way to the Sharf orbital without the passengers pulling against their safety restraints. Then the drive came back on and Julie's weight returned.

"So why did Flower think it so important to prescreen the people interested in working on Earth Two before they come on board?" Julie asked. "We've never done health checks for any of the people I hired to work in our shipyard, and they need to be in pretty good shape for those jobs."

"If somebody working the production line has a preexisting condition that makes them injury-prone, I can either correct the underlying problem or repair the failures as they occur," the Farling doctor said. "The terraforming crew going to Earth Two will be working on the unfinished continents with their only medical support coming from any Human doctors who hire on. Weeding out the ticking time-bombs upfront will not only preserve lives, it will also save lost time for the other workers who would end up caring for their unproductive colleagues."

"So you're not screening the Old Way community members who are emigrating, just the people who are contracting to finish the terraforming work the Container Prince started?"

"Exactly. I've snuck a few scans of Old Way members while visiting their campsites and they are a surprisingly healthy lot for Humans. Fresh air, exercise, and unprocessed food offer your species the best path to extending your lives without resorting to medical intervention."

"What do you have against medical intervention?" Julie asked.

"You'd be surprised," the Farling said, and offered the girl a twenty-cred piece.

"What's this?"

"Consideration."

"I don't understand."

"Offer, acceptance, consideration. When Dewey suggested we plan our conquest of the galaxy during the trip, you offered to give me your half. I want to make it an official contract."

"You're willing to give me twenty creds just in case we actually do conquer the galaxy together so you can have the whole thing?" Julie stretched out a hand. "Deal."

Dewey twisted in the pilot's seat and pulled Julie's wrist away before M793qK could give her the money. "I don't know what the catch is, but he's a lot smarter than both of us put together and he doesn't give away his money for nothing," the artificial person cautioned her.

"That seems a bit paranoid."

"I concur," the Farling said, extending the coin a second time.

"But then again, why would you give me twenty creds for no reason?" she asked.

"Never mind," M793qK said, returning the coin to his pouch.

Dewey spent the next three minutes negotiating a discount with the artificial intelligence handling traffic control for the Sharf orbital, eventually getting the docking price down forty percent. When the bookmobile entered the orbital's core and set down in the assigned spot, it was exactly between two spokes.

"Typical," M793qK said. "You saved a few creds but cost us several minutes of walking to the nearest lift tube.

"Life is a series of tradeoffs," Dewey said. "It's not like we have a lot of stuff to carry."

Julie trailed behind her two companions, who argued about the relative value of cash versus convenience all the way to the auditorium Flower had booked for the recruiting fair. A woman from Flash Events was waiting for them by the doors.

"I'm Gemma," she greeted the group, focusing on Julie. "Flower hired me remotely to handle the setup for your recruiting fair. I hope you like the decorations. There's a full theatre projection rig on the stage that I'd normally use to run Vergallian dramas for the people waiting their turn. Flower insisted on streaming something from her entertainment library."

Julie had a sudden intuition and groaned. Sure enough, when they entered the auditorium, *Everyday Superheroes* was playing. A holographic animated waitress four times Julie's height was just in the act of throwing her tray, Frisbee style, at the escaping Evil Mastermind. The giant beetle saw the tray with the rotating knives coming towards him and batted it out of the air with a contemptuous wave.

"Is that—" Gemma stopped with her mouth open, looking back and forth between M793qK and Julie. "The customer is always right. The customer is always right," she mumbled under her breath like a mantra. "Your table is at the back here, and the auditorium seats are all numbered. We filled them first-come-first-serve, as instructed."

"Thank you," Julie said, scribbling her signature with her forefinger on the tab that the event organizer held out. "There will be another group of recruiters showing up with the first shuttle to promote career opportunities on Flower. We came in advance to screen the terraforming recruits."

Dewey nudged Julie and pointed at the large banner stretched across the back of the hall which only became visible when they turned to see the table. It read, "Conquer the Galaxy."

Julie rounded on the Farling doctor and demanded, "Were you really offering me twenty creds in hopes of stealing the recruitment bonus Flower pays me for these things?"

"Purchasing, not stealing," M793qK corrected her. "And I thought it would be an inexpensive and invaluable lesson for you."

Dewey advanced to the front of the auditorium and began directing job seekers to the back, keeping an eye on the progress at the tables to minimize the time anybody would spend standing in line. M793qK rejected the first two candidates without even lifting his hand-held medical scanner, but he used it on the third and waved Julie nearer.

"See that?" he said, gesturing at a brilliant section of the man's spinal column.

"Is it a problem?" she asked.

"Where did you have your spine repaired?" M793qK asked the man.

"A mining world. The Drazen medic said it would last longer than I do."

"The work is adequate," M793qK rubbed out grudgingly. "You pass. Next."

"So you're my first sign-up today," Julie said to the former miner. "How did you happen to be on the orbital?"

"I finished a fifteen-year contract on a Drazen world and thought I'd see a bit of the galaxy before signing up for another hitch," the man explained. "After two days in a casino that felt like a few hours, I found myself short on funds and heard that the Sharf on this orbital employ us without long-term contracts. It's not bad work, but then I saw the advertisement for anybody with terraforming or mining experience to work on Earth Two, and the terms looked pretty good."

"I have to warn you that the Human Empire hasn't finalized their agreement with the Alts for planet-sharing yet, so the whole thing could still fall apart," Julie said. "Flower is guarantying employment for anybody who joins the terraforming crew if it never happens."

"Doing what?" the man asked.

"Oh, we have lots of work. There's Flower Entertainment, Flower Shipyards, Flower Foods." Julie stopped with her right index finger on the third finger of her left hand. "I don't want to make it sound like all of the jobs are working for Flower. There are plenty of independent businesses."

"I've got no problems with working for alien artificial intelligence," the man said. "So I'm set for the shuttle?"

Julie inked the boarding stamp and pointed at the back of his hand apologetically. "There are nanobots in the ink for security purposes," she said. "Flower buys it from the Gem, but it saves a lot of waiting in line."

The man sauntered off, holding his wrist bent to show off the stamp, and Julie turned back to her left to see M793qK rejecting a healthy-looking young woman.

"It's because I'm pregnant, right?" the woman demanded. "That's discrimination!"

"No, it's common sense," the doctor told her. "You're welcome to apply for a job on Flower when the second recruiting team arrives, and I have no doubt you'll be accepted. The same is likely true if you want to join one of the Old Way communities emigrating to Earth Two. But the terraforming group will be working in isolation for three months at a time, and I wouldn't approve you for heavy lifting in any case. Next, please."

Fourteen

"Were you worried that we might run out of fruit?" Vivian asked Julie, struggling to suppress her laughter.

"It's kind of a thing with Flower," Julie said. "She planted enough fruit trees on her ag decks to feed five million people and they're pretty much all producing now. That's how she ended up in business selling Harry's Fruitcakes."

"M793qK specifically warned me off those while I'm expecting. He said the alcohol content is very high, and it kind of creeps up on you."

"What do you think of the circular conference table? Flower said they're traditional at Dollnick negotiations."

"If it was much bigger, they'd have to shout to hear each other, but with the Alts being uncomfortable around us, maybe the extra buffer will help," Vivian said. "Isn't that giant fruit basket in the center of the table blocking the sightlines? Maybe we could move it, or put the fruit on platters instead so it's not stacked so high."

"I didn't think of that," Julie admitted. She quickly pulled off her shoes, climbed on a chair, and then stepped up onto the table. "I'll just push it to the side and then—"

A floating four-armed maintenance bot appeared carrying three large platters which it deposited along the circumference of the table near the edge to form an equilateral triangle. Then it blurred into motion as it redistributed the fruit from the centerpiece across the three platters before disappearing, taking the empty basket with it.

"Wow, that was fast," Vivian said.

"Flower didn't even say anything over my implant so she must be miffed at having to change it," Julie said, getting down from the table and back into her shoes.

Vivian pointed at her ear, nodded a few times, and then lowered her hand. "Sam will be here in two minutes, and the Alts and the Old Way representatives are on their way."

"Are you going to try to sit through all of the negotiations?"

"You worry even more than Sam, and no, I'm too busy with the family registry. Our Cayl mentor will be here along with whichever co-op student happens to be available. Sam wants to give them some diplomatic exposure. After talking to a bunch of academic professionals from Earth, we're sort of rethinking our approach to starting a school of government."

"So there isn't anybody in the Human Empire headquarters right now?" Julie asked.

"We have three co-op students working for us at all times as of yesterday. Flower keeps sending us new ones to break in, and with the colonists stopping by, they're keeping pretty busy."

"But I thought that other than the beta test of the human registry project you don't offer any services yet."

"We don't, but it's a good idea to stay open during business hours just to be able to take questions, and our co-op students have created a Human Empire helpdesk for living on Flower." Vivian glanced up at the ceiling and added, "You can guess whose idea that was."

"Maybe you could have the co-op students work on coming up with a name for the app."

The Grenouthian director entered the conference room preceded by three floating immersive cameras that he controlled with subtle paw movements. He circled the table, positioning each of the cameras near the ceiling at roughly the same locations as the fruit platters, and then addressed himself to the pair of young women. "Which one of you has always dreamed about working on a documentary?"

"I thought you had enough volunteers from the independent living cooperative," Julie said.

"I did, but they're fully engaged documenting the day-to-day activities of the growing number of Old Way colonists and Alts traveling with us."

"Sorry, but I have to get back to work," Vivian said. "See you later."

The director turned his large black eyes on Julie, who shook her head. "I'm the hostess. Even if I had the time it would be a conflict of interest."

"Then don't be surprised when Jorb and Razood show up behind the cameras," the Grenouthian said. "I arranged for them to be on standby since they are going to attend the conference in any case."

"After all of our time on set together for *Everyday Superheroes,* they must be better at manipulating cameras and framing shots than random volunteers."

"A little knowledge is a dangerous thing. They don't respond well to direction."

"Just don't let your cameras get too close to people's faces or Flower said she'll kick you out," Julie warned him. "I know that it's important to record history, but not at the expense of keeping it from happening."

The Grenouthian director drew himself up to his full height and crinkled his nose at her. "I see you've become infected with the instant expert bug as well. You take care of your garden and I'll take care of mine."

Samuel entered the conference room with a youngster who looked like he had just started shaving. "Julie. Brad," he made the introduction. "Brad is one of our new co-op students and we're going to rotate them through the negotiation sessions to give them all a taste. Have you heard from any aliens who want to sit in?"

"It's just going to be the usual crowd from—" Julie glanced at Brad and decided to play it safe, "—the special cafeteria where Bill works. Razood and Jorb are going to help the Grenouthian director with the cameras, and I know that Brynlan said he would be here. I think Yaem is skipping because he has too much work, and the Sharf aren't tunnel network members in any case."

"Yaem already asked me to write a report for him," a new voice announced, and Lume, the station chief for Dollnick Intelligence joined their conversation. "Will we be sitting at the table or on the periphery?"

"Flower told me to include six extra seats at the table," Julie said. "They're arranged in pairs to split the table into six sections so the negotiating parties don't have to turn all the way sideways to see each other. I put the Dollnick chair next to the Verlock chair since Bill told me you and Brynlan get along well."

"Then I shall take my seat and meditate in preparation," Lume said and headed for the table.

"Avisia," Julie greeted the Vergallian spy who ran a finishing school for cover. "I wasn't sure if you were coming. I have a spot for you next to the Grenouthian director, though I'm not sure if he's ever going to sit down."

"You're using us as living spacers?" Avisia asked.

"Just to improve the sightlines and create a little breathing room for the Alts."

"I'll take a seat next to the Alts. I received a message from our diplomatic service that Methan, the Alt's chief negotiator for the Earth Two project, wanted a Vergallian to accompany their local representatives. When we reach Union Station for the final negotiation, the local contract queen will take over."

"Who is taking care of your school while you're here?" Julie asked.

"I hired a couple of women from the Old Way as temporary instructors," Avisia said. "Their moral character and cleanliness are excellent for Humans."

"Doesn't that make for a conflict of interest when you'll be on the Alt side?"

"I had royal training in compartmentalization and the Alts trust me implicitly. I had to explain to them why my hiring Humans could be construed as a conflict of interest since they have no tradition of deceitful practices on their homeworld."

"They're lucky to have you," Julie said honestly. "Oh, here come the three Old Way reps."

"Oscar," the expedition leader of the original group of Old Way colonists introduced himself to Avisia, who responded with her name and a firm handshake.

"Jade," a woman with long black hair and prominent cheekbones went next.

"Garth," the third member of the party said, shaking hands and casting his eye over the table. "Nice fruit."

"I'm glad you all found the room okay," Julie said. "The con deck can be a bit confusing for first-time visitors."

"Dewey brought us to the door before returning to the lift tube to guide the Alts," Oscar said.

"I need to inform you that I'm here today as a temporary contract queen for the Alts," Avisia said. "The request just came through this morning. I want to assure you that all of the time I've spent in your camps in recent weeks was out of appreciation for your culture and the women's circles, not intentional preparation for the role I'll be playing here."

"We're happy to have you either way," Jade said. "Anybody who can tell a story like you while putting a perfect glaze on a pot is always welcome."

"Let me show you to your seats," Julie said, feeling for a moment like she was back working as a waitress. "You've all met Samuel McAllister, and the young man with him is Brad, a co-op student from the Open University who's working for the Human Empire."

"We're big believers in on-the-job training ourselves," Garth said. "Flower keeps sending Dewey around offering us deals to place our children in her schools. Neither of them seem to understand that we're all engaged in educating our young ones from dawn to dusk."

"To be fair, our community members who've worked a contract for the advanced species tell us that compulsory education for children was one of the non-negotiable terms," Jade said. "The aliens didn't care what adults did with their free time, but they were sticklers for the tunnel network treaty rules relating to the children of guest workers."

"That's Krey who is just taking her seat next to Samuel," Julie told them. "She's the Cayl Emperor's granddaughter and the Human Empire's mentor."

"She's been coming to our knitting circle," Jade said. "If any of us had been skeptical of the idea that some species were more advanced than others, her talent with those needles would have put it to rest."

"And here come the Alts." Julie took her leave from the Old Way representatives and rushed to greet the new arrivals. "I'm Julie, your hostess," she introduced herself.

"My name is Fanli, and he's Hethram," the Alt woman said, wincing at Julie's offer of a handshake. "We've been chosen to represent our community until Methan arrives."

"Your Vergallian advisor is already here," Julie said, letting her hand fall. "Please let me know if there's anything you want or need to have explained that Avisia can't help you with."

"Thank you," Hethram said, offering a slight head tilt in lieu of a handshake. "Please forgive any flaws in our manners but we're still getting used to Humans. You're much younger than the ones who have been visiting us."

"Is my youth a problem? Flower can send another host or hostess."

"We need to grow accustomed to Humans of all ages," Fanli said. "It's just that your energy level is much higher than the people we've been meeting for practice. The way you're bouncing slightly on your feet reminds me of a wound spring or a predator about to launch an attack."

"Sorry, I shouldn't have had that second cup of coffee," Julie said, backing away and gesturing in the direction of the two empty chairs next to Avisia. "If you'll take your seats, I'll get out of the way and we can begin."

Brynlan had just finished lowering himself into the heavy-duty Verlock chair next to Lume when the Alts reached the table. Looking around the room, Julie saw that Jorb and Razood had arrived and were energetically disputing camera locations with the Grenouthian director. Dewey remained by the door, as if on guard, and Samuel stood to address the conference participants.

"I want to welcome everybody to these talks in which we hope to get in front of any issues that might arise between colonists sponsored by the Human Empire and the Alt communities moving to Earth Two. My current understanding is that we will only be discussing living arrangements for the small continent, which is near completion. A different set of temporary rules will be negotiated separately for the terraforming workers who will be completing the work left undone by the Container Prince. Does anybody have any questions to this point?"

"I have several prepared," Avisia said without rising. "Shall I begin now, or do you have a longer introduction planned?"

"Just a word of thanks to Flower for providing this facility and the catering we will be enjoying for lunch," Samuel said. "I also have a small list of issues from my last meeting with Methan during which we signed a letter of intent for the joint project. Would you like to go first?"

"Is money on your list?" Avisia asked flat out. The Alts sitting next to her both cringed at the word.

"The current plan is to divide the small continent between our peoples to give them time to adjust in relative isolation," Samuel said. "We understand that money will only be legal tender in the human areas."

"With all due respect to members of the Old Way communities," the Vergallian inclined her head slightly towards the delegation, "I fear that Humans will discover they can visit Alt areas, stay for free, and depart with whatever they can carry."

"I know you have our best interests at heart, Avisia, but surely you're exaggerating the risk," Hethram said. "What kind of sentient being would abuse hospitality that way?"

"Most of them," Lume put in. "Well, maybe not the Verlocks."

"Thank you," Brynlan said slowly. "The Grenouthians also have excellent manners, though they might find it amusing to pretend they were going to make off with all of your goods, and then return to put everything back."

"We in the Old Way communities also host travelers without asking for payment, but there's an expectation that they will offer to help with chores," Jade said. "And we do try to minimize the use of money in our communities, but our movement struggled with an early attempt to operate on a pure barter system."

"I've spoken with traders who have visited Old Way communities on open worlds, and my understanding is that you accept both Stryx creds and local coinage," Samuel said.

The three Old Way representatives exchanged a few words, and then Oscar said, "That's substantially correct. In all cases, including with Stryx creds, we accept coinage because we don't maintain the installed technology base to deal with electronic currencies, or miniregisters to take programmable creds. In some cases, we create our own coinage from metals that have value at small weights."

"It's the purpose of this *money* that escapes our understanding," Hethram said bravely, though he did stumble over pronouncing the 'm' word. "I've been reading about the history of Earth before the Stryx arrived, and perhaps it would help explain our fears if I gave a summary of my current understanding?"

"Please proceed," Samuel said.

"Humanity began with barter, transitioned to using precious metals as a medium of exchange, and eventually switched to metal-backed paper currency to increase the money supply. Within a century of dropping the convertibility of paper currency back into precious metals, the semi-independent central banks with monopolies on the production of new money began creating so much that savers had to pay banks to simply hold it for them. Earth's economy was trapped in an endless series of asset bubbles denominated in this fiat currency, and when the Stryx judged that the next collapse would lead to the destruction of life on Earth, they stepped in."

"That's a fair summary, but how do the Alts deal with situations where barter isn't appropriate?" Oscar asked.

"This is the point I haven't figured out," Lume whispered to Brynlan.

"It would be a mischaracterization to say that Alt operates on a barter system," Avisia said. "Our academics are still conducting research on the ground, but they classify the system on the Alt homeworld as a sharing economy. The inhabitants all see themselves as members of an extended family, and their society lacks any manifestation of material competition and greed. Even the multigenerational effort to create an interstellar drive was funded, if I can even use the word, through the shared sacrifice of time, materials, and manufacturing capacity."

"Don't make us out to be pure altruists," Fanli protested. "We do have our blocks for keeping track of the time we put into different activities, even if there's rarely any call for showing them." She removed from her bag a small tan slab of a plastic-like substance with a stylus clipped to the side. "The block has a physical memory property that a chemist could explain, but the important thing is that it supports a simple search-and-recall function."

"So it's like an organic hand-held computer you use as a backup for the honor system?" Jade asked.

"I don't remember the last time I had occasion to recall my own entries, but our children do take pride in recording their contributions to society on their blocks and showing them to each other," Fanli said. "Some young parents worry this could take on the character of boasting, but the children all grow out of it."

"I'd heard of Alt blocks but I've never seen one," Samuel said. "Have you ever considered that they're a bit like an invisible fiat currency since they support your economy without being tied to some commodity or income stream?"

"You have it exactly backward," Avisia said. "The blocks are fully funded by the labor and efforts of a lifetime. Fiat currencies are backed by hollow proclamations and showered on groups who are in favor with the current crop of technocrats controlling the creation process. You could describe fiat currency as an attempt to imitate the honor system without the honor."

Oscar cleared his throat self-consciously. "I'd like to think that our Old Way communities function with a degree of altruism, but it sounds to me like you've abandoned private property," he said. "It may sound crass to you, but we tend to see people as a combination of how they interact with others and what they've accomplished, where the latter is often measured in material outcomes, such as the production of crops and goods, or the home they've built."

"The Alts aren't communists, if that's what you were thinking," Avisia said with a laugh. "I know the contract queen who has taken responsibility for their interspecies trade of musical instruments, and the quality and craftsmanship even meet Drazen standards. They command a premium price on the galactic market, but on the Alt homeworld, they're given away as gifts."

"Does that imply that there are cultures where hosts would offer gifts of low-quality goods while keeping the best for themselves?" Fanli asked. "What would be the point?"

"One always gives the best one can," the male Alt concurred. "Material things can be replaced, but the opportunity to improve the universe is a transient moment that will never repeat in exactly the same way."

"This is going to take some getting used to," Garth muttered to the other two Old Way representatives. "They're even nicer than we are."

"Obviously, I can't let them negotiate for themselves," Avisia said.

"No, I don't think that would be wise," Samuel concurred. "Perhaps we could codify some form of compensation through goods or labor for any of our colonists who accept Alt hospitality."

"But that would turn us all into merchants," Fanli said, looking distressed. "We're always happy to host guests. We're just nervous that Humans may..." she trailed off.

"Act like a Wanderer mob," Avisia completed the sentence for her. "I think a quota on Humans crossing the boundary into Alt areas might be the best place to start. Perhaps any Alts traveling to Human areas could simply avoid situations where quid-pro-quo hospitality is the rule."

"You mean we should tell our community members not to invite Alts to their homes expecting the usual exchange," Jade said.

"Vergallian contract queens are handling Alt business on the tunnel network and generating the income necessary to pay a planetary mortgage doing so," Samuel said, turning to address Fanli and Hethram. "I take it this means that it's not the principle of money you find unacceptable, but the idea of it coming between individuals in your society. Would you object to, say, picking up a small amount of coinage from the secretary of an Old Way community to pay for food and lodging while visiting our area? The secretaries could keep accounts for reimbursement by the Human Empire, and we could settle later with your contract queens."

"Wouldn't it be easier to just trust whichever Humans we encounter to present themselves to the community secretary and receive the money directly?" Hethram asked.

"You would be committing the sin of putting temptation before the weak," Avisia said. "Let's go with Samuel's idea for the time being and move on to the next item, unless the Human Empire's mentor has an objection."

"It sounds reasonable," Krey said.

Fifteen

"Here's the thing that I don't understand," Lynx said to her husband as they watched Nancy explaining to the guest speakers from the Alt and Old Way communities how the event would proceed. "If the Alts don't use money or track barter activity on their world, how can they measure their economic productivity?"

"Why are you asking me?" Woojin replied. "I know exactly as much about economics as they taught me in war college."

"What's a war college?" Em piped up from the seat next to her father. "Can I go?"

"A sort of boarding school that Daddy went to back on Earth," Lynx explained.

"You wouldn't like it," her father said. "We didn't have any alien artificial intelligence."

"No Flower?"

Woojin shook his head solemnly.

"Then I'm not going," Em declared, crossing her arms across her chest.

At the front of the room, Nancy said something to her husband, leading Jack to turn and approach the captain's family. "Third Officer Pyun?" he addressed Lynx. "Would you mind representing Flower's Paradise in my place this evening? We've been talking it over with our guests, and they don't think it would be fair for me to take part in the debate since I'm a paid employee of Flower's Paradise. Nancy will be moderating, and I don't feel comfortable asking any of our members on short notice. Besides, you know as much about what we do here as anybody."

"I didn't realize it was supposed to be a debate," Lynx said. "Are you sure the Alt speaker is prepared to, uh, argue?"

"We're told that the Alts have a tradition of debating all of their major decisions. If anything, I'm afraid you may be at a disadvantage."

"Don't worry about Lynx, she's tough," the captain said. "Are the debaters for the Old Way movement and the Alts retirees themselves?"

"They may be past our idea of retirement age, but I don't think they make a sharp break between working life and the golden years," Jack said. "We'll all know more about it by the time the evening is over."

"I'm ready if they are," Lynx said, casting a rueful glance at her husband and rising from her chair. "Try not to laugh when Mommy makes a fool out of herself, Em."

The table with four chairs at the front of the common room was missing the usual floating microphones, perhaps out of deference to the Old Way representative's limited use of technology. The audience, all retirees with the exception of M793qK and the Grenouthian director, fell silent as Lynx took the final place. Nancy introduced herself and the guests, and then briefly explained that she would be acting as the moderator for a debate about approaches to retirement.

"I originally intended to flip a coin to give our Alt or Old Way guest the first opportunity to describe their system, but we've made a last-minute substitution of Third Officer Pyun for Jack," Nancy continued. "Since she doesn't have a prepared opening statement, I'd like her to go first so she doesn't unconsciously frame her descriptions in the context of our other speakers. Does anybody object?"

The captain's wife pretended to raise her hand, drawing a chuckle from the audience. "I go by Lynx as long as we aren't in the process of abandoning ship," she said, "and I want everybody to feel free to interrupt me at any time if you think it's important. I've worked with the independent living cooperative since its inception, and I hope I can do you justice without preparation. I can honestly say that in all of my years of travel, I haven't seen a better solution for aging individuals who aren't living with their families."

"I see both of our guest debaters look puzzled," Nancy interjected. "Perhaps you can start by explaining to them why we aren't living with our children."

"Me?" Lynx hesitated a moment. "Well, for one thing, I know that you have to be sixty-five to join Flower's Paradise, with a five-year exception for spouses that allows sixty-year-olds, so bringing your families isn't possible. But without putting words in anybody's mouth, I assume you all decided to live apart from your children when you joined the cooperative."

"Some of us have families on board," a man called out. "Not too close, not too far."

"If I remember the numbers, over two-thirds of occupied cabins on the independent living deck are taken by married couples, so—"

"Tell them about the food service," Flower interrupted over the third officer's implant.

"—so, uh, and some members are siblings," Lynx said. "One of the main attractions for people living here is the availability of three meals a day—"

"A la carte," the Dollnick AI interrupted again.

"—without any commitment to a meal plan, so it's an on-demand service with no penalty for eating out or preparing meals at home. The independent living cooperative is also part of Flower's broader community, which means participation in mandatory exercise programs and volunteering, both of which are important for maintaining mental and physical health."

"Affordability," Flower said in Lynx's ear.

"The cost of living is an important factor for most people in retirement, and according to a Grenouthian documentary I saw some years ago, the inability to pay for necessary help produced perverse incentives for the elderly populations on Earth. In some countries, people who were still capable of functioning on their own were forced to commit themselves to government-subsidized nursing facilities to free up room for the next generation in a family home."

"Criminal," the Grenouthian director muttered from behind the camera he was manning.

"Don't forget the field trips," Flower prompted.

"Why do you keep starting to raise your hand, Mommy?" Em asked from her seat.

"Because a certain Dollnick busybody is kibitzing over Mommy's implant and getting her confused," Lynx replied. "But it's fair to point out that the dream of many retirees, including some from advanced species, is to see more of the galaxy. Choosing to live on Flower is akin to traveling on a cruise ship, but one that also contains a fully functioning economy that it brings along to all of the stops. And speaking of stops, I'm going to halt right here before Flower insists I tell you about the bazaar and all of the entertainment options on offer, not to mention part-time jobs."

"Thank you, Third—excuse me, Lynx," Nancy said, and turned to the Alt. "Would you like to make your opening statement?"

"I think in consideration of the burdens placed on our worthy colleague in this debate, I shall put aside my prepared statement and speak extemporaneously," Hethram said. "The best word in Humanese I can use to describe how life changes with age on my homeworld would be 'gradually.' Some of us nearing the ends of our lives may work more than others half our age who never quite found their calling, though I don't mean to imply that's a common situation. We all try to do what's best for ourselves and our families, in consultation with friends and community, of course."

"Do you have care facilities for the elderly who can no longer live alone?" Nancy asked.

"Nobody on Alt lives alone, at least not in the sense I believe you are implying," Hethram said. "Even if somebody has no close blood relatives due to unfortunate circumstances, surely there will be dozens of neighbors from the next generation who treat that individual as a second mother or father. Anybody with wrinkles is 'Grandma' or 'Grandpa' to all of the children. But it's only fair to point out that our health outcomes in aging are closer to those of the advanced species than humanity, so extended periods of disability are rare."

"And I suppose your sharing economy makes government insurance programs or saving for retirement irrelevant?" Nancy asked.

"You suppose correctly. As we age, Alts continue living as we always have. If we can't do all of the things we need to maintain ourselves, family, friends, and neighbors pick up the slack. The opportunity to help the aged is a blessing." Hethram nodded, as if in agreement with himself, and then folded his hands on the table to indicate he was done speaking.

"It sounds like a lovely system if you can, I mean, for those who can make it work," Nancy said. She leaned forward a bit to look at the Old Way debater sitting at the end of the table. "Reba?"

"I'm in accordance with my Alt friend about setting aside my prepared remarks, though I should point out that I've never participated in a debate before and I'm not that vocal in our regular public meetings," Reba said. "In fact, I wouldn't have volunteered if not for meeting two of your members, Harry and Irene, when they came with floating cameras to capture my baking for the documentary."

"I hope you're glad you came," Nancy said.

"Oh, yes. I've learned so much already, and the meal was delicious. Now, I don't want to be the kid in class who answers by saying, 'What he said,' but the truth is, our approach to aging in place is similar to that of the Alts. The main differences that come to mind are that there's a cut-off age for joining an Old Way community for singles, and most members do build up substantial savings during their lifetimes."

"You specified singles when you mentioned a cut-off age. How does that work?"

"We don't take new members over forty years of age unless they are accompanied by a family with at least one child older than thirteen who expresses a desire to join the Old Way movement," Reba explained. "The Alts don't have this problem because, well, all of them are Alts. An Old Way community can't afford to become a refuge or a dumping ground for people who realize that they're getting old and haven't planned for the future."

"And you think that forty-one is old?" Nancy asked, drawing a laugh from the audience, whose average age was in the seventies.

"It's old to start building social capital in a community that you expect to care for you when you can no longer care for yourself. Like the Alts, we all work as long as we have the capacity, because being a productive member of society is central to who we are. But as humans, most of us begin to feel our age by forty. I once read that mammals in general start to decline at three times the age of puberty. Of course, specific outcomes depend on a person's genes and their lifestyle before joining the movement, and the aging process goes much faster for some than others."

"Could somebody buy years under your system?" Lynx asked.

"I don't understand the question," Reba replied.

"Say a forty-five-year-old in good health comes along and he's willing to pay fifty thousand creds into your treasury to make up for not having worked in the community from a younger age."

"We don't allow that. Social capital has to be built up over decades, through good times and bad, and you can't substitute money for having cared for those who can't care for themselves."

"But if the forty-five-year-old joins with a young family, it's okay," Nancy clarified.

"The forty-five-year-old can join with eighty-year-old parents as long as they bring a youngster who's willing to stay and contribute for the long term," Reba said. "Before you ask, I'm not aware of any instances where somebody tried to game the system by persuading a young person to lie. While we obviously believe that the Old Way offers a superior alternative to mainstream society, relatively few outsiders agree with us."

"Hethram?" the moderator asked, seeing that the Alt had raised a hand like a schoolchild.

"Since we aren't following a regular debate format, may I ask a question of Reba?" the Alt inquired.

"Of course."

"My understanding is that the Old Way favors barter, yet you spoke of accumulating substantial savings. Are you referring to money, or property in the broader sense of farmland or workshops?"

"Most of us also end up in possession of land, a house, and perhaps a business, but I was speaking of savings in the sense of money," Reba said. "We don't close ourselves off from outsiders, and many a householder is willing to provide food and lodging to travelers and vacationers. But our main source of income comes from trading our surplus into the broader cash economy."

"Which won't exist on Earth Two," the Alt pointed out.

"Tell him we'll be buying supplies for the terraforming crews working on the other continents," Flower prompted over the third officer's implant.

"I just thought of that myself," Lynx said in frustration, and then gave an embarrassed smile when she realized she had spoken out loud. "Our Dollnick AI has just pointed out to me that the crews working on the other continents will need provisions. She's agreed to provide technical support for the terraforming project to meet the tunnel network legal requirements for experience and capabilities. Until a space elevator is completed and the Stryx connect a tunnel, both of which are years in the future, purchasing local food for work crews will be cheaper than importing."

"But the preliminary agreement the Human Empire signed at Union Station prohibited high-speed transportation on Earth Two," Hethram said with a frown. "How would the supplies be sent overseas?"

"The transportation ban only applied to the continent the Alts are occupying," Flower said, and this time Lynx pointed at her ear while listening. "Methan explicitly agreed to an arrangement where fresh produce and other goods could be brought to cargo terminals on the shore of the Human areas for delivery overseas by floaters and other low-impact modern transportation."

Lynx faithfully reproduced the explanation, and added, "My memory isn't as good as Flower's, but I believe Methan and Samuel agreed that Alt communities on Earth Two would receive advance notice of any major terraforming projects and be given the opportunity to veto any work not in keeping with their overall goals for the planet."

"We don't get any say at all?" Reba asked.

Lynx grimaced. "It's not that, exactly, but the Alts are the owners of record for Earth Two until our work crews earn equity through progress on the remaining terraforming work. The situation isn't entirely unlike the social capital you mentioned earlier, though in this case, it's humanity that has to convince the Alts that we're ready to be good and responsible neighbors."

"Please rest assured that we won't be judging you," Hethram said. "If sharing Earth Two doesn't work out for some reason, I'm sure it will be due to our failings as hosts."

Reba began to laugh and had to struggle to get control of herself. "That's the first time I've heard the 'It's not you, it's me,' breakup speech applied to sharing a planet. Let's just hope the negotiators can establish guidelines that will prevent our relationship from deteriorating that far."

"That's where I worry we'll fall short, even with the capable aid of our Vergallian advisors. You see, there are very few laws of any kind on our homeworld as our universal rules of conduct are learned at an early age. We don't understand how to go about regulating the behavior of adults through a system of rewards and punishments. I'm not at all sure that we'll be able to provide you with sufficient guidance."

"Can we count on you to tell us quickly if we stray from the agreed-upon path?" Reba asked. "A stitch in time saves nine. We may not get things right at first but we want to make this work."

"We have no tradition of correcting the behavior of others," Hethram said. "Our children learn from our examples, and there has never been a need for a penal system of any kind on our homeworld."

"I wonder if it could be genetic," Nancy said. "We tend to think of behavior as being learned rather than inherited but—M793qK?"

The Farling, who was standing in the back and looked like he was leaning against the wall because he had fallen asleep, answered immediately. "All species inherit behaviors as well as traits from parent organisms," he said through the external translation device he was wearing for the event. "But your scientists haven't discovered third-order and fourth-order coding effects so I can't elucidate beyond saying that 'junk DNA' is an oxymoron."

"I'm afraid that your reluctance to correcting our behavior will lead to problems," Reba said, turning in her chair to face Hethram. "While I see substantial overlap between your values and those of the Old Way movement, there will be plenty of areas where our views don't align. Like you, we try to teach our youth by example rather than through laying down rigid rules. We've already started explaining to the children that we will be sharing a continent with you and that we must adapt to your ways. But you can't expect them to internalize overnight what is in some ways an alien culture."

"Your point is valid," Hethram said. "We've been discussing amongst ourselves a timetable to allow you to adjust to our requirements, but we intended to wait until the final phase of the negotiations to introduce it as a modifier to the whole agreement."

"Ask him whether they have developed medical interventions for aging," Flower said over Lynx's implant.

"Why?" the third officer subvoced back.

"Because we're supposed to be debating aging, and M793qK is curious."

"—on Thursdays," Reba finished answering a question that Lynx had missed, and the audience erupted in laughter.

"I believe it's your turn to address a question to one of the other guests," Nancy said to the third officer when the room quieted down again.

"My alter ego wants to know if the Alts have developed technology to slow the aging process," Lynx said. "I seem to recall hearing that your life expectancy is longer than ours, but I don't have a number."

"It's not a number we collect," Hethram said. "The concept of assigning an expectation to the average lifespan seems a bit morbid to me. Is there some purpose behind it?"

"I believe the mathematics of life expectancy was originally developed by actuaries working in the life insurance industry, though government planners also used it to budget for future—are you alright?" Lynx cut herself off as the Alt slumped forward and almost hit his head on the table before recovering.

"An overreaction to shock," Hethram said. "I'll have to toughen up. Did you just imply that Humans gamble on their lifespans?"

"Insurance, not gambling. Well, I get that they're sort of the same thing, but you have to take into account that we don't come from a sharing economy like yours. Responsible parents often purchased life insurance to provide a cushion for a spouse and children in case of unexpected death."

Hethram considered this for a good thirty seconds before responding. "I find the logic suspect, but the intention speaks in your favor. As to your original question, we focus on the quality of our lives, not the quantity of years. Life extension, in the way I believe you are using the term, doesn't exist as a field of study in our medical sciences. Perhaps the Farling physician could give you a number that summarizes our mortality. It's probably a useful piece of information for neighbors-to-be," the Alt added, inclining his head towards Reba.

"Estimates of longevity from genetic analysis are at best educated guesses since the behavior of the organism figures strongly into how long it will live," M793qK informed them. "That said, if an Alt and a Human born today were raised to make healthy decisions throughout their lives and weren't subjected to any introduced traumas or diseases, I estimate the Alts would live approximately sixty percent longer. Furthermore, my analysis of the current Alt genome compared to samples of their ancestral species from Earth suggests the Alts have been evolving towards increased longevity over the past fifty thousand years. A million years from now your longevity should approach that of the typical Horten or Drazen today."

"How about us?" a voice called from the audience.

"Start eating your vegetables and following the exercise regime I prescribed and I'll let you know," the Farling said.

Since any semblance of a debate had been lost, Nancy began to accept questions from the audience, many of which revolved around food. Both Reba and Hethram seemed to enjoy the evening, and they often asked each other for clarifications to some point that came up in an answer. Woojin slipped out at some point to take Em home and put her to bed, and Lynx found herself fading by the time Nancy called an end to the evening.

"I'm so glad I came," Reba said to Nancy. "It was an honor to present the Old Way movement to such an engaged audience. Hethram was so forthcoming that I'll be seeking out our negotiators as soon as I get home to tell them what I've learned."

"This discussion contributed more to my understanding of our future neighbors than five days of negotiating specifics at the conference table," Hethram concurred. "I had been dreading the next session, but now I look forward to it."

"You're both welcome back anytime," Nancy said. "That's the longest standing ovation we've had since a saleswoman came in to demonstrate a portable auto-kitchen that made desserts, and she gave out free samples."

Sixteen

"I've been looking forward to this all week," Jorb told Bill. "Playing cameraman for the Grenouthian director has been monopolizing all of my free time, though at least I made my recruiting target for Earth Two."

"How about you, Beetle Boy?" Razood asked, swinging his broadsword to warm up. "Did you fill your quota?"

"I wish Yaem hadn't told everybody he was loaning me to M793qK," Bill said. "It was confusing enough being a double agent for the Sharf, and now I'm completely in over my head. The only good part is I haven't been tasked to do any recruiting yet."

"Doc must get more Human agents than he can use through his medical practice," Jorb said. "All he would have to do is show them a phony bill and then offer to let it slide if they'll just keep their eyes open and report anything of interest that happens in their neighborhood."

"Enough with the spy stuff," Zick said, struggling to fasten the last button on his doublet. "Man, I've got to stop eating all the desserts Renée brings home from her Open University classes."

"Come to the Old Way deck and pump the bellows for me," Razood offered. "You'll get a better workout than at the fancy health club on the Human deck."

"I don't go there for my health. I go to check out the women."

"But you're with Renée," Bill protested.

"I can still look, can't I?"

"If you were Drazen, that would be a good way to get your tentacle chopped off," Jorb said, gesturing with his noodle axe. "Are you guys ready yet? I'm curious to see what Flower came up with. She guarantees it's her most realistic Live Action Role Playing game yet."

"I miss the old days when she dressed us in holograms so we didn't have to buy all of this gear," Bill said, wincing as the helmet he was donning caught on one of his ears.

"The store helps pay the bills," Flower told them via the dressing room speakers. "The four of you come out ahead because you've already won so much gear on your quests, especially Zick. New players can spend over a hundred creds on the basic kit."

"Come on, I have to be back at the smithy in four hours to teach case hardening," Razood said. He strode to the door of the LARPing studio and called, "Ready."

Bill was caught in the act of pulling on his second boot and took a few hopping steps to get his foot settled before catching up with the others. The new game was visually stunning, with the entry point being a meadow that sloped upward towards a virgin forest that might have been plucked from a Grenouthian nature documentary.

"No introduction roll?" Zick inquired. "We aren't going to get a backstory about evil entering the land?"

"Aren't you the one who's always complaining about us breaking the suspension of disbelief by talking to Flower?" Jorb said. He sniffed the air and pointed with his axe. "There's a farm that way."

"What does a farm smell like?" Bill asked.

"Manure." The Drazen turned a hundred and eighty degrees. "This way is the sea, so maybe we'll encounter pirates."

"What if we prayed?" Razood suggested. "Maybe a goddess will appear and provide guidance."

"Wait, I think I heard something," Zick said, drawing his claymore.

Bill quickly employed the stirrup to draw back the string on his crossbow and loaded a bolt. Jorb began twirling his axe in intricate patterns, and the Frunge blacksmith melted into the greenery to flank whoever was approaching. The newcomer turned out to be a young maiden carrying a wicker basket, and her eyes went wide when she spotted the adventurers.

"It could be a trap," Zick hissed. "I saw this once in the professional LARPing league where the innocent young girl was actually a powerful witch and her basket was full of dark magic."

"Put down the basket and step away," Razood shouted from the woods, causing the girl to pale.

"Don't be afraid," Bill said, removing the quarrel from his crossbow and releasing the tension. "We're strangers and we're here to help. Are your lands under threat from invaders? Is there a castle with a necromancer raising armies of the dead, or maybe a dragon ravaging your livestock? We were sent by your, uh, deities to fight the bad guys for you."

"Bad guys?" the girl asked, keeping a careful eye on their weapons. "We don't have anyone like that here. Everybody gets along with everybody else and we're working together to build a better future."

"Flower!" Zick yelled, and again received no response. "So what is this place called, young miss?" he asked.

"I'm Shoshanna, and you're in Treadle World," she replied happily. "Come, let me show you the way to our village. There are plenty of opportunities to do an honest day's work for those with strong backs and positive attitudes." Shoshanna turned to the Drazen and asked, "Does that axe mean that you're a woodsman? My brother runs a small furniture factory and he's always in the market for good lumber."

"Maybe another time," Jorb said, resting his axe head on the turf. "Are you sure that your coastal trade isn't bothered by pirates? We were thinking of heading down to the sea."

"That's where I was going, to look for the snails my mother uses to make a purple dye for our cloth," the girl said. "If you have some sacks, you could gather seaweed and sell it in the village."

"I have a bag of holding," Bill said, drawing a scowl from Zick, who had returned his Claymore to its scabbard. "Razood! Come out of there. We're going to accompany the young lady and gather some seaweed."

"You must be joking," the blacksmith said as he emerged from the forest right in front of them. "What kind of LARP is this?"

"Maybe it's all crafting," Zick said. "Who would possibly pay to play a game without monsters to kill?"

"I did," Shoshanna said, looking hurt. "Flower credits our accounts for working on her ag deck and we wanted to return the favor by spending it with her."

"You aren't an NPC?"

She looked at Zick blankly.

"A non-player character. The villagers in these games are almost always NPCs, unless it's one of the crafting storylines where you build a farming community first so you can support an army and start conquering your neighbors. Is that what you're up to?"

"Everyone in here is from the Old Way movement, though we've invited the Alts to come and visit," Shoshanna said, moving closer to Bill. "Why would anybody want to fight their neighbors?"

"Zick's just used to a different kind of gaming," Bill told the young woman. "It's all make-believe. In real life, he's an anime artist and a computer programmer."

"Coder, and I write scripts too," Zick said sullenly.

"Lead on," Jorb said, pointing in the direction of the sea with his axe. "Maybe there are pirates and you just haven't met them yet."

"I've got a bad feeling about this," Razood muttered. "Flower's not responding to my pings. I think she means to keep us in here until our time is up."

"We can always just—where's the exit?" Jorb asked, squinting back towards where he remembered the dressing room.

"Exactly. She even replaced the grass we walked on so we can't retrace our steps."

"Can I ask you a question?" Zick addressed the girl, who was keeping Bill between herself and the possibly homicidal stranger. "You do agricultural work all day for a living, right?"

"I work in the kitchen and teach the younger children in the mornings, and then I'm in the orchards in the afternoons," Shoshanna said.

"Right. So why would you spend your money and your time off to come in here and do the same thing with holograms?"

"In here I'm learning to be a dyer and a seamstress. It's completely different." She looked shyly at Bill, put her free hand on his arm, and added, "It's also a fun way to meet new people. We're having a barn dance later if you'd like to come."

"I'm engaged," Bill told her.

"You're busy? You could visit another time."

"I mean I'm engaged to be married."

"Engaged to be married," Shoshanna repeated as if she was hearing the phrase for the first time. "Does that mean it's a business thing, like mail-order brides?"

"Julie was almost the first person I met on Flower when I stowed away. We've been living together for almost a year."

"So you're already married," she said, removing her hand as meadow underfoot began to thin into rougher grass mixed with a sandy beach.

"Not technically, but as good as," Bill said. "We're just waiting for the right time to tie the knot."

"How can one time be more right than another? In the Old Way, we get married before we set up housekeeping."

"Same here," Jorb contributed.

"Us too," Razood added. "Some Vergallians do the shacking up thing, but the real libertines of the tunnel network are the Dollnicks."

"That's not true," Flower's voice came out of nowhere, and with each word, the sound of the waves momentarily cut out.

"Just trying to get your attention. How long are you going to keep us in here?"

"I thought you'd enjoy yourselves. There are Frunge living on space stations who would pay big creds to come in here and work as the village blacksmith."

"That's because it's not their day job," Razood said. "The holographic quality is top-notch, but I'd rather fight pixilated monsters, if you don't mind."

"I can't support two environments in here at the same time, and I'm not going to introduce monsters to Treadle World," Flower told them. "Come out and I'll credit your account for next time."

"You're leaving already?" Shoshanna asked.

"Your LARP is very nice, it's just not what we expected," Bill said. "Will you be okay getting back on your own?"

"Of course. The only scare I've ever had in here was when the four of you showed up armed for war."

Zick was still grumbling ten minutes later when they were back in the dressing room and he popped a button trying to take off his doublet. "Leave it," he growled when Bill started after the round bit of faux bone that was rolling across the floor. "I'll tell everybody that it got sliced off in a sword fight."

"I can't believe I blew my evening off for this," Jorb said, glancing at the ceiling in irritation. "What are you guys going to do now?"

"I guess I'll try to get ahead on my independent study report," Bill said.

"You've finished all of the research?" Razood asked with surprising intensity.

"Yes, I mean, no," Bill changed his answer on seeing Jorb shaking his head in the negative behind the Frunge. "Maybe I should go to the Blue Tea Café and, uh, take some notes on customer behavior in the evening."

"I guess I can come along and keep you out of trouble," Razood said. "How about you, Jorb?"

The Drazen pointed at his ear for a moment and then shot Bill a look of irritation. "Rinka is at an Old Way sewing circle with Julie. She said they'd be along in an hour."

"What's wrong with learning how to sew?" Bill asked.

"She already knows how to sew and it's the tenth night in a row she's spent with the colonists. If it's not women's circles with the Old Way Humans, it's instrument making or doing choral arrangements with the Alts. She's going to forget she's a Drazen if this keeps up."

"Nice people are like cultural imperialists the way they suck you into their worlds," Zick said. "You guys enjoy the café. I'm going to the gym to work off some steam and check out the talent."

The Blue Tea Café was experiencing the evening rush when the three friends arrived. A waitress spotted the trio as they entered and led them to the last open table, which was on a slightly raised platform in the back with a view of the whole room.

"Are you giving us special treatment because I've started training as a shift manager?" Bill asked.

The waitress gave an almost imperceptible shake of her head and indicated Razood with her chin before asking, "Can I take your orders?"

"Hot sauce," Jorb said. "The hottest you've got."

"What would you like to go with that?"

"A spoon? Just kidding. Something crunchy, doesn't matter what."

"I'll have the daily special and a tea," Bill said. "Razood? It's on me. I get an employee discount."

The blacksmith, who had been looking back over the counter ever since they arrived, asked, "Is the owner here?"

"Fandaz stepped out for a minute but she'll be back any time," the waitress said. "She keeps a special stock of berry extracts for any Frunge who come in, if you'd like to try one."

"I place myself in your capable hands," Razood said, settling back in his seat.

"This table isn't steady," Jorb said as soon as the waitress departed, shooting Bill a wink.

"That's not possible!" The blacksmith grabbed the edge of the table and gave it a shake, but of course it was solid as a rock. Then he heard Jorb laughing and shot him a glare. "The only way these wrought iron legs are ever getting bent is if somebody uses the table to hit a Drazen over the head."

"Come on, guys. I'm supposed to be observing the customers," Bill said. "Fandaz will probably ask me what I've learned."

"Relax," Jorb told him. "She'll know why you're here as soon as she sees who you brought. And don't buy that story the waitress had about the owner stepping out for a minute. I'll bet all of the waitresses have instructions to ping Fandaz the minute Prince Charming comes in."

"You don't know what you're talking about," Razood said, but Bill thought the Frunge looked rather pleased with himself. "As long as we're all here together, I received a special communication from the home office this morning. They wanted to know if I had any insights into M793qK's character."

"My handler sent me a coded transmission with pretty much the same message," Jorb said. "I was going to bring it up the next time we all eat in Harry's cafeteria."

"Your—" Bill lowered his voice, "—intelligence agencies want you to dig into M793qK?"

"I wrote up his offer to collaborate with us last month, and I guess the analysts finally got around to reading my report," Razood said. "They usually don't pay much attention to what I send them because it's mainly Human trivia."

"Same here," the Drazen said. "It's obvious that the good doctor is up to something, but I got this gig almost straight out of the Open University, so I'm a neophyte at intelligence work. They gave me a crash course in recruitment and said not to call for help if I ever got caught on an alien world because they'd disavow me."

"Why?" Bill asked. "I thought everybody in the business knows that you guys are all on Flower under the special arrangement to let you spy on humanity in return for helping pay our expenses."

"That's true when we're spying on Humans, but there's interesting stuff being done by the owners of some open worlds," Jorb said. "So how about it?"

"How about what?"

"You must have some idea what M793qK is up to, even if it's just a guess."

"He said something about if I stick with him, I could end up owning the most popular café for spies on the tunnel network," Bill said. "I told him I wasn't sure I wanted that, but I've been thinking about it, and the spies I know do seem to spend an awful lot of time hanging around and eating."

"One fresh berry extract in soda water, one Blue Tea, and you didn't order anything to drink," the waitress said to Jorb as she unloaded her tray. "I'll be back with the daily special and the hot sauce sampler in a minute."

"So M793qK must be planning on setting up an intelligence network," Jorb said. "We know he's on the outs with the Farling hierarchy after he tried to move up and failed. Maybe he's decided to rebuild his position using outsiders."

Bill poured a little tea from the small pot into the white cup to check the color at the beginning of the steeping process. "There. Now I can say I researched something," he said. "What was that about outsiders?"

"Us," the Drazen said. "The Farlings don't have any issues with employing minions from other species. It's how they became so expert at alien biology that they dominate the cross-species pharmaceutical industry."

"It makes a certain amount of sense," Razood said. "M793qK had a good job working for the Stryx on Union Station as an emergency doctor while I was there. I always wondered why he made the move to Flower."

"I thought it was because EarthCent wanted a multi-species doctor on board," Bill said.

"The Farling doesn't answer to EarthCent, or even to the Stryx. He's as much of a free agent as you're likely to find."

"Oh, come on. I might not last very long alone, but there are plenty of independent traders who don't answer to anybody."

"There's a difference between being free because nobody is trying to stop you, and being a senior part of something much bigger and choosing to go your own way," Razood said. "The Farlings don't share the pecking order of their hierarchy with outsiders, but M793qK is probably top ten."

"Was top ten," Jorb put in. "And he didn't walk away, he was exiled, probably after the fact."

"What does that mean?" Bill asked, leaning back to make room for the waitress when she reappeared with a much larger tray.

The Drazen was too intent on the array of hot sauces and fried vegetables being placed in front of him to answer, and then the waitress put the final plate with the daily special in front of Bill. "I checked the schedule, and I'm looking forward to Tuesday when I'll be working for you," she said before moving off.

"That's the second young lady to make a pass at you today," Razood observed. "Maybe you should start wearing a sign saying that you're taken."

"I'm getting a ring as soon as we're married," Bill said.

"Through your nose?" Jorb asked, checking the temperature of the vegetable tempura with a finger. "And in answer to your previous question, the way I heard it, M793qK had to flee Farling space. There's a price on his carapace if he returns."

"But if the Farlings are as powerful in their own space as everybody says they are, what good would it do the doctor to get a handful of alien spies working for him?"

"The kind of information he'd need to plan his next move isn't something you can read in the Galactic Free Press," Razood said.

"Or buy from EarthCent Intelligence," Jorb added. He swiped a bit of what might have been eggplant tempura through a whitish sauce, popped it in his mouth, and then pounded the iron tabletop with his fist. "Oh, that's good stuff."

"I'm glad you like it," Fandaz said as she arrived at their table and stood between Bill and Jorb. "We don't serve that one to Humans."

"Here, take my chair," Razood said, hopping to his feet. The two Frunge attempted to change places, first with both of them starting around Bill, and then both of them starting around Jorb.

"It's embarrassing just watching the two of you," the Drazen said, pushing back his chair. "Now you go behind me, Fandaz, and you cross in front of me, Razood." He grabbed the blacksmith's wrist with his tentacle and pulled him through the gap to hasten the exchange. "It's like the two of you never even practice dated or something."

"That was over a century ago for me," Fandaz replied, and then her hair vines turned bright green.

"We'll be at Union Station tomorrow. You guys need to see a matchmaker before you drive us all crazy."

"They don't work remotely," Razood told him. "Everything has to be supervised."

"Which is why you're lucky to have me for a friend," Jorb said. "Samuel and I go way back together."

"Vivian's husband?" Fandaz asked. "What can he do to help?"

"His sister, Dorothy, became the official chaperone for a Frunge couple before I left Union Station."

"I've never heard of a matchmaker accepting alien chaperones," the owner of the Blue Tea Café said. "If this is another one of your Drazen jokes, it's not funny."

"There was one catch," Jorb said, letting the dramatic tension build as he swiped another piece of tempura through some green sauce.

"What?" Razood demanded, grabbing the Drazen's wrist to keep him from raising the snack to his mouth.

"You can't let anybody know about this or Dorothy will kill me, and this means you too, Flower," Jorb added.

"We all swear," the blacksmith said.

"Dorothy and her husband were married under Frunge law before they had a Human wedding."

Fandaz leaned back in her chair as the significance of Jorb's information dawned on her. "Of course. That makes perfect sense." She and Razood turned to Bill, their unspoken pleas visible on their alien faces.

"I'll ask," he said with a sigh, "but Julie will probably throw me out of our cabin."

Seventeen

"After the meeting, you and Bill are coming to eat with my family on Union Station and—" Vivian broke off to wave at an alien who had just entered the conference room, "Dring is here. My mom told me he's writing a history of our teaming up with the Alts to colonize Earth Two, so Samuel and Methan better settle everything today."

"Maker Dring?" Julie squeaked as everybody in the room fell silent.

"He rents space from Samuel's dad so I've known him since I was a baby. I'll introduce you."

"But I'm just a—"

"You're the host," Vivian cut her off firmly. "He's coming right over so treat him like you would any alien dignitary."

"I'm so out of my league," Julie muttered, but she managed five deep breaths before the Maker, whose current form was a bipedal reptile that didn't quite resemble any other species, approached.

"Dring, this is Flower's host, Julie," Vivian made the introduction.

"I'm pleased to meet you," Dring said, offering Julie a polite bow, and nodding as if he understood the girl's garbled attempt at welcoming him in Flower's name. Then he asked Vivian, "And when will your spark of new life be joining us?"

"A couple more weeks, I think. M793qK wouldn't give me an exact date because he said I'd try to plan around it and end up working too hard."

"A wise Farling."

"I'll fetch another chair for the conference table," Julie managed to say when she noticed the scroll case and writing supplies the Maker was carrying.

"That won't be necessary," Dring told her. "My tail provides balance or support as required, and sitting on it is a bit awkward. But if there's table space where I can unroll my scroll?"

"The Grenouthian director never uses his chair because he's always behind a camera," Julie said, and led the Maker to the table. "And I already put an extra chair next to Samuel for you, Vivian."

The spots around the conference table filled up rapidly, and unlike previous meetings, a number of correspondents from the Galactic Free Press and various alien news organizations sorted themselves into a media gallery. There was a quiet turf war between the aliens working cameras for the Grenouthian director's documentary and those working for news networks, but thanks to the presence of the Maker, the cameramen conducted themselves in a civilized manner.

"Don't forget to mention the launch date of our production line for commercial rentals," Flower prompted over Julie's implant.

"No," the girl responded so firmly that she accidentally spoke out loud before shifting to subvocalizing. "I'm nervous enough as is and I'm not doing commercials." The conversations in the room fell to a mere murmur, and as she cast her eye around the table to get the introductions set in her head, she realized that she'd already forgotten the new Alt's name.

"Methan," Flower said in her head without being asked. "You're staring at him."

"Welcome to the final day of negotiations for the Earth Two colonization project," Julie began. Her voice was amplified by the Dollnick AI and played through the public address system, with all of the acoustic delays in perfect synchronization so it sounded to everybody in the room as if she was speaking directly to them. "I'm sure you've all noticed a couple of new faces at the table today, and Flower has asked me to extend a special welcome to Maker Dring, who is recording this meeting for history."

There was a loud round of applause from the press gallery, and the conference participants at the large circular table all inclined their heads towards the Maker to show their respect. Julie waited a moment to see if Dring would say anything, but he was too busy grinding ink for his quill to do more than offer a blunt-toothed smile of acknowledgment.

"Today we are joined by Methan, who has been authorized by the citizens of the Alt homeworld to sign an agreement on behalf of his people," Julie continued. "Methan will be ably assisted by Affie, the contract queen representing the Alts on Union Station. Affie asked me to extend a special thanks to Avisia, the headmistress of our local finishing school, who filled in as an advisor for the Alts to this point. Are you here, Avisia?"

"She's supervising a school field trip to Union Station," the Grenouthian director informed everyone.

"Returning to represent the Alt colonists are Fanli and Hethram," Julie continued, gesturing in their direction, "and the Old Way representatives are Jade, Oscar, and Garth. I guess all that's left is to extend Flower's welcome to members of the press and inform you that you're all invited to partake in the free catering for lunch."

The applause and cheering from the press corps at this announcement outdid their enthusiasm for Dring, who dipped his quill in the freshly made ink and started catching up with a transcript of the events. Julie retreated to stand against the wall behind where the press corps was seated, and Methan turned his head towards Samuel, making it clear he was ceding the floor to the First Administrator.

"Thank you all for coming again to what we hope is the final negotiating session for the joint Earth Two colonization and terraforming project," Samuel began. "I've been in touch with Methan over the Stryxnet throughout the negotiation process and we've agreed to disagree on a small number of points involving the future behavior of our colonists. In place of perfect concordance, our goal today is to create a mechanism for conflict resolution that will allow the parties on the ground to work out any differences. Yes, Methan?"

"I believe we agreed to use the term 'misunderstanding resolution,'" the Alt said.

"Sorry. What did I say?"

"Conflict resolution," Vivian told him.

"Oops," Samuel said, "Yes, Affie?"

"I want to point out that we aren't planning on sending a contract queen to Earth Two until the economic output requires a business manager, so the misunderstanding resolution mechanism will have to take Alt sensibilities into account."

"Could you be more specific?"

"No lawyers, no delays, no intimidation," Affie ticked off on her fingers.

"The tripod of all business negotiations," one of the Grenouthians in the press corps muttered to a Horten, who nodded in agreement.

"We can eliminate delays right now if we set up a regular schedule," Garth said for the Old Way colonists. "We could build a meeting house right at the boundary dividing our areas and plan on meeting once a week."

"Do you expect to create that many misunderstandings with us?" Fanli asked in dismay.

"If we're relying on paper mail rather than instant communications, it would be better to hold more frequent in-person meetings than might be necessary otherwise."

"The Human has a point," Hethram said. "It would make sense for each of our colonies to establish a community within a day's walk of the border for this very purpose."

"That close?" Methan asked his fellow Alt. "I gathered from the tenor of the negotiations to this point that our colonists are counting on distance to reduce friction. There's space enough on the small continent for generations of natural expansion without bringing our peoples in such close proximity."

"Have the Old Way communities already chosen their initial colonization points from the maps, or is there room for maneuvering?" Samuel asked.

"As long as the meeting house is on the border near the shore, I don't see a problem with establishing a community nearby," Oscar said. "The central part of the continent is quite mountainous in some areas, and we don't want to disturb wildlife migrations through the plains any more than necessary."

"Of course not," Hethram agreed.

"The location of the meeting house is less important than what goes on inside," Affie said. "Alt debate club rules must be applied for the meetings, and both sides shall accept the ruling of a certified debate master."

"You mean we'll argue it out and a professional mediator will give a ruling?" Jade asked.

"A certified debate master," Affie repeated. "They're the closest thing to judges in Alt society."

"Hold on," Samuel said. "How long would it take one of our colonists to get certified as a debate master?"

The Vergallian shrugged to indicate that it wasn't her problem.

"Don't you trust our debate masters?" Hethram asked with a puzzled look.

"It's not a matter of trust, it's a question of perception," Samuel explained. "If all conflicts, I mean, misunderstandings, are ultimately judged by an Alt debate master, some people might question the fairness of the process."

"But why?" Fanli asked. "Our debate masters complete a forty-year apprenticeship before they can be certified for their impartiality. There's never been a case in our history of somebody purporting to be certified when they weren't."

"Humans lack your level of trust in institutions of any kind," Affie explained to the Alt colonist. "They have a poor record of abiding by the laws and judgments of their own system."

"I don't think accepting the rulings of Alt debate masters will be a problem for our communities as long as there is a path for our people to become certified," Oscar said, speaking slowly as he chose his words with care. "We govern ourselves through public meetings and debate, and

I've often thought the process would benefit from the presence of an impartial judge. My only concern is the forty-year apprenticeship."

"Perhaps we could allow rulings by journeymen debate masters," Methan suggested, eliciting an eye roll from Affie at his giving up ground without gaining anything in return.

"How many years of training does it take to become a journeyman?" Oscar asked.

"Fifteen years of apprenticeship with a minimum of twenty practice debate rulings reviewed by a master."

"Are the practice debates supplied in writing or as recordings of some sort?"

"I'm sorry if I misspoke, I'm still adjusting to Humanese," Methan said. "There are no practice debates, only practice rulings. The apprentice must accompany a master to debates and privately offer a ruling before the master announces his decision. Anyone interested enough in civic discussion to aspire to become a debate master would likely attend a thousand or more debates during the first part of an apprenticeship. Two a week isn't an uncommon pace for a journeyman in training."

"This may sound silly, but I've been building an image of Alt society being so well ordered that you would have nothing to argue about," Jade said. "What sort of issues come up at these debates?"

"Many of them arise from study," Hethram answered. "Debating clubs are the ideal place to test new ideas. Seeking peer feedback early on can save us from channeling time into unproductive paths."

"Most public lectures of any kind are followed by a debate," Fanli added. "Some have real outcomes and are taken up by large numbers of groups, like whether or not to build a bridge. Others are simply for fun, like debating which character in a novel made the best choices for the community."

"Millions of debates have taken place on Alt in recent months around our purchase of Earth Two and participation in a joint project with humanity," Methan said. "The results of those debates are the source from which I derive my authority to sign an agreement."

"I didn't realize there was that much tension in Alt society," Samuel admitted.

Affie stifled a laugh, and Methan looked puzzled. "Most debates end in a consensus before the debate master rules," the Alt said. "That's why it takes fifteen years for an apprentice attending multiple debates a week to present twenty practice rulings."

"It's important to remember that the Alts aren't debating out of pride or vanity," Affie said. "They're genuinely trying to find the best solution for their communities. They *want* to agree. It's the complete opposite of the royal training I received in debating arbitrary positions."

Oscar consulted briefly with his two associates. "We can accept the proposal, but given the youth of the Old Way movement, our public meetings often fall short of reaching a consensus. An apprentice visiting our debates would therefore have many more opportunities to issue practice rulings than in Alt society, and perhaps could be certified that much sooner. If some of your debate masters would be willing to visit our communities and attend our meetings, we could present apprentices for training."

The two Alt representatives put their heads together with Methan and Affie for a brief consultation, and in the end, it was the contract queen who replied.

"There are two issues at hand," she said. "While the Alt community currently on Flower has reached a level of comfort with proximity to Humans that none of us would have believed possible just a month ago, it may turn out to be a honeymoon effect that will end in disappointment. In that case, an Alt traveling alone for extended periods of time in Human areas would be almost unthinkable. Second, debate masters are not a professional class in the Human sense. The most active among them might spend ten hours a week attending debates, but the average is much lower. Abandoning their families and regular activities to perform as circuit judges for Old Way public meetings would not be an attractive proposition."

"Are there no Alt travelers who are also debate masters?" Samuel asked. "Craftsmen who ply their trade over a wide area, specialists of any sort, artists in search of new landscapes? Perhaps they couldn't live exactly as they would at home, but it is a new world, after all. A civilization that created its own interstellar drive must have some interest in travel."

"But your economic systems don't align," Affie pointed out. "An artist painting Human children would record her labor on her block, but how does judging Human debates benefit the Alt community?"

"I think that during the settling in period, outreach to Humans could be seen as contributing to the greater good," Fanli said, and Hethram nodded his agreement. "If we're going to get along as neighbors, both sides will have to make sacrifices, and it would be rude to ask the Humans to abide by our rules and then not to help them with the process."

"As long as our debate masters can be hosted without resort to money," Hethram added.

As the discussion slipped back into the weeds of running an economy without money, Dring's quill scratched away on his scroll, and Vivian ground fresh ink to allow him to keep up. Several of the alien reporters snoozed off in their seats, and even Julie stopped paying attention while reviewing her schedule for the rest of the week with Flower. Then the caterers arrived and began to set up a buffet, and the press corps got so noisy that Samuel had to call a pause for lunch.

"How are we doing?" he asked, slipping into the seat next to Dring when the maker set aside his quill.

"It's a bit too soon to be asking a historian that question," the Maker said.

Vivian returned from the buffet, set a plate of celery and carrot sticks next to the Maker's scroll, and then settled into the now-vacant seat on Dring's other side.

"I brought you a snack," she said to the Maker. "Has Sam asked you yet?"

"I was working my way up to it," Samuel said, and turned to Dring. "There's something I've been trying to figure out ever since last time we were at Union Station and Methan negotiated the preliminary deal to share Earth Two."

"I have it all written down if you need to refresh your memory about the details," Dring said.

"It's not that. Mom explained how all of the alien ambassadors who exchanged with her pushed the Alts and us together, and Daniel has some funny stories about what they got out of it for their own species. I have the feeling there was something more to it."

"And not just the usual thing with the Stryx manipulating everybody," Vivian chimed in.

The Maker chomped thoughtfully on a celery stalk before replying. "You must have some ideas. Why don't you make a case for them?"

"Because it seems—all right," Samuel said. "I think that the advanced species are pushing humanity closer to the Alts in the hopes that they'll rub off on us."

"That seems reasonable."

"Have you been talking with Krey?" Vivian asked. "That's her line."

"Krey is an interesting Cayl and a credit to the imperial family," Dring said. He picked up another celery stalk and asked, "What else?"

"You mean there has to be more to it than that?" Samuel glanced at Vivian. "We had some other ideas, but they aren't compatible with the first one, and now that I think about it, some of them were a bit paranoid."

"I still think it's the aliens trying to civilize us through contact with the Alts," Vivian said.

"Which sounds to me like half an explanation," Dring said, and popped the celery into his mouth.

"There's money in it for the Container Prince so he recovers his investment in all the flora and fauna he imported from Earth, not to mention the basic terraforming," Samuel said. "I guess that could have motivated the Dollnicks."

"The Vergallians must be happy with any arrangement that keeps their contract queens in the picture," Vivian said. "And you know how it is with the tunnel network ambassadors—they all owe each other favors, so maybe they were working…" she noticed Dring shaking his head in the negative and trailed off.

"Who are the principal parties to the agreement?" the Maker asked.

"I almost forgot about Flower," Samuel said. "In addition to providing terraforming expertise, she had the business of transferring—no?" he cut himself short.

"The Alts," Vivian said with a burst of insight. "The other half of the answer is that the alien diplomatic services think they'll benefit in some way from the Alts sharing Earth Two with humanity. But how?"

"Do I sense an acoustic isolation field?" Dring asked.

Samuel pointed at his ear, held a brief subvoced conversation, and nodded. "Flower says she established it to provide privacy as soon as Vivian sat down. It's a standard service she offers at diplomatic conferences."

"You've surmised that contact with the Alts could improve Humans in the eyes of the aliens," the Maker said. "Take the next step."

"The aliens think that living with our Old Way colonists will improve the Alts?" Vivian asked. "But the Alts are nearly perfect as is."

"That's it," Samuel exclaimed. "Didn't you tell me that your dad said Drazen intelligence didn't want to send any more agents to the Alt homeworld because it ruins them for working anywhere else? The aliens think the Alts are *too* nice, and they're hoping that contact with us will roughen them up."

"Nobody likes a goody-two-shoes," Dring agreed, and selected another stalk of celery.

Eighteen

"When you said Vivian invited us to dinner with her family, I thought it would be in their home," Bill said. "That meal must have cost more than I earn in a month."

"It's a good thing there aren't any restaurants that expensive on Flower or I'd be afraid to go anywhere with Vivian," Julie replied. "She told me that eating out is the only chance she gets to spend her family's InstaSitter money because it helps the restaurant economy. Otherwise, Samuel tries to get her to live on their income."

"It was a little weird meeting her father since he's also kind of my boss."

"What did he say when the two of you had your heads together?"

"He wants me to come in to EarthCent Intelligence headquarters next time we're here and talk to their Farling expert," Bill said. "Vivian's dad said that they don't have a dedicated desk because they know so little about the Hierarchy and don't have any agents in Farling space."

"Maybe you'll get a raise," Julie said teasingly, nudging him with her elbow as the lift tube capsule came to a halt.

"That'll be the day. At least Yaem used to give me bonus payments whenever I recruited somebody for Sharf Intelligence. M793qK pays me with advice, and EarthCent Intelligence just takes it for granted that I want to help humanity."

"You can complain to Vivian's mother when you see her on Flower. She's going to come on board tomorrow and travel with us until the baby is born."

Bill shrugged off the suggestion as the lift tube doors opened on Union Station's Frunge deck. "Fandaz said that she'd meet us in front of Hazint's legal shop," he said. "Is this the mercantile exchange corridor?"

"Hazint's is to your right, about a two-minute walk," the Stryx station librarian told them.

"Thank you," Julie said, not having expected an answer. "I think Fandaz said it's just past the Frunge honor court."

"I've never seen so many Frunge in my life," Bill said. "There must be thousands of them living here."

"Almost three million," Flower said over his implant, sounding somewhat envious. "Union Station has over a hundred million sentient occupants all told. I asked my Stryx mentor to patch me through so I can be available if you have questions before you sign anything."

"Did you hear her?"

Julie nodded. "And I asked her what she knows about Frunge law. She said that it's tough but fair."

"There's Fandaz," Bill said, and a minute later, they entered Hazint's legal shop in the company of the owner of the *Blue Tea Café*.

"Where's Razood?" Julie asked as they took seats in the waiting area.

"It wouldn't have been proper for us to wait together," Fandaz told her. "He's around somewhere ordering supplies and he'll come when I ping him."

"Why did the matchmaker want to meet us here?" Bill asked.

"She rents office space from Hazint's. Matchmakers and lawyers have a lot in common, and some of them work in both professions."

"I can't think of even one thing they have in common. Is it strictly a Frunge thing?"

"I'm not sure what matchmakers do in Human society, but with us, it's all about creating legally recognized relationships with obligations and protections for both sides, essentially contract law," Fandaz explained. "I checked us in before you got here to avoid any misunderstandings, and we'll be seeing Lawyer Rzard before Matchmaker Mizpah. It's very unusual to attempt two major contracts in a single visit, but they know that Flower is only here for one more day, and I asked our ambassador to use his influence."

"You know the Frunge ambassador on Union Station?" Julie asked.

"I investigated him once. It's a long story."

"Fandaz?" a Frunge male wearing the latest business fashion addressed her. "I'm Rzard."

"Thank you for meeting us on such short notice," she said, bouncing up. "This is Julie, and he's Bill."

"One female, one male," the lawyer said. "Excellent start. Shall we move to the consulting room?" Without waiting for an answer, he led them into a small chamber on the periphery of the office and closed the door behind them. "Your request is quite unusual," he told Fandaz even before taking his seat. "In the case you cited with Dorothy McAllister and Kevin Crick, their union under Frunge law was unintentional. I drew up their companionship contract, so I should know."

"But the precedent is good," Fandaz insisted.

"We just want to do this the fastest way," Julie added. "We'll have another ceremony for our friends later."

The attorney sighed. "I suppose you're already cohabiting?"

Julie and Bill nodded.

"How many children are you planning?"

"Do we need to decide now?" Bill asked.

"It's important for the distribution of your assets in case you should…" Rzard slowly raised a hand while fluttering the fingers, perhaps indicating a spouse running off or ascending to heaven.

"We don't have any assets," Julie told him. "Just what's in our cabin on Flower."

"I see," the lawyer said. "I'm getting the impression that none of this is going to apply to you, but my professional code requires me to run through the basics." He produced a large legal tab and swiped it to life. "I've never done one of these contracts for Humans before so I picked a standard form out of the primitive species library. By signing this agreement, you are committing to an exclusive relationship forsaking all others until death do you part."

"That sounds right," Bill said.

"During said lifetime, Julie—what's the family name?"

"Gold, but it's made up," she said. "We've both gone to just using the one name."

"Excellent choice, very advanced of you," Rzard said, scanning ahead and adding the name in the appropriate places. "Julie agrees to provide two meals a day to Bill and—"

"I do most of the cooking," Bill interrupted, and Julie blushed slightly. "It's my profession."

The lawyer exchanged a shocked look with Fandaz, muttered something under his breath, and read on. "Bill agrees to provide two meals a day to Julie and—who does the laundry?"

"I do the laundry and clean the apartment," Julie said. "Is it really necessary to get all of this in writing?"

"Do you want to live happily ever after?" Rzard demanded, glowering at his clients "All right, then. Bill, I mean, Julie, agrees to turn her salary over to his, I mean, her, husband for maintenance of the household, with a maximum of ten percent held back for personal expenses."

"We both work," Bill told him.

"What about when the babies come?"

"Flower offers daycare," Julie said. "She even pays bonuses to anybody who gives birth on board."

"That explains a lot," the lawyer said. "I think we can just skip to the good part. Given your unconventional approach to parental roles, you'll have to tell me which one of you will be providing consideration."

"Both of us, I hope," Bill said.

"He means the contract kind," Julie said. "Offer, acceptance, consideration."

"I kept asking, she finally accepted, and I gave her a ring."

"Do you have it with you?" Rzard asked.

Julie lifted her left hand and showed him the engagement ring. To her surprise, the lawyer used his tab to capture a close-up image.

"Are we almost done?" Fandaz asked nervously. "Mizpah is expecting us in five minutes and I wouldn't want to be late."

"No, that wouldn't be advisable," the attorney agreed. He did some fancy tapping on his tab, reread what was there, and then showed it to Fandaz.

"Can I pay with my programmable cred?" she asked.

"At the counter," Rzard said. He rose, offered Bill a stylus, and pointed to a blank space on the tab. "Sign here," he said, and then repeated the procedure with Julie. "Congratulations. The two of you stay here and I'll let Mizpah know that we're finished." He turned to Fandaz and added, "You can pay now and collect the marriage contract."

"I'll be right back," the owner of the Blue Tea Café promised, and fled out the door before the attorney.

"Are we really married now?" Bill asked Julie with a grin.

"I guess so, at least in Frunge space," she said. "I don't feel any different."

"I told you there was nothing to be afraid of," Flower said over her implant. "What's the big deal, anyway? You pick out a dress, choose a menu for the catering, and get a couple of friends to stand up with you. I'll check if the captain is free tonight."

"We'll get to it," Julie said out loud. "Don't push."

Fandaz returned and placed a flat stone inscribed in Frunge on the table. "The matchmaker may send me out when she talks to you. Just answer her questions honestly and everything will work out."

"That's our contract?" Bill asked, running his fingers over the deep engraving. "The only thing I recognize is our signatures."

"If you ever visit Frunge space and you want to stay in the same hotel room, it would be a good idea to bring it along," Fandaz told them. "You can get a custom carrying case."

"Are these two scrawls signatures as well?" Bill asked.

"Mine and Rzard's, we were the witnesses. Don't worry, it's entirely legitimate. The tab and stylus are Tharkbonded, so it goes on record with them and you can get a copy at any Stryx station."

"In case we want to start saving them up to build a house," Julie said and began to laugh hysterically.

"Wedding nerves," Fandaz explained to the tiny Frunge woman who entered on creaky limbs. "I want to thank you again for seeing us on such short notice, Mizpah. This is Julie, and he's Bill."

The matchmaker touched the marriage contract with a finger. "It's still warm," she said with a long-suffering sigh that sounded like branches rubbing in the wind. "Ping the male in question and get out."

Fandaz slipped a small leather bag into Julie's hand under the table, and then began backing out of the office while pantomiming handing something to the matchmaker. Julie began to bring out the purse, but Fandaz made a face and gestured for her to wait.

"That was entertaining," Mizpah said. "You have something for me?"

"I think so," Julie replied and handed over the small bag.

The matchmaker weighed it with an experienced hand and nodded. "Someone feels she needs to purchase my goodwill. Do the two of you understand why you're here?"

"For appearance's sake, right?" Bill replied, taking an elbow in the ribs from Julie. "Fandaz told us to be honest."

"Not that honest," Mizpah said, but her ancient features cracked into a smile. "I'm told you're friends of Samuel McAllister, which makes you second-degree relations of his sister Dorothy and her husband, the only Human chaperones of a Frunge couple in history. That experiment hasn't ended in disaster yet, so Fandaz and Razood have seen fit to impose on my good nature and stretch the very concept of proper supervision beyond any previous limits."

"I don't understand why Fandaz would need supervision," Bill said stubbornly while protecting his ribs. "She was an important government official and she's over a hundred years old."

"I happen to agree with you," the matchmaker said. "It's the young blacksmith who I worry about. Now tell me, each of you, how you know the aspiring couple."

"Captain Pyun introduced me to Razood right after I joined Flower. I worked as his apprentice until I found that baking is more my thing. That's how I know Fandaz, through her café, and I've started training with her as a manager to fill in shifts if she opens a new location."

"She's planning on opening a second café?" Mizpah eyed the bag of coins Julie had given her as if she was considering upping her fee in light of the new information.

Bill glanced at the door to check that it was still closed and lowered his voice. "I don't think she really wants another retail shop but it gave her an excuse to meet Razood. He made all of the wrought iron tables and chairs for the *Blue Tea Café*."

"Clever girl," the matchmaker said. She turned to Julie. "And you?"

"I know Razood through Bill, mainly from LARPing. I met Fandaz at her café, and I usually go once a week with my friend Vivian."

"So you wouldn't say that you're close friends."

"Not yet?"

"Why did you answer with a question?"

"Because you asked with a statement," Julie replied.

Mizpah let out a dry cackle. "You're not as naive as you look, either of you. Give me your hands."

Julie and Bill each reached out a hand and the Frunge took them in her own, prodding the flesh of their palms gently with her thumbs as if she were a butcher assessing their fat content.

"What are you checking for?" Bill asked.

"Aura," the matchmaker said. "Physical contact makes it easier with aliens. Yours is quite innocent, besides some retail shenanigans in your youth."

"I worked a pushcart with my Mom."

"You," Mizpah continued, letting go of Bill's hand and concentrating on Julie, "are complicated. I see you've struggled with some of the same ethical issues that forced Fandaz from her government posting, but you exited your prior career with an even bigger bang than she did. Am I correct?"

"I didn't know that the Frunge were mind readers," Julie said, trying to pull her hand away from the little old matchmaker, who proved to be much stronger than she looked.

"I supplement my natural abilities with a research assistant who checked the archives of the Galactic Free Press. You were quite famous for fifteen seconds a few years ago." Mizpah released Julie's hand and sat back. "I'll be blunt with the pair of you. You would never qualify as chaperones under the Matchmaker's Guild guidelines, but I owe somebody a favor and I have the station librarian's word that Flower will help keep an eye on your charges. I'm not going to bother insisting that you keep a dating calendar because the only Human chaperones I have experience with keep accidentally erasing the data on theirs with a hard reset. But you will accompany Razood and Fandaz on dates and come see me whenever your ship stops at Union Station. Are we agreed?"

"Yes," the newlyweds by Frunge contract said simultaneously, and then Bill added, "but I'm curious why we don't qualify when Samuel's sister and brother-in-law did. Is it because they're older than us?"

"You're all barely out of childhood as far as I'm concerned," Mizpah said with a snort. "Dorothy and Kevin had both a baby and a Cayl hound to attest to their suitability to guide a couple towards matrimony. Cayl hounds are understandably in short supply on the tunnel network, but if you come back with two babies, I'll give you the official test."

"That doesn't sound like a bonus."

"It would qualify you to hire out as chaperones for other Frunge, so I imagine Flower would be pleased. Now go tell Fandaz and Razood that I'm ready to see them."

Ten minutes later, the happy Frunge couple came out of the office and proceeded to the counter where they picked up another stone tablet. "I'll carry it back to your cabin," Razood told Bill. "You don't have to bring it along while you're chaperoning our dates on Flower, but keep it for the next time we visit a Frunge open world."

Julie stifled a yawn and checked the time on her implant. "Bill and I better get home if we're going to do any work tomorrow. Are you guys coming?"

"We may as well," Fandaz said. "We certainly can't wander around Union Station together without a chaperone."

One of Flower's large shuttles was counting down to departure when they exited the lift tube on Union Station's travel concourse, and the two couples were the last to board. Practically all of the seats were taken, so Razood and Fandaz went off to the right to hunt for two seats next to each other. Bill spotted what appeared to be a row of six open seats at the very back of the shuttle, but when they got there, it turned out that four of them were occupied by M793qK, who was lying down and taking the weight off his carapace. Nobody else had been brave enough to take a seat next to the alien.

"Sit, sit," the Farling rubbed out on his speaking legs. "I wanted to talk to you anyway. Did Clive debrief you?"

"Clive?" Bill asked.

"Oxford, Vivian's father, the director of EarthCent Intelligence."

"Oh. I'm supposed to talk with their Farling expert the next time we're here, but I'm probably not supposed to tell you that."

"Farling expert," M793qK scoffed. "I'll bet you—no, it's not germane. And congratulations."

"For what?" Bill asked.

"You tell him, Julie."

"We just got married," she reminded her husband.

"But that's just a Frunge formality for Razood and Fandaz," Bill said. "We're going to do it again properly with the captain."

"I take it Mizpah delivered the goods," M793qK said.

"Do you mean approving us as chaperones? Razood is carrying the other tablet back for us."

"Excellent." The Farling let his speaking legs relax and seemed to be studying the newlyweds through his multi-faceted eyes.

"It was you?" Julie demanded. "The matchmaker was doing you a favor?"

"You should come to work for me," M793qK said. "Bill's reliable, but he lacks a certain turn of mind."

"Mizpah said that I have an innocent aura," Bill told him.

"I have a question," Julie said to the Farling. "When the matchmaker said that Samuel's sister and brother-in-law were the only Humans to be approved as Frunge chaperones, did she mean on Union Station, or anywhere?"

"On the entire tunnel network," M793qK replied. "I enjoyed my time on Union Station. It's been a locus of activity since the current EarthCent ambassador arrived."

"Samuel's mother? She seemed like a normal person when he introduced us at the wedding. The only thing that stood out about her was her hair."

"When she was younger, you would have thought her head was on fire. You can get an idea of what it looked like from her daughter."

"That's right, Dorothy is a redhead too. And Captain Pyun's wife," Julie added. "I used to think that redheads were pretty rare, but maybe it was just the people I knew growing up. The Alts sure have a lot of them. "

"Less than two percent of the Human population has the mutated MC1R gene," M793qK said. "There's a connection to the genes that you and the Alts share from their Neanderthal forbears, but it's not something your scientists will understand any time soon. Come to work for me and I'll explain it."

"There's zero chance of that happening."

"What else were you doing on Union Station?" Bill asked the Farling to change the subject.

"Checking my dead drops, and picking a few things up for the Zarents," M793qK replied. "They prefer not to visit themselves since the station's core is entirely open and there are no microgravity environments onboard. You can help me unload when we're back on Flower."

"What was that about dead drops?" Julie asked, keeping her voice low. "Have you been disposing of bodies?"

"You explain to her, Bill."

"Uh, were they covered in that tradecraft manual you gave me to read?"

"Dead drops, dead letter boxes," the Farling said in frustration. "For transferring messages and small items without the risk of a live meeting."

"Why not keep them on Flower?" Bill asked.

"Because the individuals checking them would stand out like sore thumbs, and it would be obvious they came to deliver something to me. Stryx stations are the ideal place for dead drops because they are the transfer hubs of the tunnel network and everybody comes through sooner or later. Nobody has ever roused suspicion by stopping on a Stryx station."

"But Flower said that the Stryx pay even more attention to what's going on than she does," Julie said. "How do you keep it secret from them?"

"Trying to keep secrets from the Stryx would be a complete waste of time," M793qK said. "The important thing to understand is that they choose their spots when it comes to interfering with the activities of lesser beings. I make sure my operatives know which lines not to cross."

Nineteen

"Ugh," Irene said as the giant Dollnick colony ship dropped out of hyperspace. "We must be there."

"Flower usually times her jumps so that we'll be asleep, but this was a long one, and she's going to need every minute to get all of the colonists and their gear unloaded," Harry said. "She also has to check the status of the terraforming job the Container Prince was doing, and get the work crews started on completion."

"This is your captain speaking," Woojin's voice came over the public address system. "We have arrived at Earth Two and will remain in orbit for the next ten days. We'll be rendezvousing with a pair of Verlock lighters—that means ship-to-shore transports—and if everything goes as planned, Flower Transportation will be available to provide the usual tourist excursions before we leave. Business users should expect delays accessing freight lift tubes until we've finished unloading. Captain out."

"What are your plans for the day?" Irene asked her husband. "Are you still working on that strudel dough for Flower Foods?"

"If I get it right, she can sell the dough and the fruit separately as a kit so the buyers can make it fresh. Strudel doesn't have much of a shelf life once it's baked."

"I'll be back at the bazaar putting in my volunteer time today, but if you want to meet for—who could that be?"

Irene interrupted herself when the musical bell tone she had chosen for the door chimed.

Rather than using the voice command, Harry pressed the pad next to the door, and it slid open to reveal the Grenouthian director whose bulk almost filled the opening.

"Are you planning on wearing those to the surface?" the alien asked, eyeing Harry's pajamas. "They look a little lightweight."

"What are you talking about? The captain just announced that there won't be any tourist flights until the end of the week, if then."

"You aren't tourists, you're documentary crew," the Grenouthian said. "We're meeting on the docking deck at oh-eight hundred hours. Dewey is taking us down in the bookmobile."

"But nobody is there yet," Irene protested. "What's the point of sending down a documentary crew before any colonists arrive?"

"Haven't you ever watched a nature show where a climber claims to be the first-ever to set foot on a mountain top? Somebody was obviously there before him, and that somebody is the cameraman. I'll see you at the bookmobile in twenty minutes."

"We had plans—" Harry began, but the door had already slid closed, and something told him that even if he opened it again, the giant bunny would be long gone. He turned to ask his wife if she had agreed to go to the surface and forgotten to tell him, but she had disappeared as well. "Irene?"

"I'm changing into my travel clothes, and you better put on something sensible," she replied from the bedroom. "Is there anything in the fridge we can bring for breakfast?"

"I've got three pounds of strudel with different fillings I tried as an experiment. I was going to bring it to the common room."

"We better take it all. You never know who else the director has roped in."

When they reached the bookmobile, Jorb and Dewey had just finished installing a second row of seats into the back section. The area behind the command seats in the utilitarian spaceship was normally configured as an open space with special bookshelves on the sides to keep the books in place in Zero-G, but the shelves had been removed.

"I haven't installed these seats in years," Dewey told them. "It's lucky Flower has so much storage space or I would have bartered them for something by now."

"Is the director here?" Irene asked.

"He and Razood are bringing all of the cameras," Jorb said. "Where's your friend who stands in for M793qK?"

"Dave? Is he coming?"

"He knows all about camera angles so the director was going to ask him. Is that him coming now? He's a lot smaller without the Farling costume."

"Good morning," Dave called, shuffling forward in his clamp-on magnetic cleats. "I brought the hot drinks so I hope somebody brought Danish."

"Strudel," Irene told him. "Are you sure you haven't had breakfast already?"

"Scout's honor. You can check with Flower."

"All set," Dewey said, climbing out of the bookmobile and taking off his tool belt. "You may as well board and we'll leave as soon as Razood and the director get here."

"You're coming too?" Harry asked the artificial person.

"I'm the pilot, and I'll be staying to help with the documentary. Flower doesn't need any extra traffic coming in and out of the docking bay while she's maneuvering with those Verlock lighters and launching shuttles at the same time. I'm glad I'm not her."

"I thought AI liked being busy."

"There's busy and there's too busy," Dewey said, stowing his tool belt in an external compartment and sealing it before reentering the bookmobile. "Too busy at Earth Two. That could be our fight song."

"I'm taking a window seat," Irene said, heading for the second row. "Harry?"

"You know that looking out the window in space makes me nauseous," he said. "I don't see anywhere to put all of these containers of strudel."

"Keep them on your lap," Dave said, climbing in after Harry. "That's what those stackable kitchen containers are good for. I should know, I used to sell them. Coffee?"

"I guess it doesn't matter if my hands get shaky because we never actually touch the cameras."

"You're sure that the gesture controls won't jitter?" the retired salesman asked as he passed Harry a travel cup of coffee.

"They've got full stabilization filters," Irene told him. "Did you bring a tea?"

"This one." He handed a large silvery cup with a Zero-G lid to Harry, who rested his coffee on the boxes on his lap and passed the tea on to Irene.

"Anything left?" Jorb asked as he took a seat in the forward row.

"One black coffee," Dave said, pressing the cup against the tip of the Drazen's questing tentacle. "I thought you might be coming so I skipped the sugar and milk."

The back of the bookmobile popped open and Razood hopped in. He immediately started stacking the travel cases of immersive cameras that the Grenouthian director tossed to him.

"How many of those things are we bringing?" Harry asked.

"All of them," the Frunge replied. "We've got fourteen, so everybody will take two."

"Strap them down after we take off," the Grenouthian director said impatiently after giving the now-empty floating baggage cart a shove in the general direction of the lift tube. "We have to beat the first shuttle to the surface. All set, Dewey?"

"As soon as you climb in," the artificial person replied.

The bunny jumped through the hatch like a paratrooper moving in reverse. "Go, go, go," he shouted in his bass-baritone, slapping the button to close the hatch. The bookmobile immediately rose above the deck and began heading for the atmospheric retention field covering Flower's core.

"Look down at your hands or close your eyes," Irene warned Harry when she caught him with his head turned towards a porthole.

"Try positive visualization," Jorb suggested. "It's what I teach at the dojo."

"So I should imagine myself looking out a window and not getting sick?" Harry asked.

"I usually tell my students to start with a successful wrist lock and toss, but whatever works for you."

"Think about opening the oven and taking out a tray of freshly baked rolls," Irene said. "You should know that one."

"After a million times, you'd think so," Harry said. He kept his eyes closed and tried to take a sip of his coffee without success. "I forgot how these Zero-G sippy cups work."

"Start sucking on the spout and then push in the valve button on the back of the lid that allows the air to come in and replace the coffee so you aren't pulling against a vacuum," Jorb told him. "But don't forget to release the button before you stop sucking or we'll get big drops of coffee coming out of the valve."

"All right, enough small talk," the Grenouthian director said. "I won't ask if everybody knows their assignments because I haven't handed them out yet. Flower is treating this operation as a dry run for later visits when she'll be carrying more than ten times as many colonists. She's going to start by sending out shuttles with the advance parties for both the Humans and the Alts. Then she'll do one full pack in each of the Verlock lighters to see how long it takes."

"Full pack?" Dave asked.

"Passengers and cargo. Do Humans have a different term for colony ships loading and unloading?"

"Humans don't have any colony ships, other than Flower," Razood pointed out from where he was sitting on a stack of camera travel cases, the toes of one boot under a deck cleat to hold himself in place.

"So it will be pretty chaotic after the first landing, and I want to catch all of that on camera," the Grenouthian director continued. "Flower is going to spread any remaining colonists and their supplies over dozens of runs just to work out the choreography for the future when there won't be as much room for error."

"So how long exactly will we be on the surface?" Harry asked.

"I can't officially work any of you Humans more than four hours because of the Dollnick labor laws related to your advanced ages, but if you're having a good time and want to stay…"

"Flower says eight hours max, and if I don't have them back in time for dinner she'll dock my pay," Dewey called from the pilot's seat. "Now check those safety restraints. We'll be hitting the atmosphere in another minute."

In the back of the bookmobile, the Frunge looked around for another cleat, then gave up and grabbed the carrying handles of the magnetically clamped-down camera cases.

"We'll be splitting into two crews and I won't have time to run back and forth, so I'm putting Jorb in charge of the team at the Alt landing site," the director said. "He'll take Razood and Dave. I expect the Alt landing to be generally uninteresting and anticlimactic because that's the way they are."

"Thanks," Jorb said sarcastically.

"Let me take one of those boxes of strudel," Dave said to Harry.

"I have bag lunches for everybody," Dewey said. "I picked them up from Flower Catering before I started on the seats."

"Harry and Irene, you'll be with me at the Human landing," the Grenouthian said. "I'll position three of the cameras for long shots that will continuously record a panoramic view of the landing, and later I'll hire an actor to provide the dramatic voiceover. What I want the two of you to do is work as a team to focus on interesting-looking

Humans and try to capture something of their emotions—you're good at that Irene."

"I think I'm going to be sick," Harry said as the atmospheric bouncing increased.

"Sorry about that," Dewey called back, and the movement of the shuttle became less pronounced. "I was hurrying to make sure we can drop off the second crew and get back to the Old Way landing site before the advanced party arrives."

"Change of plan," the Grenouthian announced. "We'll land at the Human site first, and then you can take Jorb's crew to their location and return."

"It means you're going to lose at least forty minutes of my time. I'm not allowed to fly supersonic between locations on the continent. It's in the basic deal the Human Empire cut with the Alts."

"Beating the advance team of the Old Way communities is the most important thing. I'll manage the extra cameras until you return."

The next twenty minutes saw an active debate among the aliens about the best colonization documentaries they'd seen and what made them stand out. Harry kept his eyes closed and sipped his coffee, which the cup kept piping hot. Irene gradually joined the conversation, mainly asking questions when something seemed to contradict what she'd been taught in her Open University continuing education course for documentarians. By the time the bookmobile set down, the aliens had come to an agreement that a Verlock documentary about colonizing a volcanically active world which experienced an unpredicted major eruption as the first colonists arrived took the prize.

"But it had nothing to do with the production values," the Grenouthian director qualified his agreement. "They just got lucky with the timing." Then the hatch opened on a grassy field, and he jumped out shouting, "Go, go, go."

Razood began tossing camera cases to the director, and neither of them showed any sign that it was more difficult with Earth Two's gravity than in Flower's core. Dave got up to let Irene and Harry out, and the latter asked, "Apple, cherry, or peach?"

"Peach sounds great," Dave replied, accepting the plastic container of strudel. "See you later."

The bookmobile lifted silently into the air as soon as the hatches closed, and the Grenouthian director immediately began opening travel cases and getting the cameras powered up and floating. "You take the first two," he told Irene, and then shoved a single camera in Harry's direction. "I'm only giving you one because I've seen you navigating."

"There's nothing for me to run a camera into here," Harry pointed out. "It's all scrub grass, and the ocean is right there."

"That's why Flower picked it," the Grenouthian said. "The boundary with the Alt area is a half-hour's walk in that direction," he pointed towards the rising sun, "but even though the Alts are going to create a settlement near their side of the boundary, their main group landing today is going to the far coast."

After the fixed location cameras were in place, the director gave Harry a hasty lesson in properly framing long shots, and then called a breakfast break. They made seats and a small table out of the empty camera cases, and Irene offered the Grenouthian a piece of apple strudel. To her surprise, he accepted.

"Is this supposed to be the same pastry you served in the cafeteria last week?" he asked Harry after taking a bite. "It's crunchier."

"I used harder apples," the baker replied. "I made the last batch to use up some apples that were aging out, but that only works for banana bread. Are you sure we're safe here? I wouldn't want to die from a shuttle putting down on my head after coming this far."

"Flower would feel terrible," Irene agreed.

"Don't you see where those fixed cameras are pointing?" the Grenouthian asked, gesturing with a paw. "They're focused perfectly for the front ramp of the shuttle when it puts down."

"How can you be so precise?"

"I set the cameras to share the telemetry with the shuttle as it lands. You could say that we're the real pathfinders for this colonization effort."

"There it is," Harry said, pointing up at the sky. "That's funny. I always thought the shuttles landed like suborbitals, but it's coming straight down on its belly."

"You thought that because you never looked out the windows on any of our day trips," Irene told him. She wrapped the remaining half of her strudel in a napkin and stood up.

"We're live in thirty seconds," the director said, rising to his feet and gesturing a pair of cameras closer. "Remember, I'll take care of all of the technical shots and continuity, the two of you focus on the Human angle."

The giant shuttle put down exactly where the Grenouthian had predicted, and the front ramp folded out almost immediately. About three seconds passed, and then a mob of excited children poured forth, scattering as soon as they reached the ground.

"That's not what I expected," Harry said. "Should we try to interview some of them?"

"They look too excited to stand still," his wife told him. "Let's wait and see if any of the people we've met are along."

"They don't seem to be disembarking in any particular order, but it looks like the adults and the bigger kids are all headed for the main cargo bay."

"To get whatever they brought unloaded so the shuttle can return quickly," Irene said. "Flower is probably treating this as a time trial."

"Look, there's Oscar and Samuel," Harry said. "Let's see if we can get one of them to talk."

Irene and her husband shepherded their cameras towards where the expedition leader of the Old Way community had been talking with the first administrator of the Human Empire. By the time they arrived, Oscar had merged back into the group of adults unloading the shuttle's cargo bay."

"I feel about as useless as usual," Samuel greeted them. "Flower is so intent on calibrating the turnaround time for shuttles that I had to promise not to touch anything."

"Can you tell us how it's going?" Irene asked, maneuvering her cameras to capture the standard and reverse angles for generating a hologram.

The young man shrugged. "Everybody seems pretty happy so far. Most of the older members of the community have already experienced a division, so moving is nothing new to them. The Old Way communities have all picked different landing sites from a map that Flower provided. The group that Oscar is leading is going to settle right here, but other than the tents and supplies to hold them until their buildings and livestock get delivered by one of those Verlock lighters, the only thing they brought is the meeting house."

"If they use the same building for the school, that makes a lot of sense. They must have more children than adults."

"I should have been more specific," Samuel said. "It's the timbers and materials for completing the meeting house that they're going to set up right on the boundary. Oscar wants to show to the Alts that the community is serious about conflict—I mean, misunderstanding resolution. They're going to erect the building right up the beach, and they got Razood to cast a brass bell so that they'll know if somebody has arrived to talk, day or night."

"What's the director doing?" Harry asked, looking back towards the shuttle.

"I think he's trying to get them to reload the bell because he missed it coming off and realizes that it's an important symbol. Hey, they're humoring him."

"I guarantee you this conversation is going to end up on the electronic cutting room floor," Irene said. "He hates it when anything looks rehearsed."

"Are you going to stick around long enough for them to erect the meeting house?" Samuel asked. "I know Oscar wants to get it done today if possible. It's basically a kit, and they aren't going to receive their next shipment until tomorrow at the earliest."

"How are they going to move the—oh," Harry said, as he saw the first team of men set off along the harder ground near the beach with a two-wheeled cart that balanced a long timber. "I guess they've had plenty of practice."

"Are you staying?" Irene asked Samuel. "I don't want to bother people while they're working, and the Grenouthian director would probably be happy if we recorded your impressions since you're a somebody."

"I don't feel like a somebody, I feel like the kid who won the nepotism lottery," the EarthCent ambassador's son replied. "And I'm leaving with the shuttle so I can accompany the first terraforming crew to the big continent that's—" he squinted towards the sun and then pointed off to the left, "—over that way somewhere. All of the attention is on the colonists, but the Human Empire is responsible for getting moving on the terraforming work because that's our only immediate contribution to the purchase price of Earth Two. Flower's the one who's doing all of the high-level engineering, but we want the people who are going to be on the ground to know that we're behind them."

"Are they going to be isolated for the next six months until Flower returns?"

"She's juggled her schedule so we can get here four times a year, immediately after our Union Station and Earth stops," Samuel said. "And EarthCent Intelligence has undertaken to set up monthly mail delivery and pickup by contracting with some alien package delivery services that will visit all the continents where we're working. It's kind of funny if you think about it."

"What?" Harry asked.

"After coming all the way here in an alien interstellar jump ship, the first two permanent buildings to go up will be a timber-frame meeting house with a bell tower and a post office."

Twenty

"Why do you think Samuel and Vivian invited us all to the Naming?" Avisia asked. "I know they're friends with Jorb, but I've only met them in a professional context."

"It's the best buffet I've seen on Flower yet," Lume said, adding a spoonful of Sheezle bug larvae to his plate. "Vivian's mother must have brought all of the delicacies from Union Station." He dropped his whistle to the lowest level the Vergallian's implant could pick up, and added, "Be careful what you say around her. Blythe and her sister Chastity are probably the best-connected Humans in the galaxy."

"According to my information, they were some of the earliest students at the station librarian's experimental school, and they had Stryx backing to launch InstaSitter."

"I think that was pretty obvious from the results," Lume said. "And speaking of tunnel network machinations, congratulations on the job you did with the Earth Two negotiations before the Union Station contract queen showed up. It looks like the Humans and the Alts are off to a reasonable start."

"The only hard part was preventing the Alts from giving away the store," the Vergallian said modestly. "They don't understand the first thing about business negotiations. But those Humans from the Old Way movement are a good match for them. If that was McAllister's idea, he's even smarter than our intelligence estimate."

A tentacle reached through the narrow space between the Vergallian and the Dollnick and snagged a slice of pizza. "Samuel was always good at that sort of thing when we were at the Open University together," Jorb said. "I don't know if it was growing up with an ambassador for a mother, or his early years on *Let's Make Friends*, but he has a way with bridging between species."

"I saw you come in, and you were moving like one of your students got the better of you in the dojo," Lume said, miming a body-slam with his upper set of arms even as he deftly wielded chopsticks to add olives to his plate with one of his lower hands. He squinted at the Drazen's face and added, "From up close you look like you haven't slept in a month."

"It's the Grenouthian's fault. I was on Earth Two behind a camera the entire time we were there. But he promised me two points in the production and an assistant director credit."

"And what did you get out of working on the director's documentary crew?" Avisia asked Razood, who bellied up to the buffet by her side. "I didn't see you for over a week either."

"We agreed that he owes me one, but I spent half of my time on the surface helping the Alt blacksmith set up his new shop," the Frunge said. "We might have gotten a bit carried away demonstrating hammering techniques to one another." He glanced over at the waiting area of the Human Empire headquarters and asked, "What are Yaem and the director arguing about?"

"The Grenouthian doesn't want to go back to work at Flower Studios until he finishes editing the documentary, but he's got almost three thousand hours of source material," Lume told them. "He needs to get it down to ten parts if anybody other than a historian is ever going to sit through it."

"Why ten parts?" Jorb asked. "I've seen documentaries that must have had hundreds of parts and went on for years." He noted the Dollnick's skeptical look and amended himself, "All right, I didn't actually sit through any of them, but I know they exist."

"I'll bet it's because the Grenouthian is going to submit to the festivals," Avisia said. "He said something to me about seventy-one minutes per part being the average, so he's going to have to cut more than ninety-nine percent of what you've all shot."

"Our documentaries are presented uncut," Brynlan interjected, helping himself to a small wooden box of dried salt cod that had been added to the buffet especially for the Verlock.

"That's why nobody watches them," the Vergallian said. "Did you visit the planet?"

"No active volcanoes—boring. But I did mail my report through the new post office and paid with a one-cred piece. The postmaster nailed the coin to a beam because I was their first customer."

"I don't believe it's possible to drive a nail through a Stryx cred," Razood said. "They're pretty indestructible. And what's the point of filing a report by mail when the next ship isn't due at Earth Two for another month?"

"The postmaster bent the nail over the coin like a staple to hold it in place, and I brought the letter back to Flower with me after the postmaster canceled the stamp," the Verlock said.

"Why do you look so pleased with yourself?"

"It's possible that the director of Verlock Intelligence collects stamps." Brynlan allowed himself a slow smile to celebrate his career-enhancing gambit. "I also obtained a statement from the postmaster certifying that it was the first letter dispatched from Earth Two. Provenance is invaluable in these cases."

"Can I get you guys anything?" Bill asked the group of aliens. "Samuel delegated me to make sure you're all set. They'll be bringing the baby out and announcing her name in another minute."

"I thought Vivian was expecting a boy," Razood said.

"She was sure of it, but they asked M793qK not to tell them ahead of time."

"It's so strange that Human women can't tell the sex of the baby they're carrying without technology," Avisia said. "I wonder if that applies to Alts as well."

"Mammals," M793qK rubbed out on his speaking legs from the other side of the table. "It's a wonder any of you successfully procreate with all the messing about you do." He looked past the group of spies and added, "The McAllisters really need to find some more Human friends or that little girl won't know what species she is when she grows up."

"They know us," Bill said. "I mean, me and Julie, not all of you guys," he explained as the aliens all turned to regard him with strange expressions. "And you're all, I mean, some of you are, well, we all have two arms and legs, except for M793qK and Lume, but—"

"I know your character on *Everyday Superheroes* carried a shovel, but sometimes when you fall into a hole, it's best to stop digging," Jorb said. "And if you felt bad about being in the minority, here comes the captain and his family, so now we're about even."

The Grenouthian director and Yaem reached the buffet about the same time as the captain, now solo after Lynx and Em peeled off to sneak an early peek at the baby. Woojin made a show of counting all of the spies at the buffet and nodded to himself.

"I'm glad that you're all here," the captain said. "Vivian's mother is leaving Flower at our stop this evening to catch a liner back to Union Station. She wants to have a word with you before she goes."

"That sounds ominous," Lume said, helping himself to another serving of Sheezle bug larvae all the same. "I guess this wasn't a free buffet after all."

"Nothing in the galaxy is free," M793qK rubbed out on his speaking legs as he examined the labels on beer bottles chilling in a bowl of ice. "Don't forget to fill me in later."

"Everything is free on Alt," Avisia commented, drawing a glare from the Farling.

"Blythe included you in the invitation," Woojin told M793qK. "You may not be paying EarthCent Intelligence to be here, but you've made clear that you want to take part in our experiment. And I'm not sure it's fair to say that everything on Alt is free, Avisia. What you don't pay for in coin may come at a higher cost."

"Is that an old Korean saying?" Bill asked the captain.

"I got it from Lume," Woojin said with a laugh.

A group including Julie, Krey, Lynx, Em, Blythe, Rinka, and Fandaz escorted the new mother and her baby from the conference room, where the Drazen and Frunge had led them through the tunnel network ceremony for welcoming female additions. Samuel, who had been hovering outside the door like an expectant father, joined Vivian and the baby, and the two of them moved over to the front of the reception desk.

"I'd like to thank everybody for coming to our daughter's naming," Samuel began. "It's been a tradition in my family to name our children for loved ones who have passed on, but my siblings and cousins have already used up all the good ones, so Vivian suggested we celebrate the Human Empire's first colonization effort by giving our daughter an Alt-style name. As you know, humanity's nearest relatives give all of their children names taken from nature, such as minerals, insects, and fungi. So my mother-in-law put her foot down and limited the options to flora or fauna."

"I can see where this is going," Lume whistled softly.

"Flower decided to help by supplying a list of potential names, which I have here," Samuel continued, producing a tab, "The finalists were Azalea, Blossom, Camellia, Dahlia, Daisy, Fern, Flora, Heather, Holly, Hyacinth, Iris, Ivy, Lilly—have you spotted the trend?"

"All perfectly good names," the Dollnick AI put in over the public address system.

"And then there's the tradition of announcing godparents at the naming. Vivian and I have received help from so many sentients in our lives that limiting our daughter to just two godparents would be ungracious, so we'd like to invite everybody here today to share in our joy and become part of little Rose's adopted family."

"Oh, he's smart alright," Avisia whispered to Lume while joining grudgingly in the applause. "How much do you want to bet that we'll all be saying in fifty years that we knew Empress Rose when she was just a baby?"

"This is the sort of story we'll be eating out on in our old age," the Dollnick replied as the godparents-to-be all formed a line to get a close look at the infant and bestow their blessings.

Dewey, who had been operating one of the Grenouthian director's cameras to record the event, slipped into the end of the line behind Jorb. "What do I say?" he asked the Drazen. "Artificial people don't have any traditions around becoming godparents."

"Just mumble something," Jorb said. "That's what I always do when I'm out of my depth in social situations. Maybe touch her forehead at the same time and look like you're thinking about something profound."

"I'll calculate Pi."

Vivian's mother stood next to her daughter, greeting each of the alien spies by name, and requesting their presence for a brief meeting before she had to leave. In just a few minutes, the population distribution in the Human Empire headquarters had inverted, with all of the intelligence professionals gathered in the conference room and the civilians hunting through the remains of the buffet.

"Will Lynx be joining us?" Blythe asked Captain Pyun.

Woojin shook his head. "I'll get her up to speed later."

"Do I have to worry about her quitting?"

"Not the third officer gig, but she's been slowly losing interest in the spy game ever since she had Em."

"Lynx believes that it's all unnecessarily complicated," Lume contributed from his seat at the table.

"Part of that comes from spending so much time with Flower," Woojin said. "Neither of them is a fan of the subtle approach, and Lynx is sure she can contribute more to the EarthCent Intelligence business database by keeping up with open commerce than by recruiting undercover sources."

"I'm sure she's right," Blythe said. She looked around at the room full of alien spies and laughed. "I suppose I shouldn't be talking about our personnel issues in front of you all, but then again, you probably know about them before I do."

"My bosses know," Yaem said. "They don't tell me anything."

"So what I have to say next may come as a surprise." Blythe activated the holographic display system and a complex diagram filled with colored ovals and connecting lines sprang to life. "The report I'm about to discuss with you was undertaken by the EarthCent president's office using outside contractors and sent directly to the Union Station embassy in the diplomatic bag, so it's possible some of you may not be familiar with the contents yet."

"What's with all the strange names?" Avisia asked. "I like to think I'm fluent in Humanese, but those all look made up."

"They are made up. It's a tradition on Earth to use invented words for trademarked products as it strengthens both the brand and the legal protection. In this case, you're looking at the pharmaceutical products manufactured on our homeworld that account for over sixty percent of the prescription market."

"If the connecting lines represent drug interactions, I estimate the maximum number of medications Humans can ingest has peaked," the Grenouthian director said.

"Perhaps our Farling friend would like to explain," Blythe said, offering M793qK a thin smile.

"But you're doing such a good job," the giant beetle rubbed out on his speaking legs. "I'm curious to hear how the story ends."

"In addition to improving health outcomes on Earth, the last few years have seen a steady reduction in prescription advertising as this relatively small pool of highly effective pharmaceuticals has taken over the market. The lines on the chart show the corporate relationships, not drug interactions, and you can see that a mere half-dozen—"

"Seven," M793qK interjected.

"—seven corporations are ultimately responsible for manufacturing all of these products that, at an initial glance, were patented by thirty-one businesses around the globe." Blythe clicked the pointer she was holding and a new hologram appeared, this one showing what looked like a turtle shell with seven eggs inside. "But it turns out the seven remaining business entities themselves are shell, or perhaps I should say, carapace corporations, and all of the patents for these medications are controlled by a single trust."

"You took over Earth's pharmaceutical industry?" the Verlock asked M793qK.

"Sixty percent," the Farling replied. "I was aiming at forty-nine percent, but quality speaks for itself and I overshot."

"I thought you only sold placebos," the captain said.

"I only prescribe placebos, but physicians on Earth lack my ability to repair underlying problems so pharmaceuticals are the main tool they have to work with. I thought it was time somebody started selling antibiotics that don't kill off your biome, and pain medications that aren't accompanied by an addictive euphoria."

"Our doctors, at least the ones who weren't heavily invested in the older pharmaceutical companies, thank you," Blythe said. "And I'll take this occasion to thank you myself in front of the others for the part you played in rescuing that shipload of medical test subjects who might otherwise have found themselves dissected in Farling space. But the president's office estimates pharmaceutical sales at over two percent of the Gross World Product, of which you now control some sixty percent, and growing."

"Hey, you're catching up with Drazen Foods," Jorb said.

"Which brings me around to the unpleasant business of taxation," Blythe continued. "The only issue that EarthCent has with your pharmaceutical empire is a feat of creative accounting the president's office is still struggling to unravel. You've managed to book one hundred percent of the license fees through the Cayman Islands."

"You should be complaining to the authorities there, not me," M793qK said. "I didn't write their laws around taxation."

"And that's exactly what the president intended to do until we got word of your desire to join our little intelligence cooperative."

"Do you mean we'll all get a slice of the pie?" Yaem asked.

"We were thinking more along the lines of waving M793qK's participation fee in exchange for his agreeing to pay a fair rate of tax to improve Earth's medical infrastructure," Blythe said. "Drazen Foods offers an excellent model for giving something back."

"Drazen Foods is practically a philanthropic holding company," the Farling rubbed out, but his twitching antennae suggested that he was finding the whole thing rather amusing. "Do I get any say in how the money is spent?"

Vivian's mother was clearly surprised by this question. "Would you care?"

"If you're going to invest in improving Earth's medical infrastructure, yes, I would like to see that the money isn't all wasted."

"Then we'll be in touch. It's been nice seeing you all again, and EarthCent Intelligence looks forward to your continued cooperation."

As Blythe turned to leave the conference room, the alien spies all began to rise, but the captain shook his head and gestured for them to sit again. He waited for Vivian's mother to leave the room, and then he asked M793qK, "What was that all about?"

"When I visited Earth some years ago for unrelated reasons, I couldn't help noticing that there was a business opportunity for anyone with a reasonable understanding of mammalian physiology," the Farling replied. "The native competition was more concerned with making tiny tweaks to their existing drugs to maintain patent protection than with developing new therapies, but even I was surprised with the speed at which my proxies came to dominate the market simply by providing superior products. I suspect it would have been much more difficult back when Earth's governments were deeply involved in regulating the industry."

"I meant, why did you give in so easily?" Woojin asked. "I don't know what kind of taxes Drazen Foods pays, but I'm guessing it will mean a large loss of income for you."

"What else could I do when asked by the grandmother of my latest goddaughter?" M793qK said disingenuously.

"Who will no doubt realize by the time she gets to the lift tube that she owes you one," Lume observed.

"Or two, or ten," the Farling said agreeably. "Besides, my pharmaceutical business earns its income in eBucks, and I've had to reinvest it on Earth to avoid crashing the exchange rate into Stryx creds. I've barely taken out enough profits to pay for some lab equipment."

"I thought you told me that you build your diagnostic scanners from scratch," Woojin said.

"I do, but the necessary components don't grow on trees, at least not any trees you would recognize as such."

"And your takeover of Earth's prescription drug market wouldn't have anything to do with blocking Farling Pharmaceuticals, which is owned by your rivals in the hierarchy, from entering a profitable market?"

"Efficiency is the soul of good planning," M793qK replied.

Twenty One

"I don't think any of the spies are going to be here for lunch today," Bill told Harry. "I just came from the naming party Samuel and Vivian had for their baby and the buffet was loaded with alien delicacies imported from Union Station."

"Then maybe I'll get this prototype strudel kit finished," the baker said. "I vacuum packed and froze a batch of dough in different shapes a few weeks ago, and I thawed it out overnight. If you help me make the fruit fillings, I'll bake them up and bring them to Flower's Paradise for Irene's lecture this afternoon."

"Your wife is teaching a class?"

"Nancy, the woman who coordinates our educational programs, calls it a seminar because it's going to be hands-on. I was surprised that Irene agreed, but she admitted to having an ulterior motive."

"Maybe hanging around the Grenouthian director has rubbed off on her," Bill said. "The aliens have ulterior motives for everything."

Harry laughed as he placed a tray of vacuum-sealed dough packages on the table. "There's enough for six strudels on each tray. We'll have to make the filling for twenty-four strudels at the same time so the taste testers can compare apples to apples."

"You mean you used different recipes for each tray of dough?"

"Minor variations, but you'd be surprised how much difference it can make in how the finished product tastes after the dough is vacuum packed, frozen, thawed, filled, and baked. I don't need to get it perfect, because the kitchen techs at Flower Foods will run hundreds of tests with even smaller changes, but I want to make sure that the process is viable."

"I don't think I could ever be a commercial baker," Bill said as he started washing apples in cold water. "The main reason I want to open a café is to see people enjoying the food and drinks I serve them. I've only worked two shifts so far in Fandaz's café, but I really like all of the choices she offers customers."

"Julie might be right," Harry said. "You're turning into a good baker, Bill, but you don't have the interest in piping and presentation to become a pâtissier. And even though I see you five days a week, I can't keep track of how many part-time jobs you have."

"I'm saving my creds for the opening, though it's going to take a couple of years. When I was doing research for my independent study course because Flower wanted me to get close to Fandaz, she told me that—"

"Play that part back again," Harry interrupted, setting aside the scissors he'd just used to cut open the vacuum packs. "You were spying on Fandaz for Flower?"

"Not spying," Bill said. "Fandaz and Razood were interested in each other but they couldn't say anything because of some weird Frunge tradition. Don't you remember Flower asking me to do my independent study at the Blue Tea Café so I could be their middleman? I've already learned so much from Fandaz. She's convinced me that it would be better to save my money for a proper launch than to rent the cheapest location with third-hand furnishings."

"As long as you're talking about saving for a few years and not for a few decades, I agree," Harry said. "You have to watch it with the aliens because they have a different sense of time than we do. How are she and Razood progressing? Are you and Julie enjoying chaperoning their dates?"

Bill moved on to coring the apples and he kept his eyes on the small blade while replying. "Between our jobs and everything else happening, Julie and I had pretty much given up on going out together. But now Razood and Fandaz come up with things to do every week that we never would have thought of ourselves and Julie forgets about work for a few hours. We're meeting them this evening for dance lessons. Somebody just opened an Astria's Academy of Dance franchise next to Jorb's dojo."

"Why does that name sound familiar?"

"Astria's has locations all over Earth, and Jorb says they even have franchises beyond the tunnel network. Everybody knows the Vergallians use them for intelligence gathering, but I guess they have the best dance teachers. What are you chopping?"

"Walnuts," Harry said. "With the apples and raisins, there should be enough to complete the test batch. When you finish with those, throw a clean tablecloth on that counter and dust it with flour. I want to roll out some of the dough from each variation to try a thin crust as well as the regular pastry."

"Got it." Bill used the flat of his knife to shovel all of the apple bits into a large mixing bowl for Harry to add the raisins and walnuts, and then he headed for the linen cupboard to get a tablecloth. Halfway there, he turned back and asked, "What's your wife's ulterior motive for teaching a documentary seminar?"

"I was waiting for you to ask," the baker said, scraping the walnuts into the bowl. "She wants to make her own documentary, and since there's no budget, she plans to emulate the Grenouthian director and use volunteers. Teaching a seminar is a way to scout likely prospects."

"What's her documentary going to be about?" Bill asked, returning with the tablecloth and spreading it over a stainless steel countertop.

"I'm glad you asked that as well," Harry said with a grin. "Irene wants to do something about careers on Flower. She was hoping you and Julie would be willing to let her tag along for a few hours with a camera crew while you're at work."

"I guess we're pretty much used to cameras at this point, and if your wife wants to shoot my shift at the *Blue Tea Café*, Fandaz would probably love the free publicity. You know that Flower would be happy to have her shipyard show up in another documentary, so Julie's in."

"I'm a little suspicious that Flower is the one who gave Irene the idea." Harry combined a bowl of raisins with the larger bowl of walnuts and apple bits and mixed it with his hands. "It's funny, but when Irene and I sat down and talked about our retirement plans five years ago, both of us expected to take it easy and catch up on our reading. Instead, we're as busy as we were in our fifties."

"Speaking of fifties, fifty-three more minutes and you're done for the day," the Dollnick AI announced via an overhead speaker.

"How come you didn't put the same restrictions on Irene when she was working for the Grenouthian director?" Harry asked.

"She's a year younger than you, and as a female, her life expectancy is several years longer," Flower explained. "And the work limits from the actuarial tables wouldn't impact the time she could spend volunteering on the documentary because it was related to her Open University class."

"Are you saying that getting an education doesn't count as work?" Bill asked.

"Unpaid internships don't count, paid co-op jobs do. The Open University only sponsors the latter."

"Do you mean if I volunteer for Flower Foods I could work a full day?" Harry asked.

"No, and the same is true for Irene's volunteering at the bazaar. If you want to borrow the kitchen to make pastries for your friends, you can work around the clock, but if it's for my benefit, we have to honor the limits."

"I'd better get everything in the oven before I go, and then you can bring them by Irene's seminar," Harry said to Bill. "If you aren't doing anything else, maybe you'll sit in."

"If only," the young man replied with a groan. "M793qK is coming by later to get me going on testing a new batch of products for the All Species Cookbook."

"I thought you enjoyed that work."

"I'd enjoy it more if he stopped trying to teach me secure communications techniques at the same time."

Seven hours later, after their free introductory lesson came to a sudden end, Bill hobbled out to the lobby of Astria's Academy of Dance with the help of Razood while their dates retreated to the dressing room to freshen up.

"You did really well for a while there, and we almost lasted the full hour," the Frunge said. "How's your ankle?"

"I think it's just a sprain," Bill said with a wince. "I wouldn't be able to stand if it was broken."

"We could swing by M793qK's and—"

"No! He gave me a message to decrypt for homework and I keep getting messed up when the numerical substitution goes past twenty-five."

"There are twenty-six letters in Humanese, so you just start back at the beginning," Razood said.

"You know how one-time pads work?" Bill asked eagerly. He opened his belt pouch and produced a small pad. "We're using the top sheet," he said, handing it over, "and I copied the encrypted message onto the back of this flyer—what?"

"You know I'm not the most traditional Frunge in the galaxy, but did you just hand me a pad of paper?"

"Sorry, I wasn't thinking. I'll put it away and ask Flower for help when I get home."

"If Mizpah could see us right now you'd be disqualified as our chaperone," Razood said as he studied the flyer that Bill was still holding up. "Handing me a pad of paper while on a date. I'll be telling my grandchildren that one in five hundred years."

"So it doesn't hurt or anything?"

"Holding your one-time pad? No, avoiding paper products is just a tradition, and the message reads, 'Next time I expect you to do your own decryption.'"

"Come on, really," Bill said.

"That's what's encoded," Razood told him, handing back the one-time pad. "M793qK can read you like a book."

"But how did you do the fancy math without even writing anything down?"

"I'm not sure modular addition qualifies as math, fancy or otherwise, and don't forget to destroy the sheet now that it's been used."

"How's your ankle?" Julie asked as she and Fandaz rejoined their dates.

"Better now," Bill lied. "Where are we meeting Jorb and Rinka?"

"Next door," Julie said. "Rinka showed me a Skippers board and it's too big to unfold at a café. We'll just sit on the mats and play."

"I'll warn you now that I always win at Skippers, so if Jorb suggests a little betting to make it interesting, tell him not until you've learned the rules," Fandaz said.

Bill tried to conceal his limp as they headed down the corridor to Jorb's dojo, and after just fifty steps, he was happy to collapse on the mat next to the six-sided Skippers board that was almost as wide as he was tall.

"How many squares are on this board?" he asked.

"They aren't very square, especially as you move in from the edges," Julie pointed out.

"It's not about the number of squares, it's about getting your pieces to the center," Jorb said as he handed out the remote controls. "Everybody starts with eight color-coded pieces, and the controller lets you move eight spaces every turn. It's up to you whether to move one piece eight spaces or two pieces four—you get the idea."

"And we're supposed to advance them to the cup in the middle? But whoever goes first will win."

"Only if the rest of us allow it," Fandaz said. "But you can't advance through a space occupied by another player's piece, and if you slip through a gap of fewer than five spaces between two pieces of the same player, your piece gets taken."

"Or a gap of three spaces between the pieces of two other players," Jorb added.

"Do diagonals count?" Bill asked. All four aliens nodded. "I'm going to stink at this game."

Before the hour was up, Jorb and Fandaz were the only players who hadn't been eliminated, and the Drazen was taking a long time between moves.

"Just go, Jorb," Rinka said. "It's only a game."

"But it's *our* game," he gritted out between clenched teeth. "I can't lose to a Frunge."

"You already have, you just haven't admitted it yet," Razood said.

"I wonder if the Alts play any board games," Julie said. "It seems like it would be pointless if they're all focused on helping each other win."

"Maybe they win by losing," Bill said. "No, then they would be competing to lose so that doesn't work either. I still don't get how they run an economy where nobody is trying to come out ahead."

"Our people tried a version of the sharing economy for a while during our first robotic era," Fandaz said. Her looking up from the board was a sure sign that Jorb's position was hopeless. "Technology has a way of taking everything over if you let it, and we weren't alone in almost going under."

"You mean the robots revolted?"

"Worse, they didn't," Fandaz said. "My main concentration at university was in our early history, and my dissertation was on the parallels between species facing a post-employment economy who still have records going back that far."

"Aren't historical records permanent once we reach a high enough level of technology?" Julie asked.

"You would think so, but ask a Verlock or a Grenouthian academic for details about their societies from seven million years ago and they'll just be embarrassed. As time passes, interest fades, and eventually, physical records are misplaced or destroyed to make room for more relevant material." Fandaz paused as Jorb pointed his remote control at the board, but then lowered it again. "It's the source materials that go first," she continued. "Everybody has classic reference works that offer a survey of their history, but most of it may as well be legends because there's no supporting documentation remaining. Some scholars resort to reading ancient historical romances for clues about the past."

"But why do you say it's worse if the robots don't revolt?" Bill asked.

"Because life evolved to fight for survival," the Frunge replied. "I don't know how many species end up extinct because they replace work with automation and wither for lack of purpose, but it's more than have been lost to wars or any of the things that can go wrong with the fabric of space. The main thing that kept us going was our quest for an interstellar drive. Once we found that we weren't alone in the galaxy and that all of the successful species put severe restrictions on how they used robots, we did likewise."

"I guess humanity would be heading in the same direction if not for the tunnel network."

"Humanity would have killed itself off by now if not for the Stryx intervening," Razood said. "What most of us find amazing is that the Alts never even started down the path of over-automation."

"Is it because of their sharing economy?" Julie asked.

"Most species have experimented with eliminating money at some point or another," Fandaz said. "Some, like the Verlocks, have done it several times."

"Then why do they keep going back to it?"

"Money?" The owner of the Blue Tea Café considered the question. "I suppose because it's convenient, and it provides a handy way of keeping score for those of us with a competitive streak, which is everybody except the Alts."

There was a loud cracking noise as Jorb crushed his remote in his fist. "Oops," he said. "I guess you win by default because I can't go."

"Very mature," Rinka said, flicking her tentacle at Jorb. "Now how are we going to play another round?"

"I'm ready for bed," Julie said. "I was up early to help Vivian prepare for the Naming, and my eyes are tired out from trying to sew lines on patterns."

"You've started using the treadle sewing machine again?"

"It's kind of fun, and I already miss the Old Way sewing circle. I'm going to write a romance novel based on a fictional version of one of their communities."

"You can join a new sewing circle as soon as I pick up the next Old Way group heading for Earth Two," Flower said, speaking through the dojo's sound system so everybody could hear. "They'll be living here for almost three months, so you'll have plenty of time to work on your trousseau."

"I knew it was too good to be true when you stopped bugging us about getting married," Julie said.

"You are married," the Dollnick AI retorted. "Do you think that a Human ceremony is somehow more valid than a Frunge contract?"

"So you won't be mad if we skip the wedding?"

"I didn't say that. I'm not running a trust economy here, and weddings create work for part-time professionals like musicians and banquet hall employees."

"What kind of honeymoon package are you offering them?" Fandaz asked.

"Now we're getting down to business," the Dollnick AI said. "Two weeks of paid vacation, and I'll only contact them about work if it's an emergency."

"Who decides what constitutes an emergency?" Julie asked.

"It's fully explained in the employee handbook."

"I wouldn't know what to do with myself without any work for two weeks," Bill said. "Can I get a month at thirty hours a week instead?"

"If you wear a tux at the wedding," Flower countered. "I'm expanding into formalwear and it would reflect badly on me if you show up in blue jeans. Post the banns tomorrow and I'll add the wedding to the captain's calendar for next Sunday."

"Jeans post," Julie exclaimed. "You've got it, Flower. GenePost. That's what Vivian should call the Human Empire's family registry. It's like a postal messaging service based on a genetic database."

"Uh, did you catch the bit about where she just scheduled our wedding?" Bill asked.

"Like she said, we're already married, and I think I'll go for the thirty-hour-a-week honeymoon option myself. It's going to be weird not having Flower nagging us about getting married all the time."

"And baby makes three," the Dollnick AI said, but so softly that Rinka and Fandaz were the only ones that heard.

From the author

The next release will be a sequel to **Orphans on the Galactic Tunnel Network**. If you've read the five EarthCent Universe books starting with **Independent Living** without reading the original EarthCent Ambassador series, I recommend starting with **Destiny: Union Station.** You can sign up for e-mail notification of my new releases on the **IfItBreaks.com**.

About the Author

E. M. Foner lives in Northampton, MA with an imaginary German Shepherd who's been trained to bite central bankers. The author welcomes reader comments at e_foner@yahoo.com. He's also online at:

facebook/E.M.Foner/

Also by the author in reading order:

Destiny: Union Station

Date Night on Union Siation

Alien Night on Union Station

High Priest on Union Station

Spy Night on Union Station

Carnival on Union Station

Wanderers on Union Station

Vacation on Union Station

Guest Night on Union Station

Word Night on Union Station

Party Night on Union Station

Review Night on Union Station

Family Night on Union Station

Book Night on Union Station

LARP Night on Union Station

Career Night on Union Station

Last Night on Union Station

Independent Living

Soup Night on Union Station

Assisted Living

Freelance on the Galactic Tunnel Network

Con Living

Empire Night on Union Station

Space Living

Traders on the Galactic Tunnel Network

Orphans on the Galactic Tunnel Network

Swap Night on Union Station

Made in United States
Orlando, FL
11 November 2023